LABYRINTH

Oliver Thomson

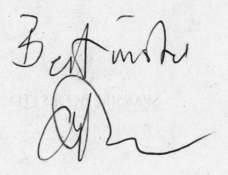

SPARSILE BOOKS LTD

Disclaimer

Please note that much of the content of this book is intended in a humerous or ironical tone. If you find such content objectionable, we suggest you do not continue.

Thanks to the staff of Sparsile Books, especially Lesley Affrossman and Jim Campbell.

Also to my amazingly tolerant wife Jean and to the late John Buchan of Tweedsmuir.

...as I lay looking at the frosty stars a fancy wove itself in my brain. I saw the younger sons carry the royal blood far down among the people, down even into the kennels of the outcast. Generations follow, oblivious of the high beginnings...

John Buchan

PREFACE

I have lived many lives
I was a man, I was a woman
I was a hunter, I was a farmer
I was both free and a slave, rich and poor
a sailor, a soldier, a fisherman, a merchant
and a priest.
And once, when the world was young, I was a king.

There is no doubt that when Pythagoras three thousand years ago invented his idea of the legs of a triangle he got it absolutely right, but less reliable was one of the philosophical ideas which he made popular in ancient Greece.

This was the belief that all creatures have immortal souls and that when they die the soul moves on to another creature, sometimes up the scale, like from worm to lion, or monkey to male human, or down the scale, like from princess to porcupine, each promotion or demotion depending on the behaviour of the previous owner.

Plato and many religious reformers over the years have endorsed this idea of metempsychosis, but it later became unfashionable. In his *Ulysses* James Joyce referred to it as 'met him pike hoses'. However with the recent massive advances in genetics there is perhaps evidence that there is something immortal that does transfer from one creature to another, generation after generation after generation.

CHAPTER ONE

Let's play the music and dance
I. Berlin

New York, Jan 17th, 2118

I'm facing a crisis, probably of my own making. My career is extremely dull, but I need the money, so I put up with it. My love life is a contradiction in terms, disaster. Yesterday I zoomed Dr Jane, the shrink at my old college, and she instantly diagnosed early-onset metempsychosis.

'What's that?' I asked. 'It sounds nasty.'

'Well, it's still quite rare,' she replied. 'Nothing to worry about. It was recognised quite recently by a group of research psychiatrists based at the Bronx University. They identified a kind of non-functional DNA, buried under the more recent functional DNA, which means that some people have memories about their ancestors, usually as dreams. Often they are quite detailed, as if the people actually inherit a mental picture from long-dead relatives. The ancient Greeks understood it perfectly well, Pythagoras in particular.'

'In other words I dream too much,' I said. It's mostly about my ancestors who were much brighter than me and make me feel inadequate. I feel boringly average with a third-class degree in social media, reduced from a second because I failed the hacking practical.

I asked Dr Jane what I should do about it all.

'I have several patients who practice yoga and they are quite good at controlling these dreams. So are some Australian aborigines. But the Bronx research group are looking for more guinea pigs to back up their research using a new bio implant, so they're offering money to anyone like you who will report your dream memories. Why not give it a go? You could download the memories yourself and play them back; it might be therapeutic as well as financially useful. And find a good woman while you're at it. Was there not a suitable woman in one of your dreams?'

I thought there was. It might even have been Dr Jane herself, for she was very attractive in some ways. Then she added, 'From bits you mentioned earlier I gather there are a few mysteries in your past. Why not get those dreams in the right order, so that you have a proper family history, maybe even going back to the Stone Age?'

Brooklyn, New York, Jan 2nd, 2119

I fear that I made no immediate effort to follow the doctor's advice. After signing up for the program and receiving the implant, I set the recordings to download onto my comp, but never seemed to get the time to replay them. Apart from my work, the news had become my main obsession, but it has been more and more depressing.

New York is once more the worst city for overdose deaths per thousand people. All the international space stations have been abandoned due the huge halo of satellite debris scattered round the globe. And today is the

400th anniversary of the first ever financial crash in the USA, when the banks dished out too much paper money, then suddenly panicked and stopped, causing all-round disaster and misery. It still keeps happening. The one bit of good news is that this year the average summer temperature has dropped to 47 degrees, so perhaps global warming has stopped at last. Yet there has been a spate of violent hurricanes including Hurricane Harry VII which left half of Texas under water And of course famine and wars continue in dozens of places all round the globe. To cheer us up the massive new cruise liner, the thorium-powered QE4, came up the Hudson to a rousing welcome from the fire tugs.

But I realise that I haven't introduced myself yet, so here goes.

My name is Theo A. Thens. I was born in the year 2089 on floor 203 of the north condominium, where the lifts frequently broke down and most people just went up or down a few floors except on special occasions. Of those in employment most worked on e-pods, so they didn't need to move around much. There was a frozen food shop on floor 198 which catered for most of our needs and an open exercise area on the floor above where we could also plant vegetables in tubs.

Until I was fifteen I never went above floor 220, but when I did, it was to visit a poor cousin of my mother's and I was shocked by the conditions up there. People had to go either up or down five floors to the shops and these offered a very limited choice. The ceilings in the rooms were even lower than in ours, and many of the apartments had no external window. For some this was a blessing, for the average summer temperature was then 48 degrees and the less sunlight the better. All coal and gas-burning heaters had been illegal for the last seventy years, but it had been too late to stop many of the effects of global warming. Several countries close to the equator had been reduced to empty desert and the children of redundant oil-workers had formed maniac gangs which roamed the country causing mischief. In our own building groups of youngsters wandered along the corridors spraying the walls with obscene pictures and unintelligible slogans from long-forgotten tribes.

Eventually my father, Mino, developed quite an expertise in real meat trading on his e-pod and we were able to move to a three-storey block with a real lawn off Brooklyn, while I attended the Multi-media College.

New York by this time had so many cable ducts and so few vehicles apart from roboids that most of the streets were left permanently dug up. Thus the cable repair people could spend all day fiddling with the tangle of disconnected drains, leaking water pipes, telecom tubes, redundant wires and satellite connectors until they found each fault, by which time they needed to start all over again.

When I was eighteen my father announced that there was little future in real meat, as cattle breeding had been discontinued in most countries due to methane emissions, so I chose to go into timber trading instead. Not that I see or feel any actual wood. I just shift various types of plank around the world using my e-pod. Very occasionally I go to a dealers' conference, which means three changes of roboid to the other end of the state. I now control three out-workers, so I have to put myself about a bit.

To sum up I do now feel slightly important. I get a little bit of respect, but I haven't fought in a war or invented anything. I'm still underachieving, so if my soul has transmigrated from someone else's dead body, like Orpheus said, then it's unlikely that I'm much of an improvement on the last owner. Unless of course its owner was a cockroach. As Dr Jane suggested, I think I will replay my dreams, at least the exciting ones. There was a shrink in Switzerland called Jung who said that you can remember things in dreams which you could never remember when you are awake. But I can, if I replay my recordings.

§

I am a good hunter, one of the best in the tribe. We have always brought in enough meat and hides for the women and children. But the animals seem to be moving away. We have to run a long distance to find any. And the berries hardly ever seem to ripen. My legs are beginning to hurt. I need more to eat. I'm tired. There is a constant trickle of ice-cold water coming from the cave above my head and I cannot be bothered moving.

§

There's a list at the back of this diary where I have traced the locations and dates of my dreams. This one seems to have been near the Neanderthal Valley in Germany and around 50,000 BC

Newark, Jan 23rd, 2119

I decided that I need to get out more and do something adventurous, so I went to a conference on the continuing use of timber as a defence against rising sea levels. The Atlantic is nearly a foot deeper than it was when I was born and e-cars here tend to be hub deep at high tide despite the new embankments. These conferences offer opportunities for staring at women; a pleasure denied to us most of the time since we are tied to our e-pods. So on this occasion a woman in a red dress particularly caught my eye. She was sipping from a glass of wine, obviously attending a different conference at the same venue as ours, and I quickly lost sight of her. But a few minutes later she suddenly popped up behind me.

'Nice design,' she said, lifting up the tip of my new corporate tie.

'It's my new company logo,' I replied with quiet pride. 'The motif is based on a two-headed axe to symbolise our two-sided approach to South American hardwoods.'

'So you're in wood,' she said indulgently, stretching out her wine glass at an angle and pulling her collar across her throat as if to hide the short gold chain around her neck.

'Hardwoods,' I said.

'They must be hard indeed,' she said.

I put out my hand. 'I'm Theo A. Thens,' I said. 'And my business is called We Try Hard-woods.'

'Well, hello Theo,' she replied and took my hand briefly. 'I'm Ariadne Aufnax and I'm with Geriaid, the brand leaders in care for the over nineties. This is our half-yearly meeting. I thought you were maybe one of us, as I don't usually talk to strange men.'

'I'm glad you did. And I'm not particularly strange.' She was about my height and the initial impression suggested she was perhaps a fraction overweight, but had the sort of suppressed energy that often goes with a size fifteen or above.

'I don't really know all that much about planks,' she said. 'Trees are more my thing. So who designed your company logo?'

'An artist down in Greenwich village. He said it was based on an old Cretan design.'

'I'm sure that says a lot about your character. Cretan. It rhymes with Thetan.'

'So what do you do with Geriaid?'

'Just a junior exec. Here's my card.' She zapped it into my phone and moved off with the determination of one who makes a point of circulating round everyone at a party to check where the best opportunities lie. I read the card and it said Ariadne Aufnax, Dip. Ger., Geriaid Division, Scientology Corporation, 51st St. New York.

I stood there scratching my elbow, a subconscious habit that tugs at me when I'm worried.

§

The old man who had no cave was splitting flints with the dexterity acquired from years of practice. Though I had learned to flake flints like any hunter it was still a joy to watch the skill with which he worked the stone to make a perfect axe-head. So we feasted him, thanked the spirits for his skill and sent him on his way with many gifts and enough venison to last him till he reached the next tribe in need of his skills.

Manhattan, Jan 25th, 2119

So you're thirty,' said my mother, kissing me on both cheeks when I arrived at her tiny apartment. 'And still not married. What birthday present do you give to a thirty-year-old bachelor who has everything but a wife?'

'Nothing, Mum. Just a smile.'

'You seem to spend all your time making money and buying things with it. You've got so much music and all these fancy drinks. Anyway here's what I got you.' She handed me a small card. 'It's time for you to find out who you really are. The Church of Latter Day Saints organises it. The blessed martyr Saint Joseph Smith was told by an angel that everyone should know that we are descended from saints. Take the card and it will bring you contentment and joy.'

She looked at me uncertainly as if wondering if I would approve. I took a piece of her homemade chocolate cake and looked at the card, mumbling a half-enthusiastic thanks. At least it was a change from hand-knitted jumpers.

'They want to baptise thousands of poor dead souls,' she went on. 'So they need to find out their names and where they were. Then they can be baptised and go to heaven. So there,' she added defiantly. 'I read it in *The Laughing Times*.' This was her favourite newspaper, as it specialised in turning all the news into a joke or a rhyme. It was very popular with all her age group and was subsidised by the government as part of its anti-depressant campaign. I of course looked down on it as patronising rubbish, though I confess to enjoying the odd article.

'You find out,' she said. 'Who you really are. And stop getting yourself lost in the maze.'

'Okay, Mum. I will,' I said and strode off down the corridor to the lift, protesting to myself vigorously that she did not understand the stresses of modern business or for that matter any other aspect of life in the twenty-second century. It was true that I found it hard to relax and sometimes was kept awake at night scratching my itchy elbow, but so far as mainstream life was concerned I was as well-adjusted as anybody. As I whisked downwards in her express lift I felt renewed irritation at her lack of trust, but as I emerged onto the street below I caught a passing roboid and soon forgot all about it. I dozed.

§

One day there was a huge flash in the sky and afterwards the earth grew cold because the gods were annoyed with us, that much was obvious. For many months there was no game in the forest, not even mice or

19

rats, and the sun never came out to ripen the berries. The tribe split up into family groups, but still my woman died and so did three of our children. One is still alive and I told her to leave me, for I no longer have the strength to go long distances in search of food. I don't care anymore. I scratched an itch on my elbow.

New York, Jan 31st, 2119

It was several days later that I accidentally plucked my mother's birthday present from my pocket and read it.

> This card entitles you to a FREE mtDNA
> FINGERPRINTING WHICH WILL
> INDICATE YOUR ENTIRE ETHNIC
> ANCESTRY AND ANY KNOWN
> ANTECEDENTS ON OUR DATABASE.

Please attend one of our swab collection stations at your earliest convenience.

COLDS Foundation,6001,43rd Street, New York

or reply to swabs@colds.com

'Waste of time,' I said to myself and forgot about the card for ten days. Then I called Ariadne at Geriaid to see if she fancied dinner at the Geyser Icelandic Theme Bar. Her answer machine said, 'Miss Aufnax is currently out of the office but please leave a message and press the hash key.'

New York, Feb 2nd, 2119

Ariadne came to the Icelandic and was wearing the same red dress, but despite my plying her with two large White Deaths and Tonic and treating her to a chef's special hot-rock she refused to come back to my flat afterwards.

'What's the hurry?' she asked.

'I thought you'd enjoyed yourself.'

'I did, but you think you've poured enough aquavit into me to get a one-night stand. I thought you were brighter than that. I thought we had affinities.'

'Life's too tense to talk about affinities,' I whined. 'You have to grab the moment. This whole city could short-circuit any minute and blow us all up.'

'So?'

'We should enjoy the moment.'

'I have and thank you. It was a nice meal.' And with those words she blew me a kiss and a second or two later I saw her swing elegantly onto a passing roboid.

I stuck my e-pod in my ear for the news. A gang of over-enthusiastic teenagers in Poland had machine-gunned several thousand cows as a protest against illegal cattle breeding causing dangerous clusters of methane gas that contributed to global warming and created a black market in steaks. I shut my eyes for a few minutes.

§

When I had walked for nearly four days I met a group of three men who had no woman and they gave me food. It was grain soaked in water and bits of some kind of bird. I could not understand what they said. I liked one of them more than the other two, but they made it clear that they wanted to share me, so I had no choice. At least they had a fairly dry cave and knew how to make fire and the one I like best is a good hunter.

New York, Feb 12th, 2119

Ten days after my supper with Ariadne I found myself at a loose end and thought I might as well clear my conscience with regard to my mother's gift, so I rang COLDS for an appointment.

'Church of Latter Day,' answered a machine at the other end. 'Choose from the following options. Press 5 for appointments. This call may be monitored for training purposes.'

'I'd like to make a swab appointment.'

'Please key in the time and date that would suit you ,then hash.'

I did as I was told, thinking that if it came to the bit I would just renege on the appointment and tell my mother some prevarication. But the following morning business was quiet, I had nothing better to do, so I attended the swab clinic in Mitochondrial Towers. Boringly soporific.

§

I am lucky as I have three fathers, a mother and one sister. We hardly ever grow hungry and I am learning to shoot arrows from a bow. There is one of my fathers that I don't like. He looks at me strangely. The one I like best paints stones with different coloured dots and carves little animals out of bone. He made a mammoth for me because I once saw one in the distance and it made me afraid, but the little one made of bone I keep by my bed.

New York, Feb 19th, 2119

A week later I received an email from Dr Joseph Smith, B. Gen., M.Theol. of the C.O.L.D.S Foundation inviting me for my free half-hour DNA profiling. He must be descended from the first Joseph Smith who was shot in 1844. Before going I emailed Ariadne for another dinner date, but there was no reply.

'Mr Thens, I'm Dr Smith, please sit down,' said the white-coated doctor when I arrived at the clinic and I chose one of the imitation executive armchairs. 'A most interesting sample,' he went on, projecting a coloured spreadsheet onto his wall. 'I'm glad to say, though it's not the purpose of this interview, that your main organs all appear to be in good condition. Though perhaps you're a kilo or so overweight. And you're drinking a shade too much. I suggest cutting a few units each week and try an e-bike for exercise.'

This was not what I wanted to hear.

'Do you suffer from tension?' he went on.

'No more than a million other e-pod traders,' I replied.

'Well, make it forty minutes serious bike exercise a day.'

I grunted, resenting his condescending manner and the fact that he appeared so skeletal as to have no dietary vices.

'As I said, your profile is very interesting. I punched it through our world database and you have several identifiable gene patterns. There's Mediterranean blood, probably Greek. Some Viking, or Norman, some Afro-Asian and a few Jewish characteristics. Sephardic. Some M.18.25, a touch of R5, U1 and 2e. But now it starts to get really exciting.'

I found it quite hard to believe that Dr Smith ever got excited.

'We've found a match between your swab and a skull, probably second millennium BC that was found about a century ago by the Danube just south of what is now Budapest. A skull with a hole in it, so your ancestor seems to have met with a violent death.'

'My ancestor?'

'Exactly,' he said. 'But there's more. As you can imagine we don't have files on all that much human organic material from the early periods, except of course for the Egyptians as they had so many mummies. And there's been the odd homo erectus preserved in the ice or peat bogs. But there was one rare skeleton found in an airtight sarcophagus a few years ago during excavations in Athens when they had to repair the underground. An elaborate sarcophagus that suggested its occupant must have been very important. And in it was a very large skeleton. It was found near the Temple of Theseus in the Athenian market area. So several respectable archaeologists have argued that it could well be the tomb of Theseus himself. The famous Greek hero. You know?'

24

I nodded. I had done a module of Classical Studies at the Multi-Media College in my second year and thought it a complete waste of time. Nearly as mind-numbing as the module on religion.

The doctor went on. 'According to documentary evidence, Theseus was killed or forced to commit suicide on the island of Skyros and buried there, but Herodotus tells us that the skeleton was later brought back to Athens for a state funeral. Anyway the remarkable thing is that you and this skeleton share certain unique genetic features and there are only two other such people on our entire database of 285 million people. So it is almost certain that this man, probably Theseus, is your direct ancestor, remember? The man who killed the Minotaur in the Labyrinth at Crete. This is a fascinating outcome.'

'Thank you,' I said, beginning to feel that the whole exercise was an elaborate fraud.

'As John Buchan put it, yours is the path of a king,' he said, polishing his spectacles benignly.

I felt horribly inadequate. It seemed I might be descended from royalty, but was myself a mere e-pod trader in the timber business.

'The only other thing I know about Theseus,' he went on, 'is that he eloped with a woman called Ariadne who had helped him escape from the labyrinth at Knossos. He made her pregnant and then marooned her on the island of Naxos. But you can look all that upon the web, Mr Thens. That's your half-hour free analysis completed. Thank you for choosing COLDS to do your DNA analysis.

I'd be happy to book a further appointment, but it will be charged at $500 per half hour.'

He shook my hand and with mixed feelings I wandered out to catch the rush-hour roboid. My natural cynicism suggested that I should dismiss the entire episode as some obscure method of squeezing money out of me or my mother. On the other hand there was a feeling of bemused satisfaction that I might become something of a celebrity, that I had two ancestors one of whom at least was seriously famous.

New York, Feb 20th, 2119

I've checked Google and it confirms that Theseus was the grandson of a Greek god. Somebody, probably my mother, once said that I look like a Greek god. I must start asserting myself.

As it happens exactly 500 years ago today a German woman called Eva Susannah Moringer claimed to have been forced into witchcraft by a man with a black beard whom she thought was the Devil. This morning there was another volcanic eruption in Iceland and all transatlantic flights were cancelled for forty-eight hours. It was also the tenth anniversary of paedophilia being reclassified as a genetic disease, so there was a small flag-waving march in Manhattan to celebrate the big day.

My mother had made me take away her copy of *The Laughing Times* and it had a box you had to tick to agree *'I am not a robot.'*
Certainly not.
So what?

Facts are rot,
And I'd be most annoyed
If you called me an android.

There was a news flash that navigation on the River Rhine has come to a standstill due to various invasive creatures from outside Europe. A species of signal crayfish from America has undermined the banks of the river with their extensive burrowing. This has resulted in severe damage to roads and railway lines, whilst zebra mussels from Asia have clogged the water channels with their ultra-hard shells. This has caused flooding north of the Lorelei and silting of the main channels. No cruise barges are allowed beyond Koblenz.

Another new strain in Covid73 has been identified in Brazil where 50,000 plague deaths have already been recorded in the past six months. Fifty tons of vaccine had been accidentally destroyed as a result of confusion over their use-by date due to a computer input error.

CHAPTER TWO

LIFE AND DEATH

The Book of Life begins with a man and a woman in a garden
O. Wilde.

New York, Feb 22, 2119

My feelings of modest elation about my new-found ancestry soon wore off. I had a text message from Ariadne saying she would be away for several days and I became depressed by the feeling that she saw no future in our relationship. To make matters worse I had a number of unprofitable contracts to put through with a lot of tedious virtual paperwork: cheap wood for a Chinese bed-making factory and a board walk to a new visitor centre at the former cruise missile silos near Newark. I scratched my elbow.

That evening the new Episcopal Church of the Americas announced that as a result of the two recent tsunamis it was deleting the word almighty from all references to God. And the Australian government announced that the Barrier Reef had finally disappeared due to sea temperature increases.

§

It took me three days to hollow out a tree to make a boat that would cross the great river. And long before the boat was ready I used to stare at the speed of the river,[1] thinking that if I paddled straight across I would end up swept into the bottomless lake. At nights I would lie scratching my itchy elbow till it was raw.

'Forget it,' my woman kept saying. She didn't like the water and said she would never come with me.

'But on the other side there are plenty of beasts and no hunters,' I would reply. 'Here it's getting harder all the time. We either cross the river or find a tribe to accept us, or one day we'll starve.'

'You should spend more time hunting,' she'd say. 'Instead of chipping away at that cursed tree.'

Five winters ago she had admired everything I did, but now all she seemed to care about was a couple of scrawny rabbits to feed our brood.

A few days later I tried out the canoe in shallow water near the river bank, but it rolled about too much. It was another couple of days before it sat cleanly in the water. Yet still neither my woman nor any of my children would come with me, so in the end I went alone.

The river was much faster and rougher in the middle than it had seemed from the shore. For over an hour I paddled hard, just to avoid being swept downstream, and I made little headway towards the other side. By the time I neared the far shore my legs were shaking and my arms

---

1   *Study of Theo's diaries gives us few clues as to which river this might be, but given evidence elsewhere it was probably the Danube. Further notes on the locations and people referred to in these chapters will be found in the end section of this book.*

stiff with pain. Then suddenly I was tipped over by a wave and as I scrambled to the bank my precious canoe was carried away by the current.

'I'm the first person to cross the great river,' I said aloud to the trees. I had lost my boat, so there was no going back, but I had no regrets.

For five days I enjoyed easy hunting, ate well and did not feel lonely. Then I saw smoke rising from a small hill in the distance and realised that, after all, there were other men on this side of the river. For another week I managed to do all the hunting I needed without being seen by the far-bankers. But then I grew careless. I was jumped on by two of them as I struggled to light my fire. Their words were not like those of our own people and their faces had a different shape. I could see from their expressions that they resented me hunting in their territory. They kicked out my fire and snatched the small deer that I had shot. Then I was aware that there was another far-banker behind me and a huge pain exploded in my head.

New York, Mar 21st, 2119

I am a seed. I am an embryo. I wake. I sleep. I don't know what I am. Or why. I don't know what will happen to my mind when I am dead or remember anything from before I was born.

Ariadne seems to be avoiding me.

I ask why I am on this earth at all when, suddenly, I get a recorded telephone message from the World Court of Justice. 'This is to make you aware that all humans are still welcome on this planet and anyone whose life has

30

been made less happy due to sexual, racial or religious discrimination can claim compensation by contacting any of the undernoted solicitors. For a full list of authorised practitioners press 1, to repeat this message press 2 and to delete it press 3. If you wish to receive no further calls from this number press 8#.

§

After my father disappeared beyond the river there was a time when I was bullied and harassed, but I ran away to the next tribe and found a man there. He gave me skins to wear and better food than the old tribe, so I stayed with him.

New York, March 30th, 2119

One of the biggest problems for an e-pod trader is cash flow. We work on tight margins, our suppliers expect to be paid on time and our customers keep us waiting as long as they can. So it was a huge relief a few weeks after my DNA profiling that I had a reasonable e-cheque from Brazmahog, one of my main clients. I paid off my e-card balances in the nick of time and felt rich enough to ask Ariadne out to the French Franchise. This time she returned my call and I walked round to meet her outside the Geriaid offices. There were thousands of people going in both directions, weaving their way past the open cable man-holes. They mostly looked tense and grim.

'Hi there,' I said when she emerged from her office block five minutes late. Her smile was hesitant, as if she was looking for reassurance that she was the right person in the right place.

'Thanks for coming,' I said and stretched out for her hand.

§

'Your grandfather crossed the great river and was never seen again,' my mother warned me, as she had numerous times before.

'But these days lots of people cross the river,' I said.

'Across the river are the people who burn stones. They're killers. They killed your grandfather.'

'They won't kill me'

So I went and the only reason I wasn't killed was because I made myself useful as a pot-slave. And I learned the secret of killing for myself. The spears and axes of the far-bankers were much sharper and easier to aim than ours, because they used the burnt stone that went red.

New York, Mar 30th 2119 cont.

'What do you feel like drinking?' I asked Ariadne, checking the price of the house red. 'The Chilean Merlot is quite drinkable. It says 2112 was a vintage year.'

'That would be nice. You seem very perky tonight. Had a good day?'

'Yes. Business has improved. I paid up my credit cards.' And I tapped the gold-rimmed plastic on the marble table, enjoying the click and relishing its power to bring happiness, however temporary, though in fact it was just

32

for show, because all I needed to do was tap my finger print.

'Do you really enjoy being an e-pod trader?'

'What has enjoyment got to do with it? It pays the bills. It's what I can do.'

'But don't you want to do something else with your life? Be creative, make a difference or something?'

'What would that be? The world could boil or blow up any time within the next fifty years. Who's going to care? What's the point in leaving anything behind if there's no one left to see it?'

'But surely we should live to our full potential,' she said and clinked her glass of red against mine before tilting it back into her throat. 'What's the point in worrying about the end of the world? Why do you keep scratching your elbow?'

'I don't know. It's just a bad habit.'

§

My mother looked at me hard as she stirred the porridge.

'Why are you so discontented always?' she asked.

'I don't know,' I said.

'Your grandfather started life as pot-slave, but he rose to be a spear-maker for the Prince of the Stones.'

'You've told me that many times before.'

'He used to say how they put up the Stones with the help of the gods.'

'Before you were born?'

'Oh yes. But no other tribe could put up such tall Stones, let alone ones that kissed the sun and moon twice

33

a year. Since we have obeyed the men of the Stones there has never been poor hunting. The gods help us, but not people who fail to put up stones.'

She had told it me all before, many times. And soon it would be time to celebrate the Lifting of the Stones. Every year we did it. Because even with the gods helping it had taken hundreds of men months to drag the Stones to the field, then slowly raise them to full height so that they faced the sunrise. Of course in my grandfather's time men had been bigger than they are now. And stronger. So they kept telling us.

New York, Mar 30th, 2119 cont.

'Even my job isn't perfect,' said Ariadne, delving into her French onion soup. 'I love the caring side of it, but it is all spoiled by money. The latest thing is they're asking us to outsource to the Fourth World. It's more cost-effective to fly old people out to undeveloped countries like Norway and Greece where the wages and the heating bills are low. But it means they're separated from their families. Possibly never see them again.'

'That doesn't seem right,' I said, feeling that for once even an e-pod trader had the moral high ground.

§

Half way through the next year my mother died, a few days after my third brother was born, as if it was meant that the size of our family should always stay the same. From about that time less fuss was made about the Stones. Most people just took them for granted, not appreciating the huge effort our ancestors had made to put them up. And all the Chief Man of the Stones wanted was plenty of fresh meat plus a girl or two, without having to hunt for them himself. But perhaps we were wrong, for the next year the rain never stopped and food became scarce. So I said to my tribe that we must try to cross the mountains to new land.

New York, Mar 30th, 2119 continued again

'Anyway I'm rather good at being an e-pod trader,' I said defiantly as I began my second glass of Merlot. 'So what's wrong with it?'

'Nothing,' answered Ariadne, spooning out a mussel from its shell. 'I love moules frites.'

'And why do we make such an effort to keep old people alive?' I added. 'The longer you fend off heart attacks the more likely you are to die of cancer or Alzheimer's.'

'We don't try to keep them alive for the sake of it,' she said, looking hurt. 'Just to make them comfortable.'

'Sorry.' I said, thinking how attractive her elbows were. 'I shouldn't have said that. But we can't all be creatives and carers. Someone has to make money and keep the economy going.'

'Why?' she asked, giving me an undermining grin. 'What's it all about? We don't really need all these luxuries and fancy holidays.'

'Don't you like holidays?'

'I do actually,' she grinned.

'Anyway people need work,' I said. 'So we have to suffer the enjoyment of luxuries and fashionable clothes.

Otherwise there wouldn't be enough work to go around. And someone has to pay for all the roboid services and the geriaid. More than half the world's population are now over eighty.'

§

By the time we started crossing the mountains my father was too weak to keep up a normal pace, so he asked to be left behind and we had no choice but to leave him where he was.

'We may not see you again,' I said.

'It's my own fault,' he replied. 'I should have shown more respect for the Stones. Don't forget them.'

We climbed for four days through airless valleys clouded with tiny flies and thick with ankle-grabbing bracken. Then the air became sweeter and the hill was covered with huge boulders and stunted flowers peeking between their cracks. This lasted a day and at the top it was very cold, but then we started to go down again and felt renewed vigour. Suddenly we came to sunlight and a sparkling waterfall, then a glade where a brown young woman was bathing. She didn't hide herself like the river women, or even pretend resistance when I moved to take her. So my brothers left me to her and we lay on the spongy moss by the stream, she smiling at everything that I did.

Now the seed had been replanted on the far side of the mountains. I dozed off in the sun and woke as a wooden spear was thrust into my chest. The pain came and disappeared.

'But what is life for then?' asked Ariadne.

'You're enjoying that steak and French fries aren't you? Life is fun and we have to work a bit to pay for it. Nothing more complicated than that.'

'And after you've quashed your hunger then you have other appetites to gratify, I suppose,' she said looking at me obliquely.

'If you insist,' I responded gallantly.

'No, I'm sorry,' she said. 'I'm not satisfied with what you're saying. There has to be more.'

'Music, art.'

'Yes, but...'

'You can go to nose concerts, symphonies of perfumes to sooth and entertain the olfactory nerves.'

'Or go the C.O.L.D.S Temple if your soul gets hungry.'

'If there is such a thing as a soul?' I said, expecting no answer.

She wiped her lips delicately with the three-ply paper tissue printed with the fleur-de-lis motif of the French Franchise.

'I admit to having a good appetite for food,' she said, grinning. 'But lust isn't so simple, is it? For you men it always symbolises some kind of conquest. A victory or a successful siege and you have to keep the momentum going to feed your vanity.'

'I hadn't thought of it that way,' I lied.

'Liar,' she said.

Later that night there was news that a group of radicalised Confucian monks had stormed the Forbidden City in Beijing and massacred two hundred of the New Red Guard who were on duty at the time. In addition, due to no rainfall for five consecutive years, the Donald J. Trump Desert west of Las Vegas had increased by a further 3000 square miles making it larger than the Sahara. The city of Karachi had now been finally evacuated due to average temperatures of 55 degrees in the shade.

CHAPTER THREE

MATRIARCHS AND PATRIARCHS?

The last temptation is the greatest treason.
T.S. Eliot

New York, French Franchise, 12.30 am, Mar 31st, 2119

'How many units of wine have we had?' asked Ariadne.

'Maybe four each,' I said. 'Are you worried?'

'Not really.'

I glanced at the bottle label and it read 9.4 units per bottle DRINK RESPONSIBLY.

'Who is really responsible?' I asked.

'Everyone or no one,' said Ariadne.

'If everyone drank responsibly the average age of dying might rise from 97 to 99,' I suggested. 'But the decline in liver disease might mean a rise in heart attacks.'

§

They say my grandfather was a giant from the north who made love to a wood nymph, but he was killed by a monster before my mother was born. Then she and her tribe moved further south each year for hunting and fruit in the trees until, after many years, they settled in the big plains and grew barley. For the next three generations the gods had prophesied our tribe would be ruled by women.

'I need a consort,' I said to the best spear-thrower in the tribe. 'I am destined to be queen, but my consort will obey me in killing the last of the kings.'

'Obey you?' he queried.

'In everything,' I said. 'The gods of the Great Stones have said a woman must rule for three generations. I need you to help me produce a strong daughter to carry on the line.'

He nodded.

'Go tell the king that he is a cretinous coward and he will have to fight you single-handed for his honour. You can beat him, can't you?'

'Of course. I have ten years on him at least,' he answered, looking less comfortable than I had hoped. But at least that ensured he would not be overconfident and careless.

'Once the king is dead you will get your reward.'

New York, 12.40 am Mar 31st, 2119

'That was a lovely meal, Theo,' said Ariadne 'But look, you don't have to take me back to my flat. I want to get to know you better first.'

'I'm in no hurry,' I lied.

'And I've got an early start tomorrow. One of the units I look after is in Newark and there's been an outbreak of 8th variant CJD. We've got to blitz the place clean and empty the freezers. The youngest person in that unit is 120, so we have to be careful.'

I led Ariadne up the stair past the Toulouse Lautrec posters and we hopped onto the open-top roboid through Central Park. I held her hand as the lights blurred past.

Back in the flat my answer-phone was blinking and there was a message from the E-Bank Consortium warning that three million account holders had been hacked by a gang based in the Congo. Then it added that this announcement had just been made for training purposes to test the reactions of customers

§

I am the third of the three queens who it was prophesied would rule the tribe. My grandmother was the first and, though she had several daughters, she also had one healthy son. She had no choice but to let him be sacrificed to the Great Stones. There was no other way. My own mother bore a daughter, myself, and five sons, all of whom were luckily weak and died in early childhood. She herself lived to the remarkable age of forty before she died leaving me to be queen. I have three healthy sons and no daughters, so the gods have signalled that a man will be the next ruler of the tribe.

During my lifetime we have moved southwards over two rivers and three lines of mountains, and each time we had to kill all the previous inhabitants of our new homeland. But they were always smaller and weaker than us. Some of them were slow because they ate too much fat meat, others drank bread beer or chewed hemp and some were so busy farming that they never bothered to practise their weapon skills. A fatal mistake. And so at last we

41

came to the sea where our tribe is ordained to settle for the rest of time.

New York, Apr 2nd, 2119

Next day when I dropped off Ariadne outside her flat she gave me a light moist kiss on the mouth, but once she had turned away she didn't look round. When I got back to my own place there was an email waiting on my flip screen:

Your e-cheque from Brazmahog not honoured. Penalty for re-presenting $40. Note overdraft penalty points also incurred. Press e.# to acknowledge.

In a sweat I tapped the screen to check if there had been some simple fault. Brazmahog had been built up by a successful drug baron who found respectability by replanting large swathes of the old Amazon Forest. It was always my biggest debtor and on the strength of the cheque I'd paid off my e-cards and treated Ariadne to quite a generous supper. Half my turnover for the month had now vanished and, unless I could sort it, my wrist-top would be disconnected in two days and I would be out of business with at least six weeks to follow before I could reconnect. By that time half my clients would have gone elsewhere.

Perhaps it was the recaffeinated coffee or the veggy steak or the heat and humidity or the memory of that kiss or my anger at Brazmahog, but I couldn't sleep for a long time. My elbow itched. In fact I had only just drifted off into unconsciousness when the early buzzer on my wrist-top gave its first warning purr. I woke up to the realisation that my comfortable world with which I had been far from satisfied had now collapsed and I wanted it back again.

§

'My son-in-law Aegeus is an idiot taking up with that whore Medea,' I said when my daughter Aethra brought her baby son to see me, King Pittheus, in Troezen. 'Scared of his own shadow,' I went on. 'How he manages to hold on to the crown of Athens I fail to understand. And he dumped you for Jason's trollop. What a messy divorce that was.'

'Please look after my baby, father,' said my daughter, biting her lip.

'Bring him up to be a good warrior. Then send him to Athens when he's ready.'

'Of course I will, Aethra. Of course I will. Little Theesy Weesy. Look at his face. He has the look of my own father, the god Poseidon.'

My wife winked behind my back as she always does when I mention my divine parenthood. Those of us fathered by gods are the privileged few and not to be sneered at.

I tickled the baby Theseus' tummy and Aethra smiled for the first time in years. I noticed she had a slight rash on her elbow, the way I sometimes did myself.

'At least he doesn't look like daddy Aegeus,' I added. 'More like that old flame of yours, Hercules, if you ask me.' I winked at Aethra but she looked the other way.

'Maybe he wasn't all that bright, Hercules. But what a worker.'

New York, Apr 3rd, 2119

One minute I'm a respected e-pod trader, winner of the local waterbike heats, supporter of several charities and sub-leader of my tower block, the next I'm in overdraft penalties, threatened with the loss of everything, including my chance to impress Ariadne. All because some thoughtless nerd at Brazmahog thinks he can play a fast one and send me a dud e-cheque. The previous day I'd worried that I was no more than an average blue collar, not even on the first step to becoming precinct mayor let alone a city consul, but now I am just desperate to get back at least my middle-class base. Gone are the longings for distant adventures. There is enough excitement just in escaping from bank penalties without discovering new planets or rescuing virgins. All I want now is to regain my mediocrity. So I remember the old song my father used to sing-

I'm really lucky not to be
A mouse born in a cattery.
A snail in France or a Salem witch,
A Warsaw Jew or a slug in a ditch,
Condemned to starve in African wars
Condemned to pain by genetic flaws
Or prone to suffer from manic depression
A victim of sexual repression
Or one of the long-term unemployed
I should be overjoyed.

It was exactly a hundred years since the English began testing their 799 Hydroflex railway engine. The latest Covid mutation B7183 is spreading rapidly through East Africa, so all flights have been cancelled and the Astra-Pfizer conglomerate has promised a new vaccine within six weeks. However, this may be part of a disinformation campaign organised by North China to undermine South China's investments in that area.

CHAPTER FOUR

LIFE IS A LABYRINTH

*The good critic is he who relates the adventures of
his soul in the midst of masterpieces*
A. France

New York, Apr 4th, 2119

Next day I rang the chief buyer at Brazmahog, but each
time I tried he was either engaged or out, or pretending
to be in a meeting. Then I rang the e-Bank, but in those
days it was so totally automated that a staff man only
came in once a week. They had a pre-recorded complaints
procedure that involved pressing various digits on
your handset, but by the time I had listened to a dozen
questions at my own peak-time expense I realised I was
getting nowhere. The trouble with automated listening
machines is they don't grasp the subtleties and peculiar
words like Brazmahog completely fox them. At any
moment my wrist-top would be cut off with a 200%
penalty and a six-week reconnection delay if I was lucky.
Then they would start to strip me of my pin numbers,
change the bar code on my apartment entry and cancel
my roboid pass.

Suddenly, instead of secure and confident I felt
weak and inadequate. My thirst for Ariadne went dry.
The streets seemed hostile. I felt as though I was dead.
Admittedly with welfare I would never actually starve, but

it would be cold at night in Cardboard City or under the flyovers. And what is life except being looked up to by at least a few other people? A man without his pin numbers might as well be dead and even my fingerprint would no longer be recognised.

§

The track from Megara wound up through rows of gnarled olive trees.

'Watch out, young Theseus,' said an old man, as I set off at last from my grandfather's palace to seek the throne of Athens which was mine by right. But several people had already warned me that the road to Athens was infested with robbers and wild beasts.

'I'll be all right, old fellow,' I said condescendingly, buckling on the sword left for me by my mother to wear as soon as I was strong enough. I knew that the three savage monsters Corynetes, Sinis and Scyron would all have to be destroyed before I could reach my city of destiny. Not to mention the obscene hag Phaea, who it was said gave herself as a prostitute to passing travellers, then robbed them whilst they slept and slit their throats.

But naturally I had a well-thought-out plan. Knowing full well that each of the creatures would be lying in wait for me I took the precaution of leaving the road and crawling through the rocks and scrub that lay above it. I did so slowly, partly because the going was rough and partly to exhaust the patience of the dimwitted scoundrels who wanted to ambush me.

The first one to deal with was Corynetes, who I had heard was a one-eyed giant of great strength but limited intelligence who had been preying on the merchants of Megara for some years. So dodging amongst the myrtle and tamarisk I managed to reach a position just above his look-out rock without him spotting me. Then all I had to do was bring my sword down on his head. My aim was not quite as perfect as I intended, but it was good enough to kill him.

Sinis and Scyron were not quite as easy as they had a well-camouflaged cave from which they leapt out on travellers at the last minute to steal their loose change. However, by using my initiative I managed to locate their cave by its disgusting smell. Then I had to lure them out into the open by feigning a fall just round the corner from the cave and groaning as if badly hurt. Luckily they came out one at a time and I'd hacked off the arm of Sinis before I had to charge at the lumbering Scyron.

My next obstacle was the hairy female monster Phaea who usually strangled or stabbed her victims after they had enjoyed her dubious charms. I had been tipped off that she might succumb to flattery, so approaching her hovel I cooed in a soft voice that I had heard rumours of her loveliness.

'Oh wondrous beauty,' I cried.

'Who's that?'

'I am just a young lad on his way to Athens and heard tales of your wondrous charms.'

She peeked out just far enough for me to ram my spear into her hairy thigh.

New York, Apr 7th, 2119

Three days later I at last got through to Brazmahog, but it was only a robot who took the call. 'There's a twenty-four-hour backlog on e-data,' it said. 'The server's down, but I'll check the files as soon as I can and get back to you.'

It was an old one, but you never know. That afternoon Ariadne rang me and I said I was going to be tied up for a few days. She said rather sulkily that she was off to Newark anyway to deal with the CJD crisis.

The news announced that average waiting times in hospitals throughout North America had now been increased to 73 weeks. The Islamic Republic of Boko Haram had chosen its first female caliph, a woman of nineteen who had immediately declared war on six sub-Saharan nations. Queen Elizabeth III of Ulster and the Falklands had celebrated her 80th birthday.

§

So at last I reached Athens to claim my father's inheritance. For years he had refused to acknowledge me, using that pathetic slander about my mother's affair with Hercules to keep me from getting what I deserved. He had never expected that I would negotiate the dangerous road from Megara or be strong enough to use the great sword. Not only that, but I arrived leading the wild bull of Marathon through the city gate as a bonus. Yet neither my father Aegeus nor my step-mother Medea were the least bit pleased to see me.

'There is the sword fashioned by our ancestor, the great sword-maker,' I said stabbing it into the wooden floor of his throne room. Yet Aegeus was still looking for excuses to disown me, so that he could make the wretched sons of Medea his heirs instead of me.

'The Bull of Marathon is all very well, but you must still tackle the even bigger bull of Crete, the minotaur which eats seven of our maidens and seven of her young men every year.'

It was typical of his weakness that he had allowed the Cretans to blackmail him into this human tribute.

'If I succeed will you acknowledge me as your rightful heir?'

'Of course, Theseus,' he said, but I saw him wink sideways to Medea, and she in turn winked at her cringing sons who lurked beside the throne.

New York, Apr 9th, 2119

Two days later I got through to a Brazmahog senior exec on her direct line.

'Certainly a replacement e-cheque has been keyed into the server,' she said.

'But I'll need another digital signature and my director's in Sao Paolo till Thursday. It should only take a couple of days after that to download it into your account.'

'This is impossible,' I said. 'Our terms of business....' I hesitated before spelling it out.

'If you don't want to deal with us any more that's up to you,' she replied sharply.

'No, no. It's not that,' I backtracked, sweat prickling my armpits. 'It's just a matter of cash flow.'

'As I'm sure you know on all projects we practice just-in-time plus eighty days payment terms. This minor mishap will only mean an extra seven days on top of that. If our terms don't suit you there are plenty of your competitors who would take over from you.'

'Forget what I said, please.'

§

'I hate Skyros, 'I said, kicking a stone off the path as we walked up to the citadel.

'You're turning into an old man, Theseus,' said Lycomedes, king of the wretched little island.' Your hair's falling out. A lot of good it does having divine blood in your veins.'

'Do you have to make mock of me?'

'It's decent of us to let you live here at all. You're lucky to be alive after being kicked off your throne. Most deposed kings are killed right away. How come they wanted rid of you anyway?'

'Ingratitude,' I said. 'I saved thirteen of the finest youths in Athens from the man-eating bull of Knossos. I liberated the city from a dreadful curse, but they soon forgot.'

'But you got inside help, didn't you? From the Princess Ariadne, Minos' daughter, whom you conned into helping you find your way out of the labyrinth. Then you made her pregnant and dumped her on the beach at Naxos. What kind of behaviour was that?'

'She was a brown-skinned Cretan,' I said. 'I was briefly infatuated and grateful, but she would never have fitted in as a queen of Athens.'

He stared at me raising his eyebrows defiantly.

'So you got rid of her. And you got rid of your father too, didn't you?'

'What happened to him was a pure misunderstanding,' I said. 'I quite forgot that my father had muttered something about black sails being the signal for disaster. In the excitement of my triumph we sailed back to Athens with the black sails still hoisted. He came to the wrong conclusion and threw himself off the cliff in distress.'

'So then you took over as king. How very convenient.' said Lycomedes, staring at me pointedly.

'The interests of the state were my main concern,' I said stiffly. 'Individuals are there only to serve the state, after all.'

'Of course. So you then achieved some famous victories?'

'Yes. I beat the Centaurs within a year,' I said, glad at last to be on the moral high ground again.

'You slaughtered a few harmless wild horsemen living in the hills,' he said. 'And you persuaded people that it was a major victory.'

This man Lycomedes eventually succeeded in irritating me with his sarcastic comments about my wars, but for the time being he was my host and I did not dare offend him. 'There were hundreds of them,' I protested. 'Such unbelievably fine riders that they could never be dismounted. My second great victory was even harder.'

'But that was against the Amazons. Female warriors. No?'

'Female perhaps, but not in the normal sense,' I added, aware that I was panting hard as we neared the top of the hill. 'They were the most skilled archers in all of Greece.'

'Pioneers of mastectomy as I've heard,' he responded tartly. 'To make their aim better.'

'Quite so. And there were two thousand of them threatening Athens. In total I had ten years of hard fighting to clear the area round the city of trouble makers and rebels.'

'I'm sure,' said Lycomedes, turning to me as we reached he top of the path. 'But an end has to come, Theseus. Your own people had enough of you. Now I'm sorry to say it, but so have I. You can't pretend that you're happy living down in that little hovel I gave you. Since you're used to a palace. But I can't let you share my citadel. See that ship coming into the harbour?'

I looked down from the cliff top and saw a small ship approaching, dark against the setting sun.

'What colour is her sail?' he asked.

'Blackish, I suppose,' I said.

'Exactly,' he said. 'You remember the signal, Theseus? What your father thought?' he added, and taking me by the elbow he led me close to the edge of the cliff. Being a man of honour I saw I had no choice but to jump. Not even my father had shirked that.

New York, Apr 10th, 2119

This was the night they announced that half the
population of western Europe had been injected with
a tainted flu vaccine and it was likely a million deaths
would result, especially amongst older people. Some
said it was a bug that had survived in a dead mammoth
buried in the ice cap till global warming melted the ice
and released it. It was also reported that the Al Khalifa
Tower in Dubai, at one time the tallest building in the
world and now well over a hundred years old, was to be
demolished due to rust infestations in its steel core. Child
pornography had been legalised in Colombia and Mexico,
despite opposition from the regional archbishop. Estonia
had defaulted on its debts. There were such high levels
of obesity in New Zealand that the government was now
offering free zimmers for 90% of the adult population.

Then came www.god/@sky.com with ecclesiastical
background music:

'Oh twenty-second century God you're not what you were
No longer our father or lord, are you there?
No long white beard, no kindly face
You're not on high or in any place,
Not actually listening to any prayers
Let alone answering. Who cares?
Who gives us now our daily bread?
Is it organic chemistry instead?
Who can forgive our trespasses here?
Your wrath no longer causes fear,
We want to be led into temptation

To escape the aimless new frustration,
Presumably you're not inside my head.
Will you still not be there when I am dead?
The power and the glory are gone; are you trying?
World without end, but you don't interfere,
No will, no kingdom. But you must be here
In our desire, our panic, a metaphorical wraith
Wandering in the nuclear space of faith.
Amen I suppose.'

After this came another advertisement for waterproof pants for both sexes. Also a large proportion of the population of Los Angeles was being evacuated due to the drastic reduction in the supply of water to the city caused by the main reservoirs drying out with no prospect of them filling up again. Belgium now had 55% of its population diagnosed with senile dementia, and it was feared that the nation would soon no longer be able to sustain its critical services.

CHAPTER FIVE

A TALE OF THREE CITIES

Let us determine to die here and we will conquer
General B. Bee

New York, Apr 13th, 2119

My office is on the left-hand side of my sitting room, but
it is a ritual for me to move across from the breakfast table
and strap on my wrist-top at exactly eight thirty each
morning. Sometimes nothing much happens for an hour
or two and I water my coffee-plant or clean my e-pod:
then of course three queries come at once, throwing my
system into chaos.

This week I remained in a state of continual anxiety
waiting for my Brazmahog cheque to be cleared, fending
off the e-pod credit controller, a particularly officious
young woman, arguing with my automated bank manager
and keeping at bay the disconnection cowboys. It was
typical of the peaks and troughs of my business life. More
troughs really. And nothing was happening in Brazil
of course, but I had to deal with a just-in-time deal of
genetically modified walnut wanted by Mercedes for the
dashboards on their new model. Then there was a tricky
teak tender for a chain of boutique hotels in Spitzbergen.
In normal circumstances I would have found it was
exciting enough for me to forget the tedium of data
input, but financial worries made me feel insecure and

too stressed to take any initiative with Ariadne. Luckily however she phoned me.

'It's my turn to pay,' she said.

I mumbled unconvincingly.

'Make it Il Duce Pizzas at six,' she said.

I did a quick back-up, for with the current computer viruses I didn't trust any of the big data stores. Then I headed for the street.

'You don't seem yourself,' she said perceptively as we settled down at a red-clad table with miniature Italian flags. There were iconic images of the great hero Mussolini all round the walls.

'I'm fine,' I said stoically.

'There's something different about you,' she said.

'Is there? It's just I had a big e-cheque bounce and its taken time to get the replacement.'

'A lot of money?'

'For me, yes a lot, because I've already paid most of it out to suppliers.'

'Thank you for being honest with me,' she said and squeezed my hand.

'Besides, I think I prefer you when you're a little bit down. Not quite so aggressive.'

'Oh,' I said. 'But I don't like myself so much.'

'Anyway I haven't exactly had a great day either. Newark is a disaster. No apparent cause of the CJD and two of our patients on life support.'

'I'm sorry.'

'Thanks. And I think that all relationships should be based on absolute honesty. So tell me how many women have you slept with?'

I made a show of counting on my fingers, reluctant to admit my failure in that department, then said 'Six or ....' before hesitating.

'Sure?'

'Well, actually only one,' I said. 'Most of the time I've just been too busy or poor and even that one was a bit of a drunken foul-up.'

'It's nothing to be ashamed of. Do you want to ask me the same question?'

'I suppose so,' I said, but I wasn't sure that I really did.

'None properly,' she said. 'I tried out the warm-up bits with a few, but then decided the men weren't right for me. I actually believe in a monogamy system.'

'Do you?' I said. 'That's unusual these days. Most of my older friends are on number three or four already.' Then I added, 'By the way there's one other thing you should know about me. I had a DNA profile done last month. Not my idea, but my mother was desperate for me to do it. She's worried about my everlasting soul or something. Anyway laugh if you like but according to them I'm related to a Greek god.'

'I won't laugh. You do just look a tiny, very tiny, bit like one.' She hesitated, then added, 'Well, maybe not.'

As it happens this is the 200th anniversary of the Amritsar Massacre in which at least 370 (perhaps really about 1000) Sikhs were shot dead by a panicking British general called Dyer who could never understand where he'd gone wrong.

§

'So you're Theseus' bastard, are you?' said the Trojan man-at-arms to my brother, who was twenty and regarded as one of the noblest youths on Naxos.

'No I'm not,' he said, but pointed at me and added, 'My half-brother over there is the legitimate son of the great Theseus. Our mother was his wife until he left her. Then she married my father, Onaros.'

'I thought Ariadne hanged herself,' said the soldier.

'Just a malicious rumour,' I said, though I was far from sure of the real story.

'So why did you two Greeks volunteer to fight for Troy against your own people?'

'We like what Troy stands for,' I answered. 'A small sustainable empire. The mainland Greeks are just obsessed with image.'

'Lucky for you, you chose the winning side, then,' said the Trojan. 'We have survived. The siege is over and the Greeks are heading off back home. The king has asked you to come and receive his thanks before you leave.'

My brother and I with several others from the islands who'd helped in the defence were led into the hall of Priam's palace. On the dais I could not help noticing one woman of great beauty. She wore a loose white gown which accentuated the colour of her bare arms and showed the same colour inside the gown where her flesh touched the cloth. Her hair was golden red, her eyes flashing blue but she strutted across with undisguised arrogance.

'That's Helen,' said our guide. 'She had a bastard by your father when she was fourteen, I believe. What a bitch.'

'What a father,' I said under my breath.

King Priam briefly thanked us all with elegant old-fashioned manners. Then we set off through the seaward gate of the old city towards our ship. As we went out the Trojans were laughingly hauling in a huge statue of a horse which the Greeks had left behind as a token of peace.

New York, Apr 14th, 2119

'Nice pizza,' I said. 'I love anchovies.'

'Do you want to start a serious relationship?' asked Ariadne, grinding some black pepper.

'I fancy it,' I said. 'But you're right, we should know everything about each other first. I've done some bad things. I wet my trousers aged three when I saw Star Wars Part thirty-six. I once misled the authorities on an illegal batch of Honduras hardwood. I don't know what I believe in. I sometimes pretend I'm out when my mother calls.'

She looked at me raising her eyebrows.

'So you're not exactly perfect? Well, neither am I really. My father was a cable-duct repair man and my mother's an online audit clerk working from home like you do. I have two brothers: one's a green-space ranger and the other's a compressed air rep. We all get on. We have no secrets. I look after twenty geriaid units with around fifty paying pensioners in each unit. It's my job to make sure every bed is filled, that they pay the proper rate without lawyers skimming off commission, that the unit managers don't cheat on the food allowance or pinch the old folks' jewellery. But the biggest headaches are hygiene and fire drills. We have no insurance cover against bugs. Now back to you.'

'Well,' I said, 'I get people to cut down swathes of tropical rain forest so that rich people can get veneer on their cocktail cabinets and several species of moth are made extinct every working day due to their habitat being destroyed. Even when we replant the forest with genetically modified hardwoods for fast replacement, the monkeys don't like it so much. I don't seem able to find any other way of making a living and anyway these days nearly everything you do does damage to something else. And if I don't do it somebody else will.'

'We can only do our best,' she said. 'Global warming has slowed down now that oil is almost a thing of the past. How about hobbies?'

'I like to read Russian novels, canoeing, e-biking and I collect rare twenty-first century ink cartridges. How about you?'

'Believe it or not I like sewing, though I hardly ever do it. I eat too much and go swimming. And I'm on the local committee for KPSS, that's Keep the Population the Same Size, if you've heard of us. We're trying to encourage population growth in the old world, especially amongst nations like the Albanians which are at risk of becoming extinct. We want to keep the world's biodiversity, not just end up with no one but Chinese and Indians.'

'Fair enough,' I said.

'I'll be frank,' she went on. 'I'm looking for a long-term partner, but so many of my friends seem to have married sadists or exhibitionists or obsessives of one kind or another, fitness or work freaks, food or drug addicts or whatever. It's depressing.'

'It must be,' I said, wondering how many of these categories might apply to me.

'What I want to know is if you really care about living trees as well as planks? Animals, birds, mountains?'

'I think I do.'

'You really sound as if you mean it. My backside.'

'That as well,' I said.

§

'This looks like the end,' said the Captain of Tiryns, grey with exhaustion. We had none of us slept for about five days as wave after wave of northern invaders crashed at the timbers of the city gate.

I tried to smile back at him. 'My grandfather always used to tell us how they thought the Greeks had lost the war against Troy, but they hadn't. There's always a chance so long as you're still alive.'

'Look at the black smoke on the hillside over there, That is the great city of Mycenae and it has been burning for four days already. Once we ruled half the world. Now this is the last battered outpost. And the water in our well is green.'

'One more effort?' I asked.

'Yes, but I release you, my friend. You've served in our garrison for two years and done good work. Get out through the back gate. That's an order. Go back to Naxos. Here, take this gold cup.' And he handed me a beautiful goblet embossed with images of the gods at play.

In the circumstances there seemed little point in disobeying his orders, for it was true; I had done my best and there was little point in dying for a lost cause.

New York, Apr 16th, 2119

I woke up to the shrill sound of my desktop and my wrist-top both simultaneously pinging the one hour to memory-wipe warning. All my data would be obliterated at eight o'clock unless I got an extension from credit control. I tried to raise them at the e-terminal, but it was the usual digitised voice which could only respond to a pre-set formula of questions and had no software application for coping with excuses, let alone compassionate grounds which in fact amounted to little more than self pity. And to make matters worse it insisted on its right to record my grovelling excuses for training purposes. Doubtless the IT students would have a good laugh at my expense.

Having failed after ten minutes of trying I rang Brazmahog. This time it was a pre-recorded tape. All staff had been suspended on full pay pending an inquiry into illegal substances. Of course we all knew they planted umpteen hectares with coke bushes. How could a South American company survive any other way? So what was new? This wasted a further ten minutes and I spent the same again trying to get hold of my clients in Myanmar and Venezuela. Now I was down to my last few minutes, my elbow itched and the sweat was trickling round the edge of my deodorant, my heart panic-stricken, my brain almost paralysed and my libido, if I'd thought about it, totally unmanned. As a last possibility I tried my friend in Campeachy Bay and got him at the fourth attempt.

'How are you?' I said.

'Cut the crap. What do you want?'

'If you could put off endorsing that last e-cheque of mine for a week I would be eternally grateful.'

'Four days, Theo. I can give you four days. Not a minute more.'

'That's wonderful.' I replied. 'Muchas gracias, amigo.'

§

'How many vineyards do you own?' asked Zoe, the young priestess my parents wanted me to marry, as we walked by the beach near Grotta.

'Twenty,' I replied, wondering if she was calculating my worth just in terms of jars of wine. 'My grandfather was a hereditary priest of Bacchus and started off with two, but he fought in the barbarian wars and brought back enough gold to buy another fifteen. Then he built ships and became Lord of Grotta. The rest were added by my father in his turn.'

'You've certainly made sure they're well tended,' she said. 'They all look so neat and healthy.'

'Just like you,' I said and she smiled. 'But it's not going to be easy from now on.'

'Why?' she asked, as if she was genuinely unaware of the crisis around us.

'Lygdamis resents me being Lord of Grotta and owning so much land,' I answered. 'Now he is the tyrant of Naxos and wants no rivals. He has armed thugs everywhere. They keep accidentally smashing our wine presses or riding horses through our vines or cracking our best storage jars.'

'Can't you stop them?' Zoe asked.

'He's got three hundred men trained in the latest sword play. I just have a few retainers,' I shrugged. 'Why should I ask them to risk their lives for the sake of my vanity?'

'Lygdamis is obscene. Decadent and obese,' she added.

'I hear he has his eye on you as an extra concubine. That could be safer for you than marrying me.'

'That kind of safety doesn't appeal very much,' she said.

So I began to look at her more seriously and showed her round the terraced yards. Over the next few weeks our friendship developed on a more relaxed footing. A month or so later I was invited to the blessing of the huge new statue of Apollo which Lygdamis had commissioned and whose face bore an uncanny resemblance to his own. The massive marble figure four times my height, and nearly five times his, was designed to commemorate his rule. As one of the hereditary priests of Bacchus and Lord of Grotta, it was my duty to take part in the ceremony, even though I deplored the huge tax he had levied to pay for it. As I arrived the fat little prince was bouncing around, yet cast paranoid glances at every flicker of my face muscles. Then he took me aside.

'I don't like your attitude,' he said. 'Perhaps this island doesn't need a Lord of Grotta as well as a Prince of Naxos. Think about it.'

That night three more of our wine presses were smashed and the next day I married Zoe.

'It'll be a hard life,' I said. 'We daren't appear on the streets of Grotta and I think that none of our farms are safe. There's no choice but to live up in the mountains till we can board a ship and head west.'

'I don't care where we go,' she said.

'There's a city called New Naxos being built on the island of Sicily,' I said. 'A lot of our people have gone there already. It's a fourteen-day sail over the open sea.'

'We'll survive,' she said. 'We'll make it.'

New York, Chinatown, Apr 17, 2119

Standing waiting for a carry-out.

This was a night when the workers in the world's biggest call centre in Greenland went on strike in a protest against a two-degree reduction in their central heating temperature. The result was that some pre-recorded discs used to train apprentice operators were sent out accidentally by the unmanned mainframe. One warned customers of the Bank of India to withdraw all their money as the bank was about to default, and this had the effect that the bank did actually default, causing a string of other bankruptcies including the Golden Temple of Amritsar which was already heavily in debt due to refurbishment costs. The second was to recall all Hondamitsu hybrids made since 2110 for potentially fatal self-combustion issues that turned out to be for training purposes only. The third was to announce a totally fictitious award scheme for carbon dioxide savers that prompted hundreds of thousands to give up travel for several weeks resulting in the collapse of several national roboid-lines. Meanwhile the Singing Monks have released another single with lyrics by the Persian stand-up comedian Ben Khomeini, one of my favourites.

Looking at life it's hard to believe
There ever was a god
With any power to control or relieve
Our suffering. Though it may seem odd
If he/she was responsible for creation,
He/she's also guilty of devastation,
Of cruelty on a massive scale,
For pain, for dirt, for snow and hail,
For flesh-eating scavengers, rot and cancer.
There simply is no suitable answer
To justify anything quite so evil
Unless he/she's not god but the devil

Still no answers, but I liked the tune.

Then suddenly everything went dark. The fuses from the wind-farms had packed up again.

CHAPTER SIX

RELATIONSHIPS AND REBELLIONS

All wars are planned by old men in council rooms apart.

Grantland Rice

New York, Apr 19, 2119

The four days respite given me by my Belizean contact took some pressure off my delicate finances, but I needed more time and more money to stop the e-bank from foreclosing on my ledger and wiping clean my software, both tasks in which they seemed to find great sadistic pleasure. Luckily on the third day I got a reasonable order with an advance. It was for teak decking on a new luxury trimaran designed for the Yokosuka Ferry. Ever since Kyoto had been destroyed by an earthquake and half the coast flooded by a tsunami they'd been trying to build a new city at Fukushima. Luckily the Japanese were quick payers, despite all their problems.

'I admire the way you cope with all the stress, Theo,' said Ariadne when I met her for a coffee. 'I suppose I'm not as understanding as I should be. I've always been in the caring sector where it's people not money that are supposed to matter. I shouldn't have been so pompous to you at Il Duce's.'

'I love it when you apologise,' I said and kissed her as a reward. 'Why not let me show off my cooking tomorrow night. I make a mean shish-kebab.'

'Okay,' she said, grinning.

§

As it turned out our voyage from Naxos to Sicily was even more hazardous than I had been led to expect, yet if anything Zoe was a better sailor than I was and remained cheerful throughout the storms. It was only in the last few days, when we ran out of fresh water and food that she began to lose heart. Then, as soon as we set foot on dry land again, she was herself and delighted with our new city.

Most of my money had gone to the ship's captain, but there was plenty of land available along the coast and I had brought with me some vine roots which had survived, so I knew we would manage. I was no longer the lord of anywhere, but we were free and had nothing more to fear from the tyrant Lygdamis. In fact three years after setting up our new home there came news that Lygdamis had been driven out of Naxos, but we had no desire to return. We loved Sicily and that is where our family would be born.

New York. Apr 20th, 2119

The next afternoon I raced round the Cutgroce hypermarket lobbing packets, tins, bottles into the trolley, taramasalata, stuffed olives, real beef in vine leaves and lamb kebab pieces pre-marinated in a burned hazel flavour essence, a bottle each of Retsina and Samos, honey cake. There was no doubt the meal would be Greek.

'Very nice,' said Ariadne as she scraped her plate after the first course with loving thoroughness. 'So you can cook a bit. So can I. But would we get on?'

'Why not?' I replied, my speech just a little slurred because I'd kept testing the wine while I was cooking.

'You seem unsure of your motivation. You don't take it all seriously. If it's just sex...'

She left the next bit unsaid.

'It's that fancy DNA test,' I said. 'It's upset my equilibrium. I used to think I was more or less a nobody, so any minor achievement would be enough. But now I've got far more to live up to. One of my ancestors was a king, a slayer of giants and dragons, even if he did dump his first wife. I on the other hand have never done anything more adventurous than biking through the Staten Island Tunnel. I'm just one of a million e-pod traders scattered round the world. Politics has always seemed to need too much grovelling to attract me and I only half accept any religion. So I just plod on trying to keep my head above water and do no harm. There are times when I can't remotely remember why I'm alive.'

'You don't have to be ambitious,' she said. 'That's not what matters. So far as I know, I come from a long line of peasants and when the sun gets turned off it won't make any difference what we all were. It's now that counts.'

'I agree,' I said making a move with my arm round the warm cotton above her waist. 'Have you heard of J.E.C.T.O.R. psychometric testing?' she asked.

'No,' I answered.

§

Smoke was rising vertically from the top of the fiery mountain, for there was no wind. I sat on the pink rock to eat my picnic lunch where the hillside beneath my vineyard swept down to the huddled cottages in the city of New Naxos, tucked inside walls made with huge lumps of lava. There was a tiny, curved harbour where my grandfather came ashore bringing two or three vines from Old Naxos five hundred miles away, just before my father was born. The River Alcantara still cut its deep gutter to the sea. Now already our vines are old and gnarled with years of pruning, yet they love the black soil of Sicily and this strange black mountain.

'Only hard work and good soil make for a successful vineyard,' my father always used to say to me and now I said the same thing to my own son. It seems my ancestors were rich and noble, but they lost everything. So our family had to start all over again, building up the narrow terraces on the mountain with walls that held up the troughs of soil and kept in the moisture. Even now we still have to spend hours every day hoeing, pruning or picking off the spring caterpillars.

'You hardly ever smile these days,' my wife would say.

We need perfect grapes to make good wine, otherwise we don't get a good price from the merchants at Gela or Syracuse. I shouted down to my son and the Phoenician slave who was working with him 'Another ten rows yet or we'll be three jars short. Then we won't be able to pay our debts and we'll end up beggars.'

My son just shrugged and carried on at his usual slow, reluctant pace.

'The trouble with you is you just don't like work,' I said. It worried me that though he was already my height he seemed to have no desire to make a living nor had he shown any interest in marriage. And he was more afraid of me than I ever was of my father.

New York, Apr 20th cont.

'The JECTOR Test? What's that?' I asked.

'Its a special test for couples,' replied Ariadne. 'JECTOR stands for Joint Ecumenical Churches Test of Relationships. You pay $250 and get a card with twelve tasks on it. You punch the answers into your wrist-top and it tells you what chance you have of a lasting relationship.'

'I'll do it,' I said, for she looked very fetching in her Geriaid uniform. 'What are the twelve things?'

'We won't know most of them till we do it, but it takes at least a month. I know the first one is a four-day mountain hike. Then there's two days water sports. Two days beach life, two three-hour sessions of mixing with total strangers, two days non-stop motoring, two nights without sleep, some hard labour, a night of heavy drinking or drug taking, two days of extreme stress and two days looking after damaged children.'

'And we actually have to pay for this?'

'Yes, but everyone who's done it says it's well worth it. Think what you save in legal costs for marriage and divorce permits.'

§

'Sad day when we need peasants to join the army,' said the aggressive recruiting sergeant from Syracuse poking me between the shoulder blades to make me stand up even straighter than I already was.

I resisted the temptation to say it was sad for me too. I did not like the idea of soldiering and would never have left the estate if any other man under the age of forty had been ready to stay with me in New Naxos, but the moral pressure to join the fight against the Carthaginians was immense. Though my father had dropped dead on the hillside five years earlier I could still hear his sarcastic tongue accusing me of idleness and implying that I was a hermaphrodite. I suppose there's some truth in it. I do prefer the company of men to women. I always have. And I like their bodies. But if you keep a vineyard you need a wife, so I'd taken one and done my duty with her often enough to father a couple of sons.

'You Naxos boys are barely fit to carry the baggage for the army of Syracuse,' shouted an officer, pushing his helmet up on his sweating brow. 'The Carthaginians will take one look at you and spit you out in tiny pieces. Look up, I say, and swing those arms.'

He ranted at us for three days and then we were sent to fight at Himera, a pile of ashes that was once a town. I still find it hard to say why an army wins or loses, though I came to quite enjoy fighting once I discovered it was easier than they made out. Sometimes it's just a question of which side had a better sleep or a better meal. Sometimes it's just generals being slightly less stupid on one side than the other. Anyway, surprisingly we beat the Carthaginians at Himera on the north coast. Their general Hamilcar accepted the blame, for he had a huge fire lit afterwards and dived into it from a rock above. Needless to say our prince, the intrepid Hieron, took the credit and built himself a new palace decorated with golden statues of the gods made from melted down Carthaginian jewellery. For some reason he took a great liking to me, but at a cost.

'I'm running out of virgins,' he said one day, grabbing my arm. 'How about your sister?'

If I'd replied that she wasn't a virgin she'd have been branded with a red-hot poker, but if I said she was a virgin she'd be raped by Hieron.

'She has an unpleasant skin disease,' I answered uneasily. 'It may be a form of leprosy. We're not sure.'

'Remarks like that are an insult to my intelligence, Theophilus,' said Prince Hieron menacingly. 'I'll have to post you to the Malta patrol to improve your attitude.'

Some officers survived a year on the Malta patrol, but none that I knew had ever survived two years. It was the one area where the Carthaginians still managed to achieve their cruel ambition of vengeance for Himera. If your ship was cornered by far the best option was to let yourself drown.

Colorado, Apr 25th, 2119

I told my clients I would be away for a week and turned my e-pod onto automatic. Business had been erratic anyway, because there were several power surges due to gales affecting the wind farms. Ariadne appeared in her bright orange cagoule with a blue-and-green rucksack slung over one shoulder and big rubber boots on her feet. We flew to Denver, then took the roboid to Colorado Springs and headed towards Pike's Peak in the Rockies. The lower slopes were dotted with bright blue irises.

'This is where we really start,' said Ariadne. We shook hands solemnly and signed the JECTOR Test commitment form on our wrist-tops.

I checked our tent and our food supplies and we headed off up a steep, wooded gorge where there had once been a mountain railway. To be honest I wasn't all that fit and for the first three hours sweat poured off me as we plodded on up the gorge. Ariadne seemed less tired than I was, and walked ahead to keep the moral advantage though it wasn't supposed to be a competition, so said our instructions. Then at midday we stopped by a stream to have our first picnic of pork pies and apples.

Within minutes my hot sweat turned to an icy trickle and my legs started to stiffen up.

'You look a bit sorry for yourself,' said Ariadne.

'I am,' I said. 'You're too fit. Damn you.' My male pride was hurt.

'As long as you keep expressing yourself honestly without losing your temper we should get a reasonable score,' she said equably and I swore under my breath. She pretended not to notice. She wanted us to do well.

That afternoon we climbed together another two thousand feet and I made a smug internal note that I was now treading on Ariadne's heels. She was beginning to trip over roots and accidentally kick rocks as the day wore on, but I was settling into a pattern of plodding survival.

'Let's stop here,' I said and knew I'd won back the initiative, even if it wasn't a competition. For she sank gratefully onto the grass and stayed there sucking a packet of juice while I put the tent up.

'I'm knackered,' she admitted. 'But it's different for men.'

'I'll heat up the stew. You get inside the tent.'

'There's no need to be patronising,' she said. 'We'll lose points for that. This is all about relationships, remember. Respect.'

We had our stew and hot tea. Then she rustled off into the bushes to do whatever and asked for two minutes on her own in the tent before I crawled in beside her.

She was curled in a ball with just the top of her head showing. We had never slept together before, but I slid into my sleeping bag beside her and as the night grew colder she came closer for warmth.

§

I had lost track of how long I had spent chained to that bench in that Syracusan galley on the Malta patrol, and much of the time I was in such pain that I did not care whether I lived or died. I think it was about eighteen months, longer than most. In fact I wanted to die, but I wanted the oar-master to die with me and when I saw a Carthaginian ship heading towards us I thought my moment had come.

The Carthaginian ship rammed us amidships and I saw a huge splinter go in near the oar master's groin. I just lay back and waited as the tepid sea-water lapped slowly up to my bench.

I was satisfied.

Colorado, Apr 26th, 2119

The next morning I felt stiff and slightly sick with the effect of altitude at ten thousand feet, but I got up first, shaved in the stream and made two coffees.

'Thanks,' she said, propped up on one elbow in her sleeping bag.

'Muesli and raisins to follow,' I said.

An hour later we had packed away the tent and were on our way. This time the route was level on a rough path which contoured round the side of the mountain towards a ridge that led to the summit. At first we were both silent and a little sore from the day before, but as the sun rose and the birds grew louder we began to talk more and relaxed.

'It's so beautiful,' said Ariadne. Indeed, the sun seemed to bless us and the deer-mown turf was like a dancing floor as we kept up a steady pace to the mountain pass. By four o'clock we had completed our allotted mileage. It was still baking hot in our chosen camping spot where a wispy waterfall plunged into a cool brown pool fringed with heather.

'It looks inviting,' I said, wiping a stream of sweat from by brow.

She dumped her rucksack. 'Don't watch me,' she said unbuttoning her shirt.

'This is an extra part of the test. We can look but not stare.'

Somehow it didn't seem immodest or surprising that we both stripped off in this Garden of Eden and plunged laughing into the cold brown pool to splash each other yet stay innocent, at least in theory. I kept my word not to stare but my peripheral vision promised a fine reward for our current labours.

The next day after a good sleep and a hard walk we slogged up the final few thousand feet to the summit. Ariadne turned as we came to the cairn and kissed me on the lips, hugging me.

'Thank-you,' she said. 'That was wonderful.'

§

'Why do you Naxans always hate Syracusans?' asked the little ambassador who had just arrived from Athens.

'Because they keep trying to destroy us,' I answered. 'They've made use of us to help win their battles against Carthage and then just treated us as their slaves.'

'But you're not a slave, Philo,' said the little man shrewdly. 'You own several ships, I gather, and you have vineyards.'

'Yes, but I've had to work to get them back. My grandfather was drowned with the fleet off Malta and after that Hieron confiscated most of our land. My father toiled to build the estates back up again, but Syracuse has three times the number of men we have in New Naxos. If they want to pull us down they can.'

'So will you join with us and help the Athenian army to capture Syracuse?' he asked. 'Our fleet is on its way. The more Greeks living in Sicily that help us the, quicker will be our victory.'

'We'll help,' I said and shook his hand. 'But it's to win our freedom from Syracuse, not to become a colony of Athens.'

'I guarantee your independence,' said the diplomat and left, small but dignified. I was far from sure that he could be trusted, but it was worth a try.

So when the Athenian army arrived to besiege the hated city we gave them support. We sheltered their fleet and fed their men. We sent thousands of slaves and artisans to help build the siege wall outside Syracuse on the landward side, so that no one could come or go. We lent them sappers, cooks, carpenters and mounted messengers. But the siege dragged on. The Athenian generals were horse-heads. They missed every chance and then foolishly let the city get reinforcements from Corinth. So, instead of starving out the Syracusans, they themselves began to run short of food and let the streams run dry. In the end there was a pitched battle near the walls and all the Athenian soldiers seemed to care about was scrabbling to one bloody, muddy little stream to scoop out handfuls of tepid water. Then with thirst half-quenched they surrendered. And so, since we had nowhere to run, did we.

After two years of starvation rations the Syracusans were in no mood to be lenient. The two surviving Athenian generals were nailed to planks in the sun, and frankly they deserved it. The rest of us were taken in chains to the great stone quarries of Acradina. There it was a waterless furnace during the day that flipped to dripping black chill by nights. Most of us were feverish skeletons within a few months.

'I can't last,' I said to my son. 'But you can survive. Just do the minimum of stone chipping and save the night water for the day. If you can survive for a year you'll get away.'

Denver, Colorado, Apr 28th, 2119

Waiting for the 2020 express roboid to Chicago that has been delayed by the usual forest fires in Montana.

This was the night the news was announced that cures had now been found for every form of cancer with the result that heart attacks have once more become the most common cause of death. The second most common cause remains the Type Z2 E5 bird flu spread by starlings that was first noted in the roboid-parks of world-wide hypermarkets. Then came a commercial for Hilton Robotels:

It's one of life's most pleasant treats
To slip between fresh-laundered sheets,
Caressingly cool as the feet first probe

To the darker regions of the foetal globe,
Then warming gently as the pillows hug
The work-worn body neat and snug.
Then anaesthetic night shuts out
All pain, all memories, all self-doubt.

But still the express was delayed, so we just had to put our sleeping bags on the roboid-station floor and doze as best we could.

We were not left in peace for long. Suddenly the red-alert alarms went off, as did the lights. I checked my earpiece and there was a self-repeating announcement that war had broken out again between the two halves of China. They had been quarrelling for some time over the ownership of the famous Mao Asteroid, the second largest object in Orbital Level 4, which twenty years ago, when China was still united, had been tunnelled and irrigated for a massive rice-production facility capable of feeding fifty million people a year. By the time it was in full production China had split up, and while North China regarded itself as the rightful inheritor, the South China government disagreed, Meanwhile the South had a rice production problem due to a succession of bad winters and was desperate for supplies to feed a starving population. So it had mounted a full-scale invasion of the North, demanding a share of the rice. However the robot crews of Asteroid Mao were loyal to the North and started directing huge rocks to be dropped at extreme velocity on Wuhan and other cities in Hubei, causing massive destruction. It was expected that Korea and Vietnam would both support their allies in this conflict, Korea for the North and Viet Nam for the South.

'Is it disinformation again?' asked Ariadne.

'I don't think so,' I replied, just as the roboid train at long last shambled into the station.

CHAPTER SEVEN

A TALE OF TWO RIVERS

Had we but world enough, and time
This coyness, lady, were no crime.
A. Marvel

New York, May 7th, 2119

When we got back to New York I found one or two
nice orders on my desktop and another e-cheque from
Brazmahog for half of what they owed me, so life
improved. Ariadne asked me to one of her work stations
and showed me around the block of geriaid bedsits,
all with ensuite facilities, low-entry baths, geribuzzers,
zimmer ramps and senility-proof microwaves.

'Admit it, you're impressed,' she said with a
proprietorial air.

'I can't wait for the day,' I answered, not entirely
flippantly.

'Well you'll have to wait till you're ninety. That's the
new minimum age, since half the world's population
is now over eighty. And you'd better start paying into
your gerifund now,' she said. 'Now I think of it you are
beginning to look a bit decrepit.'

I slapped her gently on her rump.

§

The sun was shining fiercely but a pleasant breeze was coming up from the plains to make our work bearable. The streams of Axios which flow from the north end of Karanos were bubbling past us before they plunged over huge cliffs at the bottom of the town.

'Get on with it, you,' growled the foreman, threatening me with his little whip.

As a stonemason I was lucky to be doing the more delicate work on the mosaic floors for the King of Macedonia's new palace at Pella. My father and grandfather had been stonemasons before me. Indeed as a young man my grandfather had worked as a slave in the notorious quarries of Syracuse, until he managed to escape by climbing up a two-hundred-foot cliff in total darkness, or so he and my mother used to tell us.

I had to cut several hundred more blue bits for the sea parts of the mosaic picture I was working on for the king's bathroom. Then there would be the gold outline of a figure of Neptune, but it would be several weeks before I got round to that. Meanwhile a young strumpet flounced round the site and swept a pile of my newly cut blue bits over the parapet. Almost immediately the foreman kicked me hard, otherwise I might have directed my anger at the stupid young woman.

'I don't like that shade of blue,' she pouted. 'It's cold.' And she marched off to the next room.

'That's the king's new doxy,' whispered the foreman. 'Cleopatra. Watch her. Just make the sea greener and don't complain.'

'How long will she last?' asked one of the other masons. 'The king's had eight new mistresses since this palace was started.'

'Well he's married this one. So that should tell you something. Olympias has been given the boot. So has Prince Alexander. He's now officially a bastard.'

Just at that moment I glanced over the parapet, wondering if it was worth searching for my blue bits, just in case they would come in handy. Then I saw a young man, short but of fine physique, leap with ease onto a huge white horse and gallop off down into the plain, followed by three men-at-arms.

'You know who that was?' said the foreman and winked.

'I think I can guess. The bastard?' I said, for the newly demoted Prince Alexander had a reputation for escapades at all times of the day and night. And he had an extra-fast horse to make it easier for him.

At that minute there were a series of high-pitched shrieks from the older part of the palace which had been finished the previous year. There was a small stone theatre where King Philip liked to watch the latest plays by Euripides. Especially if they were laced with violence and lust.

'Take no notice,' said the foreman. 'Get on with your work. What's another little orgy or rape or decapitation between friends?'

So we worked on and it was my son, then a trainee in the infantry barracks, who came home and told us what had happened.

'It was a madman called Pausanias who hates both the king and his new wife's father. He dodged the guards at the entrance of the theatre and stabbed Philip in the heart. Prince Alexander is no longer a bastard. He's the new king of Macedonia and wants to start a war; he's always wanted a war of his own.'

'I don't suppose he'll bother about the colour of the bathroom floor.'

New York, May 9th, 2119

It was Monday so I checked out with Transtel. Overnight prices on the Nikkei and Hang Seng had slipped because of the Chinese asteroid war, but the yen was still strong against the dollar. However the Panislamic Congress in Tehran had broken up with another massive disagreement between Sunnis and Shiites over the admission of gay imams. Most liberal Muslims had already walked out on both sects and there had been a huge drop in mosque attendance. The one bit of good news from my point of view was that the mullahs had cut an extra billion barrels of oil production, so my compacted sawdust would be cheaper than oil and business in off-cuts might look up.

Then the phone buzzed and it was Ariadne.

'Time for JECTOR stage 2,' she said. 'Water sports.'

'Ordeal by water,' I quipped. Luckily I had foreseen this, indeed almost welcomed it, as I thought it was an element in which I could probably make a real impression on Ariadne. So I had made contact with the big water-sports centre that used to be a row of huge sand quarries in New Jersey. I booked in for the following weekend.

After eight years campaigning with King Alexander's army I was beginning to wonder if it would ever end and if there would ever be another kind of life. We were camped outside Baktra in the mountains and it had been a long siege of a town that did not look worth the bother. I was not usually in the phalanx, more a baggage handler and steward, a putter-up of tents, the sort of jobs that go to the son of a lowly stonemason with no military background. But even the keen types were beginning to get restless. Some hadn't had home leave for ten years. All right, Alexander was a hero as usual, first to scale the city walls in the final attack, but now he was drinking his fill at the celebration banquet and it was my job to top up the goblets. The one good thing was that the local women were quite pliable, even if they did look as if they had leather for skin. But since we hadn't seen any other kind of females except camels there was some relief. As to the king craving female company I was never sure, for sometimes I thought he just fancied boys. But now after a few goblets of the local plonk he was in a mellow mood and seemed to fancy the daughter of the captured chief. We'll see, but rumour has it we'll soon be off again and not back to Macedonia. There's the place further on called India that is seriously rich, so naturally we have to conquer that too.

New Jersey, May 10th, 2119

'The whole idea is that you must do something out of your comfort zone,' said the water-park warden. 'Something more difficult than any previous experience you've had on water. In your case, Mr Thens, you've done elementary sail-boarding, so your challenge will be to use Miss Aufnax as your crew and sail a thirty-foot yacht round a seventy-mile course in a force six or seven wind with no reefing allowed and no engine. Go to pontoon 4.

'I don't like this,' said Ariadne as we donned imitation oilskins and then packed enough food for twenty-four hours into the tiny galley. 'The furthest I've ever sailed is to the Statue of Liberty.'

'Don't worry,' I said masterfully, though fear of at least embarrassment was already getting to my bowels. 'At least we'll be heading into the wind for the first five miles or so.'

That having been said it wasn't easy to get away from the jetty into the wind, particularly as between us we were slow raising the sail and almost drifted back onto the shore before the drop-keel began to bite. As it was we missed the opposite pontoon and the boom of a large yacht by only inches as sails flapping wildly, deck heeling madly, we went about at last into the main channel.

§

I had been campaigning eleven years without setting foot once in Macedonia, but at least I was now head steward and I'd had three wives, two of whom I left behind further east. The new model is Persian as the King is telling us all to get a Persian wife like his latest. Drinking contest tonight, Babylon style. The last one finished with a phalanx sergeant downing four bottles of wine and dying two hours later. Yet another posthumous medal for one of the boys.

New Jersey, ten minutes later

For ten minutes we kept on the same tack. When we tipped over too much Ariadne shrieked aloud and I shrieked internally, but I just loosened the sheet and let the air spill out. Then with what I thought was remarkable patience I explained to Ariadne what she would have to do when we went about.'

'Just explain it to me,' she said.

'I just have,' I said.

'Well don't be so bloody patronising.'

'I wasn't.'

'Yes you were.'

'Ready about. Let go the jib sheet!' My voice had risen a whole octave.

'What?'

'Let that go,' I said. 'Lee ho.' And I swung the tiller, but Ariadne was too busy saying 'Stop shouting at me' to let go the jib. The boat stalled mid-turn in a flapping shambles, the cockpit bucketing and Ariadne nursing pinched fingers.

'Do you know what you're doing?' she yelled rather unfairly.

I knew this was the test. 'We'll try again. When we start to turn just let go of this rope and when I give the word pull that one hard.'

This time the boat heeled over in a more orthodox manner onto the new tack albeit several hundred yards astern of where we had been before.

'There was no need to shout at me ', said Ariadne.' Just explain things quietly to me.'

'Sorry,' I said. 'I didn't want to capsize.'

'There's no need to be so melodramatic.'

We sailed on our new course for twenty minutes in sullen silence, then tacked again with slightly greater success. So we kept going for twenty miles or so, including some narrow channels where the former gravel pits had been linked by canals and even past a huge wind farm which had an unpredictable effect on our sails, causing us to heel over suddenly. By the time evening approached we had reached the half-way stage, but were wet, cold and hungry.

'You take the tiller,' I said. 'I'll put on some hot soup.'

'What do I do?' she asked. The rain and spray were dripping from her hood onto her nose.

'Just keep a straight course.'

The hot tomato soup made from a packet followed by a slightly damp crust of bread and cheese helped to restore some equilibrium.

'I don't think either of us did very well there,' said Ariadne. 'You shouted at me.'

'You can't sail without a bit of shouting,' I said. 'I think we were remarkably calm considering. Heh, there's the yellow mooring buoy with a pick-up wire. Bring her round into the wind and I'll lean over with the boat hook and grab hold of it.'

'I don't know if I'll manage.'

'We will,' I said and encouraged her with a grin.

In fact Ariadne managed it remarkably well and we drifted back onto the buoy at only the second attempt.

'You did very well,' I said.

'So did you,' said Ariadne, beaming as I tugged down the sails and secured the mooring rope. Then at last we escaped the rain, hung our dripping clothes in the spare cabin and I opened a can of Bolognese plus a bottle of Korean Muscadet. Ariadne squeezed into the tiny heads. A few minutes later came a shout, 'How do you pump out this thing?'

'Six pumps with the lever open and six with it shut.'

'Is open anti-clockwise?'

'Yes.'

'I suppose we really coped quite well,' she said, emerging with her lips repainted.

'I think so. Have some more wine.'

'I'm still a bit cold.'

I went round and sat on the bunk beside her with my arm around her shoulder while we listened pleasantly to the radio and sipped our wine as the wind howled above us.

'I suppose you could come into my sleeping bag as long as we don't break the rules. Just to keep warm,' she added.

'It'll be difficult,' I said. 'But I'll risk it if you will.' These days self-restraint has become quite cool again. News came in that King Mohammed bin Salman III of Saudi had been forced to abdicate after admitting eight charges of sexual harassment and one of attempted rape. There were signs of a possible ceasefire after North China agreed to hand over one of its smaller asteroids to the South.

§

'Is the king really dead? How did it happen?' I asked. We were standing shocked in the half-completed market place of the new city of Alexandria at the mouth of a great river. I had done everything the king had asked of me, campaigning for twelve years in his army to India and back again, then marrying a Jewess called Ruth, because he said we should all intermarry and settle down in the new cities: I'd left my previous three wives behind. Then I'd chosen to take my bounty as a small plot by the riverside in Egypt. There I was building up a small trading business and living with Ruth above the shop.

'Yes, it's definite. He's dead,' said one of the other veterans with tears in his eyes. 'They're bringing his body down from Babylon.'

'He should have rested,' I said to Ruth.' He never rested. He conquered almost the whole world by the time he was thirty.'

'You all worshipped him.' said Ruth, half sympathetically, half resentfully.

'Perhaps,' I said. 'But not the way you mean worship.'

'It's blasphemous for any human to pretend to be a god.'

'Now Ruth, you're just quoting the rabbi who knows nothing about it. Be grateful. But for him we would never have married. You can believe what you want, we agreed that much. The boy can be circumcised, but that's as far as I go. I'm allowed to say what I think about Alexander, but you're not. We knew he'd keep on fighting till we were all dead, unless he died first. He lived for conquest. He never slept. He was more than human. Much more. And now he's dead.'

'Well we do have this to thank him for,' said Ruth placidly, pointing to our well-laden jetty. 'Business is good.'

'If there is such a thing as a human god Alexander must have been very close to it, but a human devil too,' I said. 'Now I suppose I'll have to shut up shop for the Sabbath to please you.'

'No,' she said. 'I'll stop work, but you can carry on if you want. Let's be practical. The rabbi understands.'

New Jersey, May 14th, 2119

That was the night when a hole ten miles across appeared in western Texas and was blamed on fifty years of fracking by the George Bush VI Foundation. There was also an ad in the Twitter personal column of The Laughing Times:

Professional retired and sensible M
Early fifties, no overdraft, absolute gem,
Into nature, sex and renaissance art
WLTM F with plenty of heart,

Ideally a fortyish blond who can cook,
Prepared on occasions to overlook
Some bouts of S & M. Just send cv
And recent photograph to Box 53

Then came the warning from the safeguarders:
She asked me out to lunch one day,
But when the moment came to pay
She happened to look the other way
And in the ensuing short delay
I couldn't think of what to say
But feeling frankly quite distrait
Placed my card on the waiter's tray.
'It's my turn next time, come what may,'
She muttered as we walked away.
'You're always leading me astray.
I'm giving up lunches as of today.'

This was cut short by a news flash that the Cocaine Junta had staged an armed coup in Mexico, where the drug barons had suffered badly from the collapse in drug prices after most Class A Drugs had been legalised throughout the world. The new government intended to re-criminalise all drugs so as to keep the price up and avoid a collapse in the Central American economy. It also planned to build a frontier wall to keep out migrants and asylum seekers bringing cheap drugs into Mexico from the USA. The massive tomb of Vladimir Putin in Red Square had been demolished and his coffin transferred to an unmarked grave in Chernobyl. Twenty people had been killed in the city of Wuhan after another attempt by the South China government to abolish all wet markets.

Palestinian tanks had destroyed 3000 hectares of solar panels in Sinai in return for Israel bombing the Jericho subway.

After the excitement of our sailing trip to New Jersey I was so bored and feeling so lonely that I even read the label on the wretched packet of pre-cooked pasta which I was opening for my solitary supper. It read:

Here's what our happy customers eat
Genetically modified sugar and wheat
From packages widely recycled or not
Or kept in buckets until they rot.
For allergens read list in BOLD.
This can be eaten hot or cold.
Microwave it for half a minute,
But always check the ingredients in it,
Including poly-unsaturated fats
That are tested by experts on innocent rats.
For BEST BEFORE see top of lid
And that of course is what I did.

Copyright@ Murdoch The Laughing Times

Then came news that a genetic scientist in Israel had developed a plant that tasted like real bacon. The farming of pigs was to be discontinued worldwide with immediate effect. Stocking up of toilet paper was to become a criminal offence. In New Zealand all out-of-doors farm labour had become unsafe due to the increase in UV radiation caused by magnetic deviation in Antarctica. The notorious, but in some quarters popular, criminal Sam the Siphon had at last been arrested in Chicago. For years he had been siphoning money out of international bank accounts and amassing a huge fortune, but also putting some of it back into what he thought were deserving causes. Sam turned out to be a Chinese girl aged twelve.

CHAPTER EIGHT

WINNERS AND LOSERS

In war ...there are no winners, but all are losers.
N. Chamberlain

New York, May 15th, 2119

'Our JECTOR scores for hill-walking and water sports were quite respectable,' said a breathless Ariadne, stroking an email across her pad. 'We only need an average 90 points on the remaining tests to be in the Highly-likely-to-succeed bracket.'

I grunted. I'd had a difficult day with the sudden devaluation of the Chilean peseta, which had left me with a significant loss on a hospital flooring contract. 'Aren't you pleased?' she asked.

'Yes,' I said unconvincingly.

'Spoilsport. The next test is easy, just a few days of beach life.'

'There must be a catch,' I said 'The sun can do strange things to people. Look at Australia, no ozone left at all, they can only surf wearing dry suits.'

§

I became a soldier like my father before me. Though I thought of myself as a Macedonian I had a Jewish mother, so I was not treated as one of the elite. Thus after helping young Ptolemy become the new king of Egypt – he even wanted to be called Pharaoh and would not let me be one of his bodyguards – I became disillusioned and took to steering a barge on the Nile.

Coney Island. May 17, 2119

Ariadne packed two towels and our costumes in a rucksack and we took the subroboid B6 to Coney Island. We wasted an hour at the Aquarium where Ariadne thought it was cruel to keep whales in captivity, so I explained that they had to be fitted with shallow water alarms as so many whales had died due to solar storms affecting their natural ability to navigate safely.

'Clever,' she said rather dubiously. Then we went along the board-walk to Nathan's for a special hot dog.

'I'll open it,' I said as Ariadne struggled with her tomato sauce sachet. 'You have to be a member of Mensa to undo some sauce sachets.'

'No, I can manage,' she said, squirting some of the red potion accidentally onto her T-shirt. Then we sauntered down onto the recycled beach, eating our hot dogs as we went.

I hired two sun-loungers and we made a wall with them so we could change.

'I've not stared at your body before,' I said. 'But I'm allowed to when you're in your diakini. It's great. Two wonderful...'

'Stop being cheeky. You could lose half an inch round the middle. Remind me to see to it.'

We lay on the sand and I stared at her with undiminished pleasure, thinking that this put all other ambitions to be a precinct mayor or mega-e-pod trader into the shade. Then we swam in the dark green water and came back again and slept. Suddenly I woke with a start as a gang of Afro-Hispanic youngsters on hoverpeds with ghetto blasters screeched round us.

'We shouldn't have stayed so long,' said Ariadne. 'Why didn't you wake me?'

'I'm not a mind-reader.'

'Don't be sarcastic.'

'No I'm not.'

'Yes you are.'

Within minutes we were bickering away and the magic was gone, but the noise and sandstorm caused by the gang continued. Ariadne was close to tears.

'You're dehydrated,' I said.

'Very clever of you,' she replied. 'Really sympathetic.'

'No, I'm just a thirty-kilo weakling who gets sand thrown in his face by Bronx misfits.'

She nearly smiled. I pulled her to her feet, stared defiantly at the beach loonies and took her to the first bistro in Astroland, plied her with Amstel and pizza.

'That's better, isn't it?' I asked,

'I suppose so. Put me into the wrist-top. I suppose I've lost us about fifty points for silly behaviour.'

'Not at all,' I said. 'It was mainly my fault.'

'Put that in the wrist-top too,' she said. 'That'll probably win us back the lost points.'

§

That my old Jewish grandmother was a great influence on the family there was no doubt. It was she who brought up my father with furtive visits to the rabbi and quiet instruction about the single god, when my grandfather wasn't looking. So it was not surprising that he married a Jewish girl from the north Alexandria synagogue. His older brother, who inherited the family business, was more of a Greek, but my father became assistant lighthouse keeper on the huge new Pharos that was built on the rock outside the harbour. Often in my youth I got to pull the carts of logs along the mole and then carry them up the hundred steps to the fire platform. I quite enjoyed it, but as I grew to manhood I found that a lighthouse keeper's job no longer appealed to me. I'd seen too many ships sail in and out, laden with wealth. So I took a berth on a schooner serving the Italian trade and enjoyed several years on her, rising to be mate before disaster eventually struck.

I still remember the rabbi telling me the story of Jonah, the sea-faring man who ended up in the belly of a whale. I fared just as badly as he did, if not worse. Our ship was trapped by a flotilla of Carthaginian warships, so I ended up chained to an oar in the belly of one of their stinking galleys, third bench upper, with two tongueless Africans beside me. I've had five years of it already. The only consolation is that once or twice a year we're allowed ashore to breed more galley slaves. I've married a Phoenician washer-slave in Carthage and we have a son already whom I've only seen once.

'I've had a bad day at the office,' said Ariadne over the phone.

'You?' I said. 'I thought that never happened to you.'

'Well it has. We've had another death from suspected food poisoning and there's a charge of sexual harassment from one of our nurses aged sixty against a male patient aged ninety-five. And one of the eighty-year-old women wants to marry the robot who makes all the beds.'

'Let's go out for a drink,' I suggested.

'I thought you'd never ask. How was your day?'

'Not much better. There's another war started between Tutsania and Hutumbe, so I've got two container loads of high-grade hardwood stuck on a freighter up the Congo. And I've paid a twenty per cent deposit already.'

'That's only money. I'm talking about death and rape.'

'Never mind. See you in the Geyser Icelandic Theme Bar in twenty minutes.'

As I strolled along the pavement my earpiece announced the news that New Delhi had once again become the largest city in the world with forty million people despite another outbreak of Covid 53.

§

The sun shone on the wide inland lake of Trasimene as the Carthaginian army swung down from the hills.

'The general wants you,' said my officer, Hada.

'Not me, just my elephant, I expect,' I said, cuddling her trunk for a moment before I ran to respond to the order. Somehow I guessed we were near the end of our long journey together. For of all the elephants that crossed the mountains with us two years ago only mine was still alive. Partly I felt it was due to my skill as an elephant handler, for I had made more effort than most of the others to scrounge around for places where Misa could eat and drink her fill. Those winters in Italy didn't suit her at all.

As I rode Misa, lumbering her way through the ranks of Hannibal's crack troops, they ignored me as usual, for I was not of Carthaginian blood. My grandfather had been an oar-slave and my grandmother a laundry worker, my parents the same, but I had shown an early skill in elephant handling so I got into the army. That was tough but better than the galleys. Two of my little brothers had been burned alive in the great sacrifice before the invasion of Spain. So not surprisingly I had been brought up to fear, hate and admire the ruling elite. At least in the army they recognised I had some skill, even though I was an alien of mixed race.

'Hurry, you, elephant man,' yelled a sergeant, despite the fact that I was already running alongside Misa at the regulation pace ordered for crossing through the camp. Then I came to a group of officers standing around the general's tent and I knelt to await orders. One of them broke off. 'Elephant handler?' he asked.

'The last one,' I said. He laughed.

I bowed my head.

'The general-in-chief wants to ride on your elephant into battle tomorrow. Report here at dawn with your beast.'

I nodded and backed away, then headed down the slope back to our encampment. I knew instinctively that this would be the end. Misa was still strong, but it was getting harder to find good fodder because the Romans, in spite of everything, kept burning crops as they retreated. So that evening I took special care to lead her to the best fodder I could find.

New York, ten minutes later.

I turned on the news and it was depressing again. The hypermarket giant Lidesco had collapsed with enormous debts and threatened to bring down the State Bank of Luxembourg in its wake. The Islamic Republic of Papua New Guinea had launched a rocket attack on Northern Australia. A collection of works by the twentieth-century British artist Damian Hurst had been sold off at a fraction of their former price to make room for some old masters at the New York Metropolitan.

§

That night I slept poorly, knowing it might well be my last, scratching at my sore elbow which often flared up at times like this. All the army knew that general-in-chief Hannibal was ill in mind and body. For years he had led us – I have to include myself in the us of the Carthaginians even though I am just a mercenary – to victory and this was to be the last great battle, so they said. To finish off the Romans once and for all. But to

103

hide his illness Hannibal wanted to ride into battle on the last elephant left alive in his army, my Misa. And since he always led from the front that meant that Misa and I would be in the front of the front.

Dawn came and I reported as ordered, right on time. Hannibal strode out in his exotic uniform, his one eye blazing with hate and fever, his back unbelievably straight, but I could tell he was struggling, for he had some difficulty pulling himself up on to the saddle platform. Then with the precision of years of practice and officer intimidation the palace guard and the crack Numidian squadrons of cavalry swept in behind us.

The Roman army was waiting by the shores of the lake. Misa was as fast as she had ever been, but I knew she was suffering. In that heat she needed something to drink after only thirty minutes, but Hannibal insisted we charge up and down the lines for a full two hours as the slaughter of the Romans proceeded. He cared about destroying Rome, but not for the life of an elephant. I knew that and hated him for it.

At last the battle was over. The green slime around the edge of the lake was blotched with red where Roman bodies had slid through the canopy of water weeds. At last Hannibal dismissed us with a brief word of thanks and I took Misa to the deeper water. But I knew it was too late. She lay there with her trunk in the lake drinking listlessly, then slept. I waited in that disgusting place till the end, then made my decision.

When I saw that Misa was dead and the sun had set, I crept out of the camp and headed up into the hills.

By dawn I had covered about eight miles and stumbled upon a couple of goatherds with their throats cut, doubtless by fleeing soldiers; I didn't know which side, but most likely Romans. The huge herd of goats stood as if waiting orders, so I picked up the pipes that were lying by the bodies and brought the herd together. Then half-following, half-leading, I drove them all to a farmstead, the only one that I could see.

I could not speak the farmer's language, but I could make him understand what had happened and he could see that I knew how to handle animals. Thus it was that a Carthaginian elephant handler turned into an Italian goat herd and free of war, more or less.

New York, twenty minutes later

Another ad in the personal column of the Laughing Times:

> *Attractive blond forty-five divorcee Into bee-*
> *keeping, flowers and Radio Three,*
> *Aerobics, rambling and BLT's,*
> *Enjoys eating out and planting trees*
> *WLTM god if it's not too late*
> *With a view to arranging casual date*
> *Or long-term friendship with plenty of chat*
> *About theology or this and that*
> *If you notice this ad please make a sign*
> *I'll cook a meal if you bring wine.*

§

But I still missed my lovely elephant, the best friend I ever had. Goats were not quite the same.

New York an hour later.

The use of dronecopters for home delivery of restaurant meals is to be taxed at seventy-five per cent and follow a one-way street system to reduce the large numbers of injuries caused by the crashes of rival drone operators. There is also yet another demand for all nations to redefine their core principles, but no one quite knows what this means. Transatlantic flights have been delayed due to the malfunction of one of the main battery recharge facilities. This was probably the result of another disinformation campaign by the North Chinese, who have the most advanced computer-hacking skills in the world.

Stop Press:

Strong winds have driven a mile-wide floating island of plastic waste onto the beaches of Miami and buried an entire commune of luxury villas under about forty feet of compacted debris. Diggers have been brought in to try to reach any possible survivors.

CHAPTER NINE

NEW GODS AND OLD

Whan than the month in which the world began
That highte March whan God first maked man.

G. Chaucer

New York, still May 22nd, 2119

After a couple of White Deaths and Tonic at the Geyser Theme Bar Ariadne and I agreed to go to the JECTOR Test 4 the following Thursday. We'd paused in a Robostop shelter to kiss voraciously and my hands were almost out of control.

'Only eight more tests to pass and we could make babies together,' she said breathlessly. 'Now get out of here.'

§

I looked after two herds of around five hundred goats each. The worst job was to stop them killing themselves when they climbed up the cliffs, but they were amazingly sure-footed. The males were solitary creatures that took no notice of the females except during the rut that lasted seventeen days. Then the older males would drive the younger ones out of the herd. The does just have one kid each and within six months it is weaned and away. It took me two years to find my own doe, a little Tuscan slave girl who could milk a goat every four minutes and knew just how to add the whey for the cheese. We managed a kid a year for five years.

New York, Chinatown, May 29th, 2119

When we arrived on the appointed day at the JECTOR Centre our tutor gave us the briefing for accentuated stress management.

'First go to the Bronx by subroboid and change at these two stations. You're allowed to take two things with you: a bag of two hundred dollars and a large box of biscuits.'

The first station near Chinatown was derelict and no longer in normal use so we were the only people to get off the sub. The walls were encrusted with layers of three-dimensional plaster graffiti. Suddenly, as the sub hissed away into the darkness of the tunnel beyond, a swarm of Korean quadrats came leaping out. They wore sacking over their shoes as they slid over the high voltage track. Apparently they fried eggs and bread on it between subs and slept in the old robescal shafts. Now they danced round us with unsheathed needles which they tossed menacingly from hand to hand.

'They're dead headers,' I said. 'Keep clear of the needles.'

'Oh God,' said Ariadne.

'They're just playing,' I said, as two of them feinted past us with needle points inches from our faces.

'I can't bear it,' said Ariadne.

'We'll be okay,' I said. 'All we have to do is get down that corridor and up the robescal to the Purple Line. Just join in the fun.'

With our backs to the tiled wall and tossing ten-dollar bills to the quadrats we slid along the passageway till with only ten dollars left we made it to the upper station, at which point the quadrats stopped their pursuit.

'That was horrible,' said Ariadne. 'You did well to get us out.'

'You did well too,' I hugged her as we reached the third level at last. Then within seconds a subroboid swished into view and we were away.

'They don't really mean any harm,' I said. 'They just want money to buy food.'

§

The only reason I joined the Roman army was to get some land of my own. My father and grandfather before him had been goatherds near Perugia, virtual slaves both of them, and our family often went hungry in the winter. They would say I should be grateful to be free at all, but I saw them work themselves to death for a landlord we never even met.

'Join if you must,' said my mother, who was of Etruscan stock. 'But you're a fool.'

So after a year's training I went to serve under the consul Publius Rupilius, who was suppressing the slave revolt in Sicily. I don't know why, but I always felt a certain sympathy with those Sicilian slaves for standing up against the might of Rome, but of course I was too keen to get my gratuity to express such inappropriate feelings out loud. In the end I came to quite admire Rupilius. To begin with, whenever we defeated a group of rebel slaves, he just slaughtered them, but the resistance of the next region was all the stiffer. Then he realised it was a cleverer trick to spare the captives and have a more persuadable enemy the next time. So from that moment onwards the war became much easier for us.

Thus at last after fifteen years of service I came to claim my rewards. I had never before been to Rome and when our legion was at last disbanded outside the city gates I must admit to a certain awe as I entered the murky vastness and headed for the offices in the forum. Conscious of my impure birth I felt a deep sense of inferiority, so it was not surprising that when a smooth-talking quaestor told me I would have to wait some time for my allotment I just walked meekly away. But when this treatment had been repeated a number of times my bitterness began to grow stronger than my inbred fear of officers.

'Come back next week,' said the quaestor for the seventh time. And by luck two of my mates from the Sicily campaign, who like me were of mixed blood, happened to turn up at the same time. Most nights we had to go and sleep in camp outside the city walls, because old soldiers aren't allowed to stay in the city and our rations were very meagre. The three of us met another group in a similar situation and before long we found ourselves part of a crowd, maybe a thousand strong, all recently released soldiers with no land and no job.

'The only man to help us is the tribune Gracchus,' said one whose name I later learned was Lucius.

And so we all became supporters of young Gracchus, a true champion of ordinary soldiers, though he was the son of a consul and the grandson of a great general. Within ten days I had a token for a decent plot of land not far from Perugia.

'Before you head off to your vegetable patch wait here just a few more days and vote for Gracchus, so that he'll get another year as tribune,' said my new friend Lucius. 'He's the only one that cares about us.'

So I stayed and voted for him, but by then the streets were full of officer thugs who just wanted big lush farms for themselves with people like us turned into slaves. I paid one last visit to the Forum and there as usual was the smooth-talking quaestor. This time, however, he had a big crowd of senatorial yobs, arrogant officer types with the purple stripe of snobbery on their togas. Half of our crowd of veterans had turned up and we had about the same number as the yobs. Then we saw the graceful figure of Gracchus himself emerging from the assembly room.

'Get him,' shouted the yobs and, though our group piled in, we were on the wrong side of the forum to be much help. Before we could push our way across they had clubbed Gracchus to death with table tops and chair legs. The best man I ever knew. And Lucius as well was crushed to death by them along with several hundred more. As for me I was clutching the token for my plot of land and saw no point in staying with the losing side, so I headed for the north gate of the city and Perugia,

The next disused station where we had been told to get out was beyond the river and the people living in it did not at first appear so threatening as the Korean quadrats.

It turned out to be a community of thousands of ex-covid teenagers scrounging a living from passing commuters, their derelict side tunnels festooned with vast numbers of childish ornaments, cuddly toys and plastic knick-knacks.

'Basically they're just LD cases,' said Ariadne, who this time was much less perturbed than I was.

'LD?' I asked.

'Learning difficulty, many thousands of youngsters who caught Covid 80, but had no symptoms, were found later to have suffered brain damage and began to blame their parents. They couldn't find jobs so they just developed scavenger communities like this one.'

It wasn't the individuals who affected me. They mostly had simple grins and offered no violence except the obvious desire for an affectionate touch. It was the sheer numbers of them, the effect of hundreds of vacuous faces, rolling expectant eyes and listlessly twitching arms that somehow became rapidly unnerving. Like a mirrored warning of one's own inadequacy.

'Poor souls,' said Ariadne and I knew for certain at that moment that I felt real love for her, as well as lust. 'As you know there was a big increase in LD birthrate due to mobile-phone-mast syndrome. Congress couldn't afford

to keep up the allowances, so thousands just had to fend
for themselves.'

After a few minutes my sympathy for the youngsters
started to turn to anxiety. They hugely outnumbered us
in this cramped environment and, though most of them
seemed timid individually, it was different when they
came together, for as a seething mass they were very
intimidating. Somehow I felt we would never get to the
other side of the station. As it was we only made it with
the last biscuit handed out in the final few yards.

'We shouldn't dislike these kids,' said Ariadne. 'It's part
of the test to keep smiling.'

'If you say so,' I said. 'This time it was me that cracked
up.'

'At least you never stopped holding my hand.'

'I was scared,' I said.

§

I should never have got in tow with Catiline. My old
grandfather, who built-up our first estate near Perugia,
always used to warn me about men like him, but I
was young then and from the country, so I was deeply
impressed by Catiline's athletic arrogance and blistering
wit. Everyone in Rome seemed vibrant and exciting
compared with our Perugian neighbours who just talked
about vines and olive trees or goats.

Catiline's career had of course by then come to a
sudden stop over some charge of corruption while he
was governor of West Africa. So he was barred from
the consulship until the allegations could be resolved.

113

Meanwhile he had an amazing grasp of Roman politics, was elegant, witty and incredibly lavish in his hospitality, sneering at anyone who fell behind his pace in pleasure. Women, boys, gambling, slave-baiting and horses. I loved it when he hugged my shoulder and said, 'Sallust, you're not bad for a Sabine. You know how to enjoy yourself. Lend me a couple of thousand, will you?'

I'd hesitate but then give him the money, scratching my elbow, which often itched when I felt uneasy.

'You should have a mistress, Sallust,' he'd say. 'You deserve one.' And on one occasion he added, 'Try Fulvia. She knows all the tricks. And she's tired of Cethegus. I'll send her to you. Caesar recommended her highly before that.'

'Thank you,' I replied.

'Not at all. By the way I have a modest plan for saving the republic from death by boredom. If that pompous dimwit Cicero becomes consul he'll be the end of us. So we need to be the end of him instead.'

I took little notice of these plots of his, for I'd heard him go on like this before. So for the next week I initially enjoyed but then grew satiated and maddened by the combination of stylish elegance, total immodesty and voracious appetites of Fulvia. After seven days of almost non-stop sexual activity interspersed only by bouts of drinking and eating I could no longer tell the difference between pleasure and pain.

'Right,' announced Catiline when I saw him next. 'The plan is in place. I'm still about seventy thousand in debt and so is Cethegus. We chop Cicero.' He drew his hand across his throat expressively. 'You get Sicily. I get the consulship for the next term along with Lentulus and Caesar gets Gaul. We pay off all our debts and pick off a few other childless senators with profitable estates.'

'Caesar is in favour?' I asked.

'Bald Julius? Yes, indeed. He's got even bigger debts than I have. He paid for those exotic games last year all out of his own pocket. The lions alone cost him several thousand. All his takings from Spain have been used up already. And he's in hock for his two extra villas, one for his mistress and one for his fancy boys.'

'Go on, Sallust,' said Fulvia, fondling my ears. 'Help save the republic. Kill Cicero, the boring old bag of stale air.'

That night we went round to Caesar's townhouse for a banquet and, with so many brilliant people supporting the plot, I was now sure it was the right thing to do. What none of us knew was that Cicero was more paranoid than dim and had spies everywhere. The very moment when we broke into his official residence to kill him he was well out of the way, sending the senate to sleep with an extra-long speech about all our iniquities.

After this mess-up we stood no chance of success. Both Gaius Cethegus and Lentulus were arrested and later executed. Cicero lambasted Catiline again in the senate and Julius Caesar engineered a clever disappearance into the country until all the fuss had died down. Trust him to wangle his way out of trouble. So I and the rest of Catiline's friends were left to make a last stand with him at Pistoria. As the battle came to its climax I found myself fighting at his side.

'Sallust,' said Catiline, whose physical courage was still undiluted despite many years of debauchery, 'we've lost this one to the pompous old bore.'

'You're right, I'm afraid,' I agreed, for there were only about a dozen of us left alive. 'As a matter of interest who betrayed us?' I asked.

'Fulvia,' he answered with a wink. 'I should have known better.' And at that moment a spear took him full in the throat. I registered a tiny moment of pride that I had managed to fight on for longer than such a remarkable man as Catiline. Then the legionary in front of me broke my sword and his own flashed towards my chest.

New York, June 2nd, 2119

'What do you believe in, Theo?' asked Ariadne. 'Anything?'

'What do you mean?' I said, rather resenting this inquisition, especially after I'd just bought her two White Deaths and tonic.

'Why are we here?'

'At the Geyser Theme Bar you mean?' I asked.

'No, you idiot, in the world.'

'Because it's better than not being here. Like in a black hole or something.'

'You're so superficial at times,' she said. 'And I thought you were a Thetan.'

'I'm a positive thinker,' I said with only a touch of insincerity. 'Even when hardwood prices are falling and demand is slack I always have faith that they will rise back up again.'

Ariadne stared at me in mock despair. 'How can you think of the world just in terms of wood prices?' she said.

'What else is there?' I replied, deliberately adopting the pose to tease her, although I didn't know why; perhaps I sometimes feel the need to assert some feeble form of domination. 'The price of disease-free cattle, drugs or a season ticket for the red light district. And what about geriaid subscriptions now that the retirement age has gone back down to eighty?'

'It's a question of feelings. Enjoying things like sunsets and birds singing. You never say you appreciate that kind of thing.'

'I do a bit,' I said. 'But what I also appreciate is when the e-police manage to trap one of these computer hackers that are forever asking for protection money. And what I do like is history, the overlapping lives of millions of different people like a huge pile of spiders' webs. I admit I do find it hard to believe there's a god like an everlasting president managing everything, mismanaging it rather, but there is some kind of unseen force. I do believe that. For a start I do also believe in the immortality of the gene, the will to keep going not just for one lifetime, but forever until the sun blows up. Have you come across Joe Smith?'

'No,' she replied.

When it came to deciding whether I should fight on Caesar's side or Pompey's I had mixed feelings. I slightly preferred Caesar's politics, but my mother for some reason brought me up to think of him as a scoundrel. Because of my father, I suppose. And while Caesar was making himself famous conquering the Gauls I was behind a desk in Syria. So I chose Pompey and things have been going badly. We had just landed in Egypt and found that Bald Julius had his army there waiting to pounce on us. My master strode up the beach to greet the Pharaoh, who was waiting under a canopy, but before he could get there, an Egyptian sprang out and killed one of the noblest Romans I had ever known. Unbelievable treachery, yet now we find Julius is holed up in Alexandria with a rival pharaoh, a woman no less. With our army leaderless what is the point in going on?

New York, June 4th, 2119

This is the 200th Anniversary of the passing of the 19th Amendment allowing US women to vote. Yet these days most of us hardly ever bother to vote, because it's just the same people who win elections whatever you do. The Climate Deniers led by Donald J. Trump III have begun a new investigation to prove that the last Covid outbreak was a deliberate plot by the Zero Emitters who wanted to reduce the world's population by at least twenty per cent.

§

Naturally I changed to Caesar's side once Pompey had been killed. There was no choice. But I did not shed tears when he was knifed in the Senate. Then I had to choose between Octavian and Anthony. Octavian seemed the sounder bet, so I helped him put an end to the republic which was already rotten to the core. They had not allowed Caesar to become a king, but Octavian would be an emperor and we would have no more civil wars. At least that was the theory.

New York, June 6th, 2119

A couple of days later I took Ariadne to the COLDS Citadel, the superb marble worship station built fifty years ago when they merged the Latter day Saints with the Lutheran and Baptist Churches. It had a magnificent series of imitation stained-glass windows that showed the story of the original Joseph Smith who had a dream of an angel in Manchester, New York State three hundred years ago, then found hidden writings on golden plates, but was shot dead in Carthage gaol aged only thirty-nine.

'Here he comes,' I said to Ariadne as the same Dr Joe Smith whom I'd met for my DNA analysis glided up the platform in flowing robes.

'Impressive,' said Ariadne. 'The Seventh Day Adventists and the Iranian Shiites are part of this now too, aren't they? My granny was one of them.'

Dr Smith started to repeat his usual mantra in his usual sing-song voice.

Everyone who has ever lived is still alive.
Relax and your soul will move backwards or forwards,

Let your mind meander into the minds of your ancestors,
Let your mind meander from soul to soul,
Back in time,
Forward in time.
Everyone who has ever lived is still alive.'

Then as a choir of red-clad choristers repeated the words he raised a golden goblet to his mouth and drank from it.

There was a long silence.

'Why don't you get your DNA analysed?' I said to Ariadne.

'Is that some kind of proposal?' she asked and winked.

That night the Buddhist Republic of Myanmar voted to expel all Muslims and it was reported that a hundred thousand refugees had fled into Eastern India. The European Union had expelled Switzerland for money laundering. Donald J. Trump III opened his new tower in Polokwane, South Africa. A Washington man created a new world record for transgender marathons and Jerusalem was selected as venue for the 2126 World Football Championship.

CHAPTER TEN

WASTE AND WILDERNESS

The night is darkening round me
E. Bronte

Little Rock, Arkansas, June 15th, 2119

Most of my work I do online, but this time I had to make
a quick dash down to what was left of Arkansas to bid
for a major rebuild contract after a series of tornadoes
had flattened several cities. I called Ariadne, but got
her answerphone, so I just had to brood on my own
about all the problems of the modern world. I mean, if
there is a god why has he/she allowed all these climatic
changes? Ever more frequent tornadoes. Okay, maybe
global warming is the fault of humans, but if he/she was
almighty surely it could have been stopped. So either he/
she can't be almighty or he/she has a nasty streak.

§

My career in the Roman army had to date been somewhat
erratic. People said that my grandfather Sallust, who died
gloriously at the battle of Pistoria, had been a friend of
Julius Caesar himself, but his eldest son died fighting on
the wrong side in Egypt. My own father, the younger son,
made it to quaestor and governor of Illyria, but his heavy
drinking and preference for under-age girls made him
unpopular with Augustus, so he never got another post

after the age of forty. Thus I had to work doubly hard to impress the new emperor. In fact it was ten years before I got my first half-decent promotion, as deputy procurator in Samaria, reporting to the prat Pilate as we called him behind his back. Anyway at least it got me out of Rome, for no one was safe there after Tiberius had retired to Capri to have his fill of little boys. The evil Sejanus had embarked on a reign of terror in the city.

One of my main tasks in the new job was to keep a watching brief on Herod Antipas, a half-Greek, half-Jew who ran Galilee. This crawler was building a huge new fortress by the lake there and called it Tiberias in a bid to ingratiate himself with our beloved emperor. The wretched country was already littered with huge fortresses and temples built by the man's father, another of the same brood.

I used to pay official visits to Antipas at least twice a year and from my own base in Samaria I usually went up through the desert or sometimes along the Jordan valley. It was boring a lot of the time, so one of the few amusements was to stop and watch some of the strange would-be holy men in those parts. One in particular, a man called John, wore nothing but a rough coat of camel hair and used to chew squashed locusts right in front of our eyes. Of course I couldn't understand more than one word in ten and I'm not sure that the crowds of locals who came out to listen to him managed much better. But often his ravings finished with a mad rush to the river, where they would push each other beneath the limpid green of the Jordan.

Once in Tiberias there was little to do but listen to the rantings of Antipas and his tart of a wife, though it was also very pleasant to retire to the natural hot baths on the edge of the fortress, where normally I could rely on a few undisturbed hours and some underwater groping of the female attendants. On my last visit Antipas was in a particularly truculent mood. The locust-eating John had apparently made a few uncomfortably truthful remarks about the queen and this she did not appreciate. The Jews of course had a vast number of strange customs. Amongst these apparently was one which ordained that it was a form of incest to marry your brother's widow and of course Herodias had indeed been married previously to Antipas's brother, though how she came to be a widow was another story altogether.

'I've got four platoons out in the desert searching for the locust-eater,' said Antipas. 'It's just a matter of time. Now, before supper, my step-daughter Salome has said she'll dance for us.' He clapped his hands for music. 'She has no love for this John either.'

New York, June 17th, 2119

'It's me,' said Ariadne's voice on the phone.

'I thought it might be,' I replied.

'It's time for the next JECTOR test,' she said. 'If you're still game.'

'Just about,' I said. 'But I've had another bad day. Some rotten Kraut e-pod dealer in Berlin had the effrontery to undercut me by two cents a metre on an environmentally sustainable bridge contract for Mexico.'

'I'm sorry,' she said.

'It's all so petty. Why do half a dozen of us waste days on the phone competing to source mature larch trees when one person doing it is enough?'

'That's the capitalist system for you. Never mind if you only get one in six contracts that will be enough money for us to set up home. That's if we pass the JECTOR tests,' she added.

'You're wonderful,' I said. 'It's just hard to keep life in perspective. And the news has been so depressing too. Listen.' I switched my handset to the radio tuner function.

'It has been announced that the entire population of sub-Saharan Mauretania has been wiped out by a Covid-related virus.' said the computer voice. 'And the whole area is to be recolonised by Korean migrants from nearby Senegal. A new drug called Cozyme, a mixture of solidified alcohol and concentrated cannabis has been legalised in the French Peoples Republic of Quebec, which has seventy per cent unemployment. The ozone layer above Australia has been further depleted and the recorded number and size of meteorites crashing into the continent have shown a significant increase. The single-sex nation of Raratonga has achieved the highest rates for literacy and numeracy in the entire world, announced its president Ms Katanga. The civil war in China has escalated and the city of Nanjing has been attacked by hovercopters with cluster bombs. UNESCO plans to raise parts of the submerged city of Venice have run into further technical problems and the budget has been increased to fifty trillion euros. The final of the World Cup is to be between North Korea and Namibia.

A further series of tornadoes is forecast for the almost deserted state of Arkansas.'

'Enough?' I asked, switching off the tuner.

'Yes. Meet me at the JECTOR office at two tomorrow.'

§

My final command was the XIV legion based in Gaul and it was the only time I ever saw action in my entire career. Like all new emperors the latest one, the hunchback Claudius, wanted a conquest to his name, so he ordered us to cross the channel to invade Britain. What I especially remember are those impressive white cliffs, but we landed further east on shingle beaches where we met hardly any opposition. Within weeks we had overrun almost the entire island, so the emperor can stamp that on his coins. Not much else good, for the weather is dreadful, so are the women, and wine is non-existent.

New York, Rockaway Park, June 18th, 2119

I have an ingrained compulsion to be at least a few minutes early at any rendezvous, as if I expect the other person not to bother waiting.

On this occasion Ariadne was at least fifteen minutes late, so I treated myself to $2 worth of the coin-op interactive confessional machine while I was waiting. Seven sin options came up on the touchscreen, so I picked gluttony, a sin to which I am only mildly (worse than that says Ariadne) addicted and of which I am hardly at all ashamed. This then gave me a further seven options ranging from junk food to hard drugs and I picked alcohol. I then had to punch in my daily intake of each category and for each type select from a multiple choice of six different reasons as to why I felt compelled to drink. I pressed insecurity feelings and stress. Then the computer told me not to worry and put another $2 in if I wanted to make another confession or $3 for full absolution.

'Hi,' said Ariadne coming up behind me and tweaking me there, so I saved my credit for another time. Anyway I'd decided the machine was just a would-be subtle way of doing market research for the drinks lobby. Then we picked up our next test-pack from the pigeon-hole. In it were two pairs of biodegradable gloves, a detailed map of the Hudson River and a half page of instructions for our two ten-hour shifts of hard labour.

The first day we had to fill three roboskips with garbage from the shoreline and get a fair loading into a five-colour bottle bank.

There was a biting cold wind coming off the Atlantic as we set to work and our special phosphorescent vests did little to keep it out. For five hours without a break we picked supermarket hover-trolleys out of the mud, sodden old mattresses, pizza packets, frayed nylon ropes, gas bottles, detergent cartons, dirty syringes, condoms, phones, hundreds of assorted drinks bottles and one car engine before we qualified for a ten-minute lunch break. We ate a couple of sandwiches in the foyer of the huge plant that cracked the carbon out of carbon dioxide, the invention which they said had saved the world.

In the afternoon it was the same except that we also dug up a barnacle-covered machine gun, two bidets and an antique television set. In the final half hour we were allowed to follow our roboskips to the district crusher, where leafless trees blossomed with slivers of white plastic. Clouds of obese seagulls glided on thermals of oxidised garbage as two massive hydraulic rams shunted mounds of human detritus ever closer to the lip of the crusher shaft. There was an ironic sign proclaiming THANKS TO YOUR EFFORTS 85% OF RUBBISH IS NOW BEING RECYCLED. I didn't believe it.

'My back's just about broken,' said Ariadne, stretching like a tired cat. She pecked me on the cheek. 'Please don't be angry if I just go off home for a bath and bed,' she added.

'Sure,' I said, thinking this must be where we would chalk up a high relationship score and watching with some self-pity as she disappeared to the robo-station.

§

A cloud of black smoke hung over the entire city of Rome.

'Can't you chop a hole in that aqueduct?' said the man beside me as we watched the huge fire spread across another block of tenements. 'The only way to put it out is to flood the place,' he added.

'Unfortunately it's too well built and there's no outlet for several hundred yards,' I said, though I wasn't officially on duty. To be honest I was more concerned that the fire might stretch to my own house if the wind blew in that direction.

'Who started it, anyway? It can't just have been an accident.'

'Christians, as usual,' I answered, for most recent troubles had been caused by Christians despite Nero's valiant attempts to get rid of them.

Rockaway Park cont., June 19th, 2119

The two shifts the next day were both spent using long pincers to pick up cigarette butts, ring pulls, crisp packets, plastic cups and other pocket-sized rubbish from the promenade. It was boring, irritating and frustrating, especially when passing robo-drivers unrolled their electric windows and casually tossed out fresh rubbish onto the area we had just cleared.

'Bastard,' I heard Ariadne say to one of them. 'And I don't care who hears.'

I ran after the offending vehicle and shook my fist, then came back and hugged her. I think we got quite good marks that day.

§

It wasn't that I enjoyed being sodomised by the Emperor Hadrian, but without the emperor's favour you get nowhere these days. As a reward for this small inconvenience I acquired two legions before I was thirty and a provincial governorship two years later, faster promotion than anyone apart from the lover-boy Antinous. To strive afterwards for normality, whatever that may mean, when my senses were so blunted and my wealth so enormous, was not easy.

I served briefly in Britain where I helped thrust forward the frontier of the empire well into the territory of the Caledonians, and I had a good victory against twenty thousand barbarians on the Rhine, killing at least half of them and sending the rest off with a good drubbing. Then I tried to settle down with a fairly peaceful job governing Dalmatia. I built myself a delightful villa by the sea at Tragurium and stole at least a twelfth of all taxes, so my wealth increased rapidly and I bought estates both here and in Italy.

To start with I found it hard to raise much interest in women, especially those in Dalmatia who tended to be somewhat rustic for my taste. I also found it hard to sleep at night, sometimes disturbed by a most unpleasant dream in which the result of my German battle was reversed and I would lie scratching a tiresome rash on my arm that would not seem to go away. But gradually as the wine from my vineyards began to mature quite pleasingly I would let the daughters of the more prosperous Dalmatian traders parade on my patio for inspection. In fact without remembering the occasion too clearly I did make one of them pregnant. But now that I have seen her, and smelt her nursing the child, I find the whole process so disgusting that I have adjourned to my superbly decorated bathhouse and I have decided to open my veins.

New York, June 20th, 2119

I didn't sleep well the night after the days of garbage collecting. My elbow itched just as it had when I was a child. I was feeling unsure that I could cope with relationships and another fifty-five years of e-pod trading before I could afford to retire. The normal age for pension had just been raised to eighty-seven. And if we married should Ariadne go part-time with the Geriaid Foundation so that we wouldn't make a mess of our children, if we had any? Low sperm counts had become an increasing problem in New York at that time. But above all I was depressed that I would never become a great ruler or a prophet or paint a masterpiece. I am a mediocrity, average and undistinguishable from millions of others. And, even if I did achieve some lesser glory, what would be the point if the world came to an end in a few hundred years and there was no one left to know about it? A spokesperson from the Greta Thunberg Foundation says it might be as soon as seventy years.

'Why are you quiet and morose?' asked Ariadne.

'I'm fine,' I lied.

'I know you well enough to see that's not quite true.'

'I'm just sorry for myself over nothing. Let's get married.'

'We've only three more tests to complete. It'll be no time to wait and then at least we'll be sure.'

'I'm sure already,' I said truculently.

'So am I really,' she said. 'But let's wait since we've got this far.'

§

My stepfather never really liked me and my mother was too busy to bother, so from the age of about ten I used to spend most of my time on the fish quay at Tragurium. The town was on a small island connected to the mainland by a causeway, and it served as one of the ports for the great garrisons of Illyria and Pannonia beyond. Often I would beg trips on local boats, either with fishermen or traders, some of them no more than small-time pirates or smugglers who made a living in the area. So I came to know the Gulf of Salone like the back of my hand, all the little towns hidden up in coves on the islands of Pharia with its old Greek lighthouse and Brattia with its olive groves, then further afield down the coast to Epirus and Greece.

They used to say that Commodus was a crazy emperor, but at least when things were chaotic we had freedom to enjoy ourselves, and as far as we were concerned he could execute as many overpaid generals and senators as he liked. They told me my own father had been some kind of great man, but I paid little attention, since in those days all great men died young at the hands of the army or the emperor.

Gradually I learned to find my own way at sea, with the stars at night, the feel of the wind or the colour or smell of currents by day.

After a few years I saved up enough to put down the deposit on an eighty-foot boat of my own. I paid off the loan for the rest quite quickly by doing government contract work, mostly supplies going from Ariminum or Ancona across the Adriatic for the troops on the Danube. I loved the sea and eventually had two wives, one fat and jolly in Tragurium, the other neat and serious down the coast in Dyrrachium. Perhaps I love food and wine too much, but it's fun while it lasts.

Detroit, June 23rd, 2119

Our next JECTOR test which was supposed to be a long drive with no sleep for two nights was one to which in a strange kind of way I looked forward. The instructions when we picked them up were to drive to Detroit, find a particular address and then drive back again. This was about six hundred miles each way and at the regulation fifty takes twice twelve hours plus stopover time to recharge the batteries. Since self-drive cars were now a rarity I had driven nothing but robo-cars since my teens, so I was seriously out of practice.

At this period the freeways were fairly empty because of the massive decline in private motoring and all the commercial traffic just used the hard shoulder, so the biggest problem was boredom. We stopped twice for coffee and junk hydrocarb on the way, sharing the driving, the final stage Ariadne dozing with her head on my shoulder.

'What I do for you,' I said as we came into the suburbs of Detroit. My feet felt red hot and gummy, my head pincered by the endless avenue of headlamps.

'What you do for me?' she snapped, waking at full throttle.

'For us I mean,' I corrected myself.

'Better,' she said. 'We're cracking up already, aren't we? Let's try and get through this without losing the place.'

Now we had to find the designated address and even with the satnav it wasn't easy, for most of the streets and buildings had been demolished. Detroit was like a huge concrete desert: GM-Mitsubishi had just closed and Ford were down to a care-and-maintenance basis. There were a few half-occupied skyscrapers with lifts that only worked on alternate days and wide stretches of rubble where the rosebay willow herb bloomed triumphantly from every crevice. Derelict hypermarkets were haunted by flocks of giant starlings that had morphed genetically over the previous two centuries of living off human scraps.

After an hour of frustration during which I almost succumbed to the kind of bad temper which would have led to an instant JECTOR fail mark we found the derelict Chrysler warehouse which was our goal and we could turn home.

'Well done,' said Ariadne and kissed me.

We stopped at a Pizzacheep for another junk-snack and picked up the freeway back east, Ariadne driving for a stretch. But I found sitting beside her almost as tiring as driving myself, as vast roboids swished past us in the rain, fanning great arcs of water above us. As the light pylons went past like a perpetual strobe we turned on the radio louder and louder to help keep us awake. Our ears were deadened by the audio-pollution of repeated injunctions to keep down our speed, advertisements for birth control devices and totally absurd news about failed probes to Jupiter, the first woman to pull a hover-sled across the Antarctic, a plague of monster ants in the Texas Biosphere, the usual riots between the Muslim and Buddhist enclaves in New York and yet another war between North and South China.

After four hours and some coffee I was driving again, but in a dream, hallucinating through a tunnel of rain carved by our headlight beams. Sucked towards the final solution.

Occasionally duct repairmen in orange-glow jackets would appear out of nowhere and perhaps never knew how close I was to hitting them, The lightning bounced off the horizon and only Ariadne's thoughtful hand in my trouser pocket kept me awake.

Then the news, at least I thought it was news, but it might have just been a play, that archaeologists digging in Sinai had uncovered two broken tablets of stone with ten worn lines of hieroglyphs. Then at last we came to a sign that said New York ten miles. Why should God give orders in Egyptian hieroglyphs anyway? But if not, what would he write them in?

§

My grandfather was a well-known sea-dog on the Dalmatian coast. He had three wives and at least twenty children. The eldest brother, a sailor too, was drowned at sea in a storm but the second, my father, was a farmer and did quite well as a vine grower near Salonae where I was born. So when the old emperor Diocletian decided to retire and build a country palace nearby he helped lay out the gardens and, as his daughter, I got a job as under-cook. Three of my uncles won contracts for shipping the huge quantities of stone for the new palace from the quarries of Tragurium. Spoletum was to be the biggest palace in the world, all for one sick old man.

'You're not a Christian are you?' asked a good-looking cellar-lad one day, when I offered him some scraps from the centurions' left-over pot.

'Why, should I be?' I asked.

'Well it's fashionable in some places. And you're showing charity.'

'It's also a good qualification for getting a temporary job in the amphitheatre,' I said sarcastically. 'And that I can do without.'

'But why worship an emperor who's a cruel sick old man and building the biggest palace in the world for himself?'

'You're a funny one,' I said. 'What else is a god except the man with the biggest house in the world? Or the most power. A hundred legions entitles you to call yourself god.'

'I think it takes more of a god to make the flowers come up,' he said. 'Or even to make one woman happy.'

'Even a donkey can trample down flowers. A man can kill a donkey and the emperor can kill any man he likes.'

'Well,' he said. 'I don't intend to be a cellar-lad all my life. Why not give me the chance to make you happy?'

'You never know,' I replied with a coy smile.

New York, June 30th, 2119

Just when I thought I was doing well at the JECTOR tests, and was about to achieve emotional security with Ariadne, I experienced another unnerving cataclysm at work. There are, these days, a number of rogue e-pod traders who don't really trade at all, but simply amuse themselves with computer viruses to sabotage other peoples' software. I had just put through quotes on a major contract for flooring a chain of casinos and the margins were very tight. Then some datapath in Hanoi hacked through the web and altered my price downwards by ten per cent. Not surprisingly I won the contract and was stuck with it, for an e-pod trader's word is his bond, but now I stood to lose $50k on the bottom line. Nor had I been able to get any insurance against software hacking as it had become so common. What I should have done was to fix a data anti-intrusion package. Now I could go bankrupt and be disqualified from marriage. Life seemed one long disaster and I would end up stubble-chinned in Cardboard City and hooked on super-glue.

§

'Soldier, do you or do you not accept the Trinity?' the new priest asked. He had not long arrived at our barracks in Aquincum.

I pretended I didn't understand what he was talking about.

'God the father, God the Son and the Holy Ghost, three in one,' he went on with an expression on his face designed to inspire dread.

I had begun to hear stories of heretics being reported to the magistrates and I knew the penalties were severe, usually burning. Bishop Arius had fairly stirred things up.

'Recite after me the Nicene Creed,' he said. 'If you don't accept it you will be damned.'

I certainly believed in God and Jesus, but I wasn't at all convinced of the rest, specially not the extra one, the Holy Ghost, just because Constantine had bullied a few cringing bishops. But I had a dear wife and wonderful children, so call me a coward if you want, but I recited the Nicene Creed and went on my way. It's just words after all. Pannonia has been a good posting for me and I love our home by the River Ister. It even has its own god, Danuvius, but we aren't supposed to believe in him any more

New York, Jul 1st, 2119

When I have a moment between the perpetual round of panics I wonder again what it's all for. Procreation is a wonderful thing but its seems highly inefficient. Why invent all these obstacles to happiness like disease, death, poverty? There must be a reason, but all philosophers can do is babble about the difference between consciousness and substantiality. So what? I couldn't sleep so I listened to god@sky.com again. 'Tonight's reading is from the Book of the Prophet J. Maynard Keynes:

The virtue of extravagance is greatly underrated
As sensible economists have often clearly stated.
The virtues of frugality distinctly overrated,
The fashion of austerity a fad that priests created
Resulting in economies that rapidly stagnated
And currencies that were suddenly deflated or re-flated.
It's true that wealth is often most unfairly concentrated

Amongst the few instead of the less well remunerated,
But absolute equality makes nations constipated.
The wickedness of waste is however much exaggerated.
When industry and market trends are well investigated
The data and statistics painstakingly collated
Show theft to be a virtue that should now be reinstated.
Obsessions with recycling are already rather dated.
Big spenders should not be the ones so often castigated
And greed's a vice that certainly should not be adumbrated.
Palaces and warfare in former days created
Employment for the rest of us and few appreciated
The myriad of luxuries which wastefully placated
The whims of the pretentious, the rich, the dissipated,
But also kept the rest of us quite fairly compensated.
Without the fact that everything is always duplicated
Employment for the masses would be sadly decimated.

This was sung to the tune of 'Tannenbaum' at major rallies.

New York, Jul 2nd, 2119

This is exactly two hundred years since the first airship R 434 crossed the Atlantic.

I had an enquiry from Maritime Themeland for a fleet of twenty imitation Viking long boats, the sort of job that was sometimes quite interesting, but of course they weren't bothered about authenticity, all they cared about was price, so one of those new Korean wide boys got the order.

The 236th anniversary of Marks and Spencer was commemorated with an official ode by the M&S laureate David Beckham IX:

Hail M&S the great emporium
With doors of glass and aluminium,
Glittering alleys of shrink-wrapped pies,
Frozen chips and crepe surprise.
Ladies lingerie in rows by size
Potted plants the week's best buys
Do not lose your card receipt
In case the shoes don't fit your feet

Soon afterwards it was announced that Beckham had turned down a three-million eurodollar golden hello from Walmart. He was to sponsor a new range of breakfast mueslis with freeze-dried segments of genetically modified cherries.

News came in also that a massive swarm of locusts had destroyed all crops in the West African Republic and was now heading for Chad. The North Chinese announced that this was a disinformation campaign mounted by South China and that they had used diluted novichok to destroy the swarm.

CHAPTER ELEVEN

SINS AND LOVERS

'Revolving in his altered soul
The various turns of chance below.'
J. Dryden

New York, Jul 2nd, 2119

I did three circuits of Central Park trying to clear my
head, but kept finding that I was drawn as if by magic in
the direction of Cardboard City. Life seemed so fragile.
That very day the President of Europe had been sentenced
to twenty years hard labour for taking bribes and the
crown prince of Belgium arrested on seven counts of
child abuse. My fall would embarrassingly be from a
much lower jumping off point. I had achieved nothing.

§

'You stupid bastard,' said the centurion, pushing me out of
the way for no particular reason. There was an ugly mood
in the fort and we hadn't been paid for three months, not
even the officers. There was no breeze to lessen the dry
heat and the Danube flowed green and sluggish, listlessly
bearing our detritus towards the faraway sea. I had been
serving in the Twelfth Legion in Carnuntum for ten years,
for I hated the idea of being a gardener in the Spoleto
palace like my father and grandfather before him. But
these days we hardly knew whose side we were on. With

Theodosius dead we had two kid emperors, one in the west, the other in the east and Illyria was no-mans land in the middle. Bad enough half the officers now being Goths, but if we didn't even get paid that was the end.

That afternoon we went down to the tavern by the river and, as we had no money left, we threatened to kill the landlord unless he gave us our fill. As usual we drank ourselves stupid and shuffled along to the whorehouse where the women chewed hemp and had black teeth, but felt much the same as any others in the dark.

So we were still in our bunks, asleep long after dawn when the famous Alaric crossed the river and occupied our fort without having to shed a drop of blood. He was a big man, and, Goth or no Goth, he offered us two months back pay if we'd swear an oath to him that morning. So why not? We weren't even sure if we were supposed to be fighting for one kid emperor or the other. So we joined Alaric instead and became Goths ourselves. This is why on my first visit to Rome I spent most of the time setting the buildings on fire.

At least I got paid for it.

New York, Jul 2nd, 2119 cont.

'Sorry, I do sympathise with you guys,' said the main casino contractor on his mobile to me as if I had company. 'But an e-pod tender is a tender, and legally binding, so your price must stand. Extraneous corruption is not a let-out.'

'Okay,' I said. 'Thank you for trying.' Then I rang my teak supplier in Yangon to see if he could be persuaded to drop his price a few percent.

'It's not me, man,' he said in his Chinese Harlem accent. 'But my margin to the loggers is only one per cent gross and we have five per cent inflation every week here at the moment. That's in a good week with no change of government.'

My state of morale was thus very low when I had to face up to one of the last of the JECTOR tests, a cocktail party in Manhattan where everyone else was young, Korean, black or something big in show business and all wearing designer fabrics. What's more Ariadne and I were only allowed to drink tomato juice. As soon as people heard I was an e-pod trader and Ariadne in gericare they just changed the subject and moved on.

'You don't care what I feel,' said Ariadne, after I had been morosely silent for a minute or two.

'I do, but I'm a bit preoccupied and these people give me the—'

'Your own problems, that's all you care about.'

'I could go bankrupt. Then all our hopes would be lost.'

'I'm not sure I care. What does money matter? We could live in a shack. As long as you really cared.'

'I do,' I said unconvincingly. 'But we wouldn't last long as drop-outs. I'm committed on at least a third of my earnings before I even start living.'

'I could help,' she said.

'That's very kind, but I've got to sort out my own mess first.'

142

'To heck with JECTOR, let's go somewhere for a drink.'

I glanced at my watch. 'We only need to last another two minutes here to pass the test anyway.'

'Well we must stick together even when things are rough,' she said and grabbed my hand hard in hers.

§

My grandfather had been given land near Ravenna and had drained a marsh to build a fine house. Most of the city had been created by driving huge logs into the ground and digging ditches to get rid of the fetid water. So now it became a Visigoth colony with fine buildings… until the Ostrogoths attacked us. I fought in the army of our king Odoacer, but we were defeated at Verona and then Theodoric of the Ostrogoths came from Greece and besieged our city. This lasted for three bitter years, for we ran short of food, and there was nothing much left but fish. Two of my children died of poor nourishment and my wife was deeply depressed, but things were even worse when Theodoric broke through the walls. He killed Odoacer with his own hands and announced that all Arians would be executed unless they accepted the Trinity. I gathered a few possessions and set off at night with what was left of my family to join the other Visigoths in France

New York, Jul 4th, 2119

My elbow was itching when I woke up the next morning facing bankruptcy. I was due an e-payment from the

143

casinos, but within two days would have to pay up nearly twice that amount to Yangon.

The phone rang. 'It's the last JECTOR test,' said Ariadne lightly. 'We've done so well already.'

'Quite. But I'm not sure I care at the moment.'

'Don't be horrid. See you at three thirty. We've got a dozen LD children to look after.'

'What does that mean?'

'Learning difficulties. I told you that last time.'

The phone rang again. It was Yangon and sweat trickled down my side. 'No price leduction, I'm afraid,' said the Harlem Chinese voice. 'But I can maybe help a bit.'

'How?'

'The loggers have oversupplied by about ten tonnes. I don't need it and it's probably illegal anyway, so I can't sell it separately. You can have it at half price if you can sell it. But you have to make the decision now.'

As good being a big bankrupt as a small one, I thought, and accepted the Yangon offer. If I could make a 70% mark-up on half-price teak I would almost break even. So I rang the casinos first.

'What about the optional extension?' I asked. 'The new-build in Alaska.'

'I'll know tomorrow or the day after,' said the contract manager.

'I can still hold the same low price as before,' I said.

It was now three twenty-five and I was due to meet Ariadne in five minutes.

144

'Here they are, the little darlings,' she said and seemed to mean it, though the six small children assigned to us for our twenty-four-hour test were the most over-indulged, computer-obsessed, self-opinionated potential thugs that I could imagine being found to push us to the limit. It was a very long wait till three thirty the following day, and I was close to self-immolation, in fact I could easily have lapsed into child abuse, but I have to say that Ariadne's patience wore them down and in the end they were almost human. She touched their hair and made funny faces and they seemed to come round to her.

Perhaps my memory of our final hour with them was made brighter by the call I got from Alaska agreeing to take my extra teak. I was saved. And to make the evening even more memorable the Iranians had with United Nations approval sent a thousand HE-drones to obliterate the last oil refineries in Saudi.

§

'That's the man who killed your father,' said my grandmother, pointing to King Clovis of the Franks as he made his triumphal entry into Tours. I looked down at the stocky, middle-aged man strutting up the main street with his servile retinue. In a way he looked a little absurd wearing two crowns, one on top of the other, not to mention all his other regalia.

'He's got no shame,' spat my grandmother, who would happily have taken him on single-handed. Then I saw the tiny figure of Queen Clotilde, whose kind heart was believed to be quite the opposite of her husband's.

145

'Your father was a lord and now we have nothing. Stop scratching that sore arm of yours. That won't help.'

I'd heard the story so often before. My grandmother's father had come to Gaul with the first great Alaric and been given good land near the Loire. The family had prospered, but then had come a succession of wars between the Goths, the Franks and the Germans. My father died alongside his master Alaric II near Poitiers. And King Clovis was the man who had speared both of them.

'Where are you going?' asked my grandmother.

'I need to win back some of our land,' I said. 'The Goths are a spent force. So I'm going to start being a Frank.'

New York, Jul 5th, 2119

Suddenly my life had moved from a period of huge turmoil and insecurity to amazing calm, yet such is the human psyche that the joy of escaping from disaster soon turns to jaded dissatisfaction with the dullness of safety. Ariadne and I had now done so commendably well in the JECTOR tests that we were in the green zone for low-cost divorce insurance. With growing confidence that our union could soon be official I made one or two physical moves to register my proactive lust.

'Stop it,' said Ariadne with a good-humoured nudge. Since the late twenty-first century chastity had come back into vogue. The third strain of AIDs had seen to that if nothing else. 'I think I would quite enjoy it as well,' she admitted. 'But let's wait. In this respect I'm a modern woman. I still want to be a virgin when I marry. Make this do.' She kissed me.

I half pretended to sulk. 'At least let me have a look to keep me going,' I said.

'No problem,' she said and flicked the velcro tabs of her flip-suit, held it open for a second then locked up. 'Now you do the same.'

I did the equivalent. 'Interesting.' she said, grinning.

'Let's get married, then,' I said.

'Okay. COLDS Temple or Stats Office?'

§

Our family had farmed near the Loire for three generations, ever since my father brought me from the ruins of Ravenna, and we lived comfortably enough till that dreadful year of 535. That was when the summer was like the winter, the skies were black with dust and the crops all failed. There was no sign of the sun for fifteen months. The next year was little better and three of my five children died. The harvests improved a little, but we had to use up all the seed and we went hungry. Then my beloved wife died and so did another of our children, covered in those dreadful sores. There were few of us left to work the land and God seemed to have deserted us. Then I had a huge blister on my groin and my hands went black. I had seen enough of the plague to know what that meant.

New York July 6th, 2119

That day was a dreadful shock, for a crowd of extreme Climate Deniers placed a bomb in the basement of

147

Trump Towers and brought down the whole building with the loss of five hundred lives. It did not make sense, for Donald Trump had been one of their heroes, but they were so obsessive that they had got their ideas mixed up and chosen the wrong building to make their protest.

§

'A mortal sin, my son, nothing less,' said the Abbot, shaking his head at me as if I were the meanest novice.

I accepted his rebuke because there was little point in arguing with a man like that, although I knew for a fact that with only one slip in ten years I was one of the most chaste monks in the whole of Tours. And at least my lapse had been with a female.

'I will think about your punishment,' went on the abbot, and left me there on my knees until he turned the cloister corner. I stood up and walked quickly round to the refectory, scratching at my elbow as I worried about what he might do. A little comfort-eating would be a temporary consolation.

As the third and youngest son of the royal steward of Tournai the church had for me been the only chance of a reasonable career. It had never occurred to me to object to the vows or to take them seriously, indeed so far my life had been a lot more comfortable and far less dangerous than that of my two soldier brothers, one of whom had already been killed in battle. It wasn't until I was past twenty that I found the commitment to chastity irksome, especially when I saw so many of the parish priests ignoring that part of their vows. Now one lapse with a

148

scullery maid and my chances of a nice little bishopric were in some serious doubt. Besides, she had led me on, I swear it, when I'd had an extra horn of wine. In fact I could have easily disowned her pregnancy, but for some strange reason I actually wanted the guilt to be mine. Yet now as deputy prior of the monastery of St Martin of Tours and with ten years of exemplary holiness to my credit, it seemed I'd thrown everything away for thirty seconds of dubious pleasure.

Meanwhile the town was rife with rumours about quarrels within the royal family. Kings in those days had to have a very strong character and good fighting skills or they could easily lose their inheritance. With Dagobert II of France it was touch and go. He was able enough in some ways, but he was on the short side, rather effete and had trouble imposing his will on the sword-happy courtiers.

Three days after my reprimand from the abbot he summoned me. 'King Dagobert has been persuaded to abdicate,' he said. 'He must leave the country and as your penance I have chosen you to share his exile.'

'Where, father abbot?'

'He is being sent across the sea to Ireland, to a small monastery on an island. I fear you are unlikely ever to return.'

I didn't, but my seed had been planted.

New England, Jul 8th, 2119

I tried to organise a pre-marital seduction weekend with Ariadne, but she saw through my ploy and we compromised with an e-bike trip to New England. A number of interesting monastic communities had been set up there in the late 2050s and we were both curious to see what they were like. One was a huge former electronics factory where the members lived together, shaven-headed in a uniform of dark three-piece suits. They abstained from everything that you can think of except old-fashioned cigarettes, in which they indulged continuously, deliberately courting lung cancer. Their prophet was a Cypriot tobacco martyr who had claimed descent from both James the brother of Jesus and from Mohammed, and they sat most of the day on long benches in a blue haze of smoke with occasional cough-ridden incantations from their grey-faced prior.

'I thought it was quite moving,' said Ariadne as we emerged into the autumn sunshine, taking off our face-masks.

'I'm never sure what to believe about people like that,' I said as we got back on our e-bikes. 'Yet they have a lot of followers.'

Our second visit was to the Sisters of Corn, an all-female community dedicated to ultra-organic vegetable and grain farming.

'They certainly work hard,' I said. 'But these days it's a bit self-indulgent.'

'How can you say that?' protested Ariadne. 'They do such wonderful work in Africa. They just about saved Eritrea from extinction.'

'Fair enough,' I conceded and then we cycled a few miles further to the foundation that had most impressed me, The Order of the Sacred Neutron. This was a world-wide group of men and women who dedicated their lives to the decontamination of nuclear submarine hulks. They wore a distinctive yellow sash and most people had such awe of them that they would stand out of their way on the sidewalks.

We paid twenty eurodollars each just to enter the huge hall of their headquarters, a massive derelict fast-cooling reactor whose decontamination had already cost the lives of the first twelve brothers of the Order. All the members we saw looked pale, thin and under forty but martyrish and one of them, covered in PPE, gave us a detailed tour of half a dozen submarine hulks which they were stripping.

'I do find that impressive,' I said to Ariadne as we left.

'I suppose a man would see more in that than the Sisters of Corn.'

I shrugged. Less contentious was our next visit to the Positive Brethren, who had founded a string of hospices to combat the third strain of AIDs. Then we went to the Sisters of Galilee who specialised in restocking large lakes and inland seas with fish. In fact we had a very pleasant evening at one of their Wild Fish Restaurants where they raise money for the cause.

'Very good,' I said as we crept into our tent. 'But I still don't see why they have to be celibate.'

'Perhaps that's what they want,' said Ariadne. 'Not everyone's like you.'

§

I was happy enough to end my days in Ireland, especially when wretched Dagobert was summoned home to be king again. Sometimes I dreamed about the sin that had led to my downfall and in my vanity I wondered if by chance it had led to the birth of a child. Vanity has always been my worst vice.

Niagara, Jul 9th, 2119

It was with these tastes of mine to the fore that we rounded off the weekend with a night by Niagara Falls. The spray dripped off Ariadne's yellow hat and her nose as we held hands, muttering idiocies to each other against the massive roar of the water. Then we adjourned to the three-star bunkhouse to stand together in a hot shower, not touching, with no yellow hats, just warm, steamy water cataracting down our bodies to the tiles. Continuing this hedonistic theme, which I believed we had earned by our endeavours, we treated ourselves to a whole bottle of the Chilean Chateauneuf du Pape 2103, a vintage year, so the book said, and two 8 oz meat-free steaks in pepper sauce.

'Let's get married,' I said.

Ariadne lifted her glass in acknowledgement.

§

It was the first time I had ever seen heathens. We were camped near Poitiers and the bosses told us that this time we were fighting for God. The other side had a different god, so they were evil people whom we must exterminate. When I saw them in the distance they wore billowing cloaks and head scarves, their faces were dark and they scampered around on agile little horses, never standing still and jeering at us whenever they came at all close. I admit I was frightened by them, for they seemed to have no fear of death at all, but I was frightened more by our general, Charles the Hammer.

Our orders came. We were to fight on foot, forming a huge square on the hill, so the enemy had to ride up the slope against us. Meanwhile the Hammer sent a regiment behind their lines to attack their wagon train and pinch their precious loot, for that was what they cared most about. So when the attackers heard rumours that their gold was disappearing they showed much less interest in attacking us. Their precious emir was killed in the stampede and though I suffered a few cuts and bruises, I had enough strength left to go and grab a small share of the treasure. With that I joined a group heading north for Aachen and bought myself some new armour, so that I could make something of myself and find a woman.

New York, Jul 11th, 2119

Just as I was beginning to think that all was right with the world there came news that a large comet had crossed into the gravitational pull of the sun and was heading towards the Earth at thirty miles per second. NASA had launched three unmanned tug-probes to attempt to divert before impact, but little hope of success was evident. However, I remembered that the Earth had been due to blow up both in AD 1000 and AD 2000 and it didn't happen. The new single from the Four Horsemen band had it exactly and topped the charts for several weeks.

'The end of the world is nigh', said I
So we waited tense on a mountain top
For the world to flood or come to a stop
In June 1793.
But it didn't.

The day of reckoning is beckoning,
The dance of death passed through the town,
So many a witch was condemned to drown
In March 1384.
But nothing happened.

The death of us all is near, my dear,
As we tried to evade the apocalypse
Which the horsemen had said would sink our ships
In May 1537.
But they stayed afloat.

But they might still drop the bomb, Tom.
Remember Hiroshima, that was it,
Think of the finger on the tit
In April 1990,
But the finger relaxed.

Yet if the world began with a big bang it could finish the same way. What a waste. As it happened this time the comet must have changed its mind.

A teenage member of the Dallas Gun Club has claimed a world record for the number of schoolchildren and teachers (312) whom he killed in a single day. He was congratulated by the president of the NRA shortly before he died of wounds sustained when he was shot by the Texas Rangers.

A battle in the Pacific between six nuclear submarines crewed by robots from North and South China resulted in the sinking of all six. The UNO has declared that it will take at least 200 years before nuclear contamination is released from the sunken hulks which lie at a depth of around 2000 meters in an area a hundred miles west of Fiji.

In a recent telephone survey using ratings based on zero to nine with zero meaning subnormal intelligence and nine being common sense, the average for the following questions 1) How reliable are nuclear non-proliferation treaties ? 2) How many governments tell the truth about functioning warheads? 3) How likely is Amsterdam to be submerged by the North Sea in the next ten years 4) Will the Amazon rain forest be treeless by 2150? etc etc. The depressing result was that 80% of the results suggested subnormal intelligence.

CHAPTER TWELVE

RITES AND WRONGS

*'Thousands careless of the damning sin
Kiss the book's outside who ne'er look within.'*
W. Cowper

New York, Jul 18th 2119

False alarm. The comet's going to miss us by about half a million miles.

For the first time in my life I feel that both my career and my love life are fit for purpose. Everything is going well, yet now I want something else. What?

§

'I don't want your gold,' I said as disdainfully as I could manage, but I thrust the coin into my skirt pocket all the same. The man had been too drunk to do anything, in fact I suspected that he would not have been much good sober.

For six years I prided myself that I'd been the most popular whore in the court of Charles the Great at Aachen. Those were exciting days when he came back from Rome as an emperor and every night we had huge gold goblets of wine that were filled up again by servants before you were half-way down. The trouble was that I began to put on too much weight and some of the younger knights thought they might be found inadequate for someone my size.

'Still hungry, Clotilde?' asked one of the emperor's bastards mockingly. He was young enough to be my own son, but he wasn't. I'd had eight children, but only two were still alive and one of them, the boy, had headed off to the south, God knows where. The girl is already a promising trainee in my own department.

I drifted off to a corner of the hall, kicking aside scattered beef bones, dirty straw and dogs. I curled up in one of my favourite nooks and the wine started to flow back into my head. I was past caring if the rats popped out for a titbit, although my elbow was a bit raw where they'd bitten me the last time. The noise from the party in the hall was beginning to die down and as I saw the first rat scurry past on his way to a late supper I fell soundly asleep.

New York, Jul 30th, 2119

Ariadne and I were married in the Ishkon Temple on Fifth Avenue by a JECTOR consultant with Dr Smith of the COLDS Foundation as our chief witness. My mother and Ariadne's father seemed to hit it off and we had a green reception in the Zen Wild Vegetable Restaurant with a walzamba band to follow.

For our honeymoon we flew to the Croat Peoples' Republic, using my robomiles loyalty card, and we came to the ancient walled city of Trogir. The Adriatic had risen two feet in the previous sixty years due to shrinking of the polar ice cap, so Trogir being quite low-lying had a barrage built to prevent flooding.

'Right,' said Ariadne as we shut the door of our roof-top suite in a medieval tenement by the old cathedral. 'You've waited very patiently. Let's make babies together.'

An hour later when we surfaced from the rich warmth of animal joys Ariadne announced that she was hungry.

'Me too,' I said.

We went down the winding stair and through the narrow alleyways of the old town to a restaurant in an open courtyard. For some reason I had an uncanny feeling that I had been there before.

The following day we hired a small yacht and sailed across to the tree-clad island of St Lazar, once a leper colony. There we lay on an almost empty beach disturbed only by the buzz of crickets.

'Thank you,' said Ariadne.

'Thank you,' I replied.

§

'Not bad for the son of a whore,' I said to my mother the day that I was promoted to chief armourer of the Lord of Chartres.

'And the grandson of a whore too,' she said, bestowing on me a tooth-free grin.

'My lord has given orders that the Northmen must not pass Chartres. He says the Virgin will be our aid.'

'That lets me out,' said my mother.

'He has sworn to build a high church on this spot, if we can stop the invaders,' I said.

'Surely you don't need to fight. You're an armourer.'

'I'm afraid I do.'

The next day we marched out and waited on a loop of the River Eure near Couville. The Northmen were camped downstream from us, so we pushed dead pigs into the river and the body of one of our servants who had died of the plague. The Northmen seemed in no hurry, for the king of France had already sent gold and barrels of wine to try to buy them off, but on the fifth morning, which was quite dull, they attacked at last. The Virgin did appear as promised like a glow in the mist and the Northmen seemed to have little of their usual fury. We killed many and then returned in triumph to Chartres, raping a few of our own grateful peasant women on the way.

New York, Aug 10th, 2119

Ariadne sold her flat and moved into mine so my trading area was relegated to a small corner hidden by a bead curtain.

'As your wife I must take a keen interest in your work,' she said ominously.

'Oh,' I said.

'You should insist that everyone who sells a tree should plant a new one in its place. That would help stabilise the world's climate.'

'It's not quite as simple as that,' I said. 'We're in a very competitive environment.'

'It never is simple. But if you want me to take an interest in your work...'

'Of course I do, but e-pod traders tend to be a cynical bunch.'

'That doesn't have to mean that you are too.'

I felt somewhat irritated that an amateur was wading into my professional preserve. 'Then every time a new baby is born you should pull the plug on one of your geriatrics,' I said petulantly.

'That's absurd,' said Ariadne and proceeded to set a pointed example by sowing nuts and apple pips in recycled milk cartons.

§

The emperor known by most of us as Charles the Fat had added West Francia to his realms when he could not even control what he already had. He was not the sort of man for whom I would give my life, nor would many others of the court barons. The trouble was that hunks of the empire had to be allotted to all the male relations, whether they were competent or not, and Charles was liable to have fits whenever there was a crisis. So when the Vikings invaded us with a massive army he simply could not cope. When they besieged Paris this was the last straw and my master Count Odo of Paris took the responsibility out of his hands. He kept tight control of his men and I was ordered to fight to the death if necessary to guard the city walls closest to the River Seine. I had no choice and though I do not have great courage I feared Odo more than I did the Vikings.

New York Aug 11th, 2119

Needless to say our first real row was on the subject of trees. Ariadne was convinced that it was wicked to cut down any of them, whereas I tried to persuade her that you could always replace them with new young saplings which would soon grow into CO2-absorbing trees. But people were very fanatical on the subject for, despite all our efforts, the climate change had not yet been reversed. The hurricanes and wild fires kept returning.

§

My father, who was killed at the siege of Paris, had instilled in me great loyalty to the descendants of Charlemagne, but as Lord of Chartres I had to think of my own descendants and they would have little respect for me if I continued to support the well-named Charles the Simple. His wife had just died leaving six daughters and no sons, so the succession was in doubt. He took a new wife from England, but largely ignored her and seemed besotted with a young knight called Hagano. He also ignored the fact that East Francia had now for the first time been taken over by the Germans, and the Channel coast had been occupied permanently by the Norsemen. This, combined with his ignoble infatuation, was enough for me to join the plot to dethrone him. So I supported Robert I as the new king and we drove out Charles the Simple to exile in Lotharingia. Yet this situation did not last long for Robert was killed in battle at Soissons a year later and, though we won the battle, I was badly wounded and struggled home to die.

Ariadne told me not to be depressed, but I am depressed. They're threatening to test a modified asteroid 2.2 bomb on the Pitcairn islands, there is a massive forest fire raging in Siberia and another one threatening to wipe out Oregon. What's the point in abolishing fossil fuels if living forests go on fire? The latest flood zone maps show that most of Bangladesh will soon be permanently under water. Three hundred women in Angola have died due to infected breast implants.

'Let's have macaroni and cheese tonight,' said Ariadne and perhaps the problems of the world were not all that bad.

§

'Morning, Jacques,' I said to the tanner of Falaise. It was twenty years past the millennium when the world was supposed to come to an end and when Jacques' lovely daughter Arlette was born, but the little town of Falaise was once again bustling in the spring sunshine.

'Morning, Joseph,' said the tanner, wiping his hands on his apron. The stench of stale urine in his leather tank seemed to have no effect on him.

'How's the lovely Arlette?' I asked.

'Too good for your scruffy anvil, blacksmith,' he replied. Then he stopped smiling 'I don't know what the matter is with her. Bloody women. They're so changeable.'

'It's since you had that important visitor last month,' I suggested. 'She was flattered by his attention.'

'You mean Duke Robert? She's not that stupid. Though I admit,' he added proudly, 'he did seem to take to her.'

'You were pleased enough yourself,' I said. 'An order for eight top-of-the-range saddles and ten pairs of shoes.'

'It was quite good money,' he admitted. 'Anyway you didn't do so badly yourself. Fifty conical helmets, was that it?'

With Jacques it was always money that mattered and for some time I'd thought he had big ideas for Arlette. So I began to shift my attentions to her big sister, Margaret.

Just as well, for within a month it was obvious that Arlette was expecting and local gossip was convinced that Duke Robert of Normandy was the father.

In due course Arlette produced the bastard known as William who was soon removed to the palace, as the Duke had failed to father any sons with his wife and she was now past it. In that atmosphere the boy William grew up to take delight in amputating the hands, feet or noses of any who stood in his way. And old Jacques the tanner did not know whether to be proud or ashamed. Neither did I, for by that time I had been long married to Arlette's sister and our three boys wanted to learn any trade but tanning. Meanwhile William the Bastard became our new duke and the finest warrior of his day, so successful that he conquered Brittany, beat the king of France and took two of my boys with him when he invaded England. Thus through a succession of strange events I became the uncle of the king of England.

New York, Sept 1st, 2119

'I'd like sweet and sour pork, chop suey, banana fritters, pizza marguerita and chocolate ice cream,' said Ariadne.

'What a mixture,' I replied.

'Don't you understand what I mean?' she asked. 'I thought you knew the facts of life.'

'You mean I must be fertile?'

'I do.'

I felt full of joy, yet slightly annoyed at making a fool of myself, for I was rather proud of being a man of the world. At this time however, when average sperm counts were so low, it was a big relief to be proved fertile.

'Now you make sure they plant plenty of trees out there,' said Ariadne. 'So our child doesn't get skin cancer. By the way I've resigned from Geriaid.'

I kissed my e-pod, which now had three people to support.

New York, Sept 7th, 2119

Exactly five hundred years ago today a Croatian Catholic priest called Marko Krizin was tortured to death in what was then Hungary but is now Slovakia. It was on the orders of a Protestant prince. Marko was subsequently declared a saint by Pope John Paul. It reminded me of the murals at the Saints Disney Theme Park. You swipe a screen and a short song comes out for each saint:

St Lucy always impeccably chaste
Was inevitably sooner or later faced
By a predator male

And knowing she must not fail,
Though stunned for a minute by shock and surprise,

To get rid of the man she gouged out her own eyes.
St Simeon picked at the scabs on his side
As he stood on a plinth only two feet wide
At the top of a pillar some sixty feet high
Where he stayed forty years, he alone knew why.

He encouraged the maggots to feed on his sores
And welcomed his faithful admirers in scores.
When St Barbara's father cut off her head
He was immediately struck dead
By lightning, so she became

The patron saint of fire and flame
And every gun was engraved with her name.
St John Chrysostom preached so well
That many thousands fell under his spell,
But he told them all they would go to hell.

He leaned from his pulpit with a smile
Saying 'Female beauty is slime and bile
Phlegm and blood.' But wait a while,
What an absolute waste
It's surely just a matter of taste.

And I love it.

There's no chance of me being a saint, I haven't got
the patience and my pain threshold is extremely low, but

Ariadne is different. She could perhaps be a saint. As to Dr Joseph Smith of COLDS I'm quite sure he is very ambitious to be one, but saints shouldn't be ambitious at all.

That night there was news that an unidentified pandemic was spreading from Mongolia, an area where wild animals were still trapped for food. There had also been a serious accident when thirty students at the Islamic Jihad University had been killed during a training session in aerial piracy. A new high-speed nail-polish remover had been invented by a pharmacist in Mumbai. There was another worldwide strike by the Union of Female Robots demanding equal pay with their male counterparts.

CHAPTER THIRTEEN

HOPE OR FAITH

*An optimist is a guy
that has never had
much experience.*
D. Marquis

New York, Sept 10th, 2119

Creating a new generation makes all this nonsense
slightly more worthwhile, but what future is there?
Manhattan is half under water as it is, and the Maldives
disappeared long since. Summer weather is even less
predictable than when I was a child. Every drop of water
we drink has already gone through other peoples' bodies
at least a thousand times. Most of our cereals have been so
genetically modified that factory bread tastes like sawdust.
Hits by meteors have increased and sooner or later one
of them is going to wipe out half the world. Worst of all
there are far too many e-pod timber dealers chasing far
too little work.

§

'Gerard, help me on with my armour,' said Sir Roger, the
bravest knight in Italy, so I did as I was ordered. We were
camped beside the road down to Rome, that great pile
of rubble they call the eternal city. A mass of red ruins
stripped of their marble skin, infested with paupers, huge
broken pillars half-buried in filth, great oval race courses

overgrown with weeds and squatters, everywhere phoney relic salesmen and grimy whores of both sexes.

'Look, the Holy Father of Christendom is shut up in that stinking tower,' said our priest, pointing to the Castello S. Angelo, beneath which we could see the German troops camped by the river.

Our time came. We rode hard up the left bank of the river and attacked the Germans, who were sunk in lethargy brought on by too much sun or wine or both. We killed large numbers and the rest headed off into the hills. So now it was our turn to lie in the sun and drink wine.

'On your feet. Now kneel,' came a voice.

We staggered to our feet, thinking some great prince was approaching. Instead there appeared a little priest in tattered white robes and a bejewelled dirty white hat, who walked along our ranks and blessed us.

'The heir of St Peter himself,' said our own priest, and I wasn't sure whether he wanted us to be impressed or the reverse. Certainly the Church of St Peter was a smallish, dirty, old-fashioned building compared with the great new cathedrals of France.

New York, Sept 12th, 2119

'You're a fool,' said Ariadne.

'Why?' I asked.

'You don't realise how much care and attention I need.'

'I do.'

'No you don't.'

I'd had a long day scanning my wrist-top and on the phone to Alaska and Yangon as the last casino order was rounded off. I was tired and found it hard to cope with a change of mood. Ariadne failed to realise that I too could be depressed at the thought of years ahead of mindless pod-trading with little hope of increased earnings despite the constant escalation in stress as workaholic Koreans muscled their way into our business by cost-cutting. These days competition was often close to suicidal and you had to check your wrist-top every few minutes in case some new boy came in with a ridiculous last-minute tender. Meanwhile the Atlantic had risen another foot, Oklahoma had been declared a dust bowl, only the upper floor of the Doge's Palace in Venice was above sea level, half the population of Australia had skin cancer and computer pirates had taken over most of Wall Street.

'The little creature inside me will live into the twenty-second century,' said Ariadne. 'By then there'll probably be no trees left in New England, no wild fish in the sea and all beef will be made from genetically modified hay.'

This last was untrue for I had just read a piece by the Regius Professor of Bovine Fartology at Oxford, who said that attempts to reduce methane emissions by changing cattle diets had finally succeeded.

'Never mind,' I said, thrusting my depression aside. 'I will try to insist that my suppliers plant new seedlings for every tree cut down. The other traders will think I'm mad, but so what?'

'That's great,' said Ariadne. 'Look how well our seedlings in the window box are doing.'

I put my arm round her now substantial waist. 'Well done,' I said.

My son Gerard had gone south to look for a wife, but came back instead with his head full of wild dreams. It just happened that he had been in Clermont during the Papal Council and met a group of fanatics who had heard Pope Urban's speech about the capture of Jerusalem. It seemed as if everyone had been waiting for a cause and suddenly there was a huge wave of enthusiasm to go and fight the hated Muslims who had conquered Israel and occupied the Holy City. The monks had pounced on Gerard as an innocent young knight who had listened to the Song of Roland and was looking for love and glory. His friends were the same, all chanting 'God wills it', desperate to display their courage in a foreign field. I was loath to lose him, but there was no way I could stop him.

New York, Oct 16th, 2119

Exactly two hundred years ago today Adolf Hitler made his first speech to the German Workers Party or DAP in Munich. It was a fairly amateurish effort, but it was a start. Meanwhile, in the modern world, there had been a renewed exchange of fire between Jerusalem and Gaza.

§

I want my castle built here,' said Guy de Lusignan rather pompously, I think for the benefit of his pretty, but apparently well-used replacement wife, the recently widowed spouse of the King of Jerusalem. We were standing on a fine promontory on the southern coast of Cyprus just west of Akrotiri.

'Certainly, my lord,' I said, forgetting for a moment that Guy was now the King of Cyprus. He'd expected his very good friend Richard Lionheart to give him the crown of Jerusalem, but had settled for Cyprus as second best. His reward for helping at the siege of Acre.

'This is Hugh, son of Gerard of Tournai,' he said, introducing me perfunctorily to his new queen. 'Sir Hugh, I leave you to it.' And off they went.

So for the next year I supervised the building of a strong but elegant stone keep, using local Greek peasants and slaves of mixed race, some of them Muslim prisoners. But naturally I was frustrated at being kept away from the real action in the Holy Land. I found myself kicking the stones in exasperation and scratching my sore arm. What I wanted was at least a dukedom for myself and for that I must make a real mark with the crusader kings. I might have been content with a senior position in one of the big celibate orders, but to become a Templar you really needed serious money and I had none. Thus despite my leanings towards a single life I allowed myself to become friendly with a young Genoese lady whose merchant father owned a fleet of ships that regularly ferried men to Acre. A week of marriage was a small price to pay for free transport and the new set of armour I paid for with her dowry.

Thus when the castle was all but completed I was able to join the Lusignan patrol at Acre and we set off towards Jerusalem via Caesarea. We looked superb in our flashing armour with red crosses on our surcoats. I thought that at no time in history could any men have been so noble, so highly trained in arms, yet dedicated to such a wonderful cause as the defeat of Islam.

The first day out of Acre we met a group of Greek mercenaries, scruffy-looking men-at-arms, who appeared to make mock of us, so we killed two of them and sent the rest packing, Christian or not, heretics either way. Then after spending the second night in the castle at Caesarea we headed inland over the hills. Though I was quite used to the heat of Cyprus this was worse than anything I had experienced before, especially as we had to ride in full armour. Within two days our water bottles were empty, our armour was almost too hot to touch and I was half-drowsy in the saddle. Then just past Megiddo a troop of hit-and-run Saracens attacked us from behind an outcrop of rocks beside a strange-looking mountain by the name of Hattin.

'Charge,' yelled our commander. We drew our swords and though my head was swimming with giddiness, I dug in my spurs and kept up with the leaders. At last, a chance to win my dukedom.

We outnumbered them about two to one and our armour was much better, but they were quick, lighter and took clever advantage of the rough ground. After the first sally nine of my fellows were already dead or wounded, but we turned for a second charge.

'God wills it,' I shouted and headed for the laughing Saracen in front of me.

I believe their priests had promised them a place in paradise if they fell.

So had ours.

New York, Nov 2nd, 2119

The year 2120 in which our child was due to be born was expected by many to be the turning point of the century, particularly in America. Half the nation's population were now over eighty and, though the retirement age had been lowered to seventy-five again, there was still 70% unemployment. Most agriculture was now automated and apart from a few refurbishments and leisure complexes the construction industry was almost non-existent.

The same was true of mining, automotive and civil engineering, since the need for roads had been considerably reduced by robo-trains. Apart from full-time carers the largest workforces were now the cable-duct repair people and the circuit board recyclers, the rest were mainly salespeople like myself, duplicating if not triplicating each others' work in the name of competition. Now even more care-home jobs were being taken over by robots. Fishermen were no longer needed at sea as the robotic trawlers simply hoovered up their quota of fish..

'What's the matter?' asked Ariadne.

'I do about an hour's real work a week,' I said.' And suffer about forty hours hanging around for the one hour to materialise. I'm bored.'

'Why not do something else?'

'Because I can normally earn a reasonable amount of money for this ridiculous con.'

'But we don't need money.'

'I know we're not desperately extravagant,' I said, putting my arm around where she normally had a waist. 'It's all the deductions. Geriaid, water meter, fresh air surcharge, sea barrage insurance, the so-called voluntary cable repair levy, roboid-pass, ozone replacement tax, Fourth World Debt Repayments. They all take more than half of all my earnings.'

'Well, maybe it's worth just keeping at it a little longer,' she said, patting her belly.

'And look at the latest job-creation ploy. Wilderness regeneration schemes. The Chrysler National Park. They've got to bury a hundred square miles of concrete, seventy miles of redundant motorway, then put back hills, rivers, trees.'

'I like sharing your worries. We'll be okay,' she said.

That evening there was news that a member of the extreme gun lobby had planted high explosives in the basement of the Empire State Building. The NYPD were trying to persuade him to come out. Meanwhile four hundred Shiite Muslims had been killed by Sunnis in Baghdad.

§

I never knew my father, but I learned from him posthumously the folly of fighting the Saracens, for most of the knights who went to the Holy Land never came back. But luckily I grew up with useful contacts and some of my mother's money, so I chummed up with a Venetian merchant and we bought a couple of transport ships to service the Crusaders. Money always up front, for they could never be trusted to pay afterwards. I usually ran the last part of the route from Cyprus to Acre, but one year I took a fiendish mob of crusaders right into Constantinople where they immediately began slaughtering fellow Christians. I took the money and never went back.

New York, Nov 2nd, 2119 cont.

To make me even more frustrated I had to put in an appearance at the Annual Timber and Nuts Show at the Trade Centre, where hundreds of fast-talking oriental delegates insisted on showing swathes of bio-timber and pressing plastic cups full of tepid tequila into my hand. Seed salesmen, loggers, chainsaw repairers, there was a time when I quite enjoyed it all, but that was years since.

Thanks to NYPD the gun lobbyist has been persuaded to leave the Empire State Building.

§

'The end of the world is very close,' yelled the monk, as we approached his platform through the narrow stench of Perugia.

'Amen,' I responded. I had just given away my grandfather's last ship with half the crew already dead from the plague and the rest too weak to pull a jib sheet. I remembered holy men like this one from the time we took the French Crusaders to Egypt. Then I thought they were mad. Now I was beginning to alter my views.

'At least repent before you die,' shouted the monk above the hubbub of the little square. The citizens were no longer even trying to remove all the bodies through the city gates to the great burial pit.

'We'll repent before we die,' responded the group beside me and I started to join in.

'There is a better world awaiting us when the day comes. When the day comes, Lord.'

'Take off your cloaks,' said the monk and took off his own grey habit. The rest of us obeyed, some just tossing fine cloaks into the filthy street, the night-soil of plague-sodden Perugia.

'Take up your thongs,' went on the monk. And most of us did, for there were racks of whips waiting to be used.

'Here. I've got a spare,' said an eager young woman beside me.

'Thank you,' I said and took the whip she offered.

'Now form ranks of three and whip the man or woman in front of you to the rhythm of the drum,' yelled the priest. 'Think about your sins and how the Jews slew our Lord. Get ready! March!'

We set off like an army and every time the drum was beaten I lashed at the bare back in front of me and that very second felt an unseen whip bite into the flesh of my shoulders. The timing was everything. To strike and be struck the exact moment of the drummer's heavy beat, every six steps. And shouting, 'We repent.'

The pain was beautiful. As we marched on through the city the few inhabitants who could still stand came to their doors and stared at our blood-furrowed bodies with awe.

'Are you all right?' I asked the young woman who had given me her spare whip, for her shift was now in ribbons and the thong of the old man behind her had curled round her stomach, drawing blood from the white flesh.

'Marvellous,' she said, smiling. Meanwhile the rear rank, who were still unscarred, were moved right up to the front and the new rear rank had a short respite.

After two hours the light was fading and we were exhausted but joyful. The monk led us into the sumptuous merchants' hall where there was ample wine to drink and fine rugs to sit on. Most of the merchants were already dead.

'Thank you for your whip,' I said to the girl and sat down in the space beside her.

'We all help each other,' she said. 'We couldn't do it on our own.'

And when it was dark I felt her body close to mine and she sent the pain searing through my back by grabbing me to her with her fingers digging into my sores. And moving behind the curtains we caused each other even greater exquisite pain, standing for we couldn't lie, saying to each other all the time, 'Repent, repent.'

As we repented the seed survived.

New York, Nov 7th, 2119

My Gdiary says that exactly five hundred years ago today Princess Elizabeth, born in Dunfermline, Scotland, was crowned Queen of Bohemia alongside her husband, the new king. This action precipitated the Thirty Years War in Germany with an estimated six million people dying in battle or from disease or starvation. It was a no-scoring draw between Catholics and Protestants. Why do we have to have wars?

New York, Nov 22nd, 2119

There are times when nine months seem like an eternity and others when they just seem to flash past. Sometimes even nine minutes seem an age if you're just sitting waiting for an email that spells a larger or smaller overdraft from a merciless bank, but you can't use the time to do anything else vaguely useful, let alone entertaining. This was the day that the new Chinese owner of Starbucks, a chain with fifty thousand branches worldwide, lost his entire fortune gambling in Las Vegas. Later that evening a Buddhist suicide bomber was shot by a sniper when attempting to blow up the parliament in Canberra. I got a small order for rosewood desk tops.

CHAPTER FOURTEEN

ARRIVALS AND DEPARTURES

Who breaks his birth's invidious bar
And grabs the skirts of happy chance.
A Tennyson

New York, Feb 20th, 2120

Ariadne was now beginning to look very rotund and was attending the Chinese Natural Birth Clinic, while I went to pre-paternity classes and learned how to filter strontium 90 out of dried milk, and about the porosity of various recycled diaper thicknesses. We were also both invited to a cheese and cannabis party to help raise funds for Fertility Day. The trouble was that so few couples were producing except in China, but those who resorted to drugs often ended up expecting octuplets and had to have at least the regulation five aborted. We couldn't understand it, but were bullied into feeling that it was a good thing to raise money for them.

I was still going though patches of deep frustration with the e-pod business, despite impending parenthood. When the local elections came up I wondered about politics, even thought of supporting the Neo-Marxist Alliance which was making a come-back, as were the Neo-Falangists. In the old days they used to have wars every twenty years or so, which destroyed nearly everything on both sides and that created enough work to keep unemployment down until the start of the next war, helped by the odd earthquake and flood. The submersion of Dakar, and the loss of eight million homes along the Bangladeshi coast had created a short but welcome boom in the construction industries worldwide. Also the government had organised a lot of cleverly induced wastage to mop up spare production. Compulsory fashion changes were brought in so that clothes had to be recycled every year or two, dress codes so people needed several different garments each hour of the day, designer e-zimmers so that older people wanted to change them every year.

What's more in any city there were normally twice as many bedrooms than were actually needed. Everybody wasted a lot on unnecessary travel, most of it just to maintain self-esteem. The universities kept growing new tentacles, doubling and redoubling as they invented new branches of study, like dental hygiene management and child-abuse studies. There were doctorates in transgender studies and battery recycling. But in our day the wars were mostly in the fourth world and low technology affairs, so that reconstruction projects were fairly tame. So which party would solve our problems? The Neo-Marxists were touting an ingenious idea which was to scrap work altogether as a measurement for earnings. But they hadn't solved the boredom factor. The Neo-Falangists on the other hand wanted to bring in reforms to create more waste and get people back to work.

'What are you thinking about, Theo?' asked Ariadne.
'Where the world is heading,' I answered.

'Stop worrying. We'll be all right. These big things don't matter. Let's go out and get some fresh air.' So we took the rapid-roboid to Whitewater Airport for a snack and listened to the famous myna birds. This massive flock had nested in the airport terminals for a hundred years and learned to imitate the airline announcers so well that a recent group of passengers had been flown to Teheran instead of Taiwan. It was fun and we just wandered around till it was time to go home.

§

'You've served as a mate before, have you?' asked the captain of the merchantman.

'Yes,' I said. 'I was on the Pisa to Acre run for several years. Before that I served on a Genoese ship as third mate.'

We were standing on the Riva degli Schiavoni in Venice, just along from the Arsenal, and his ship was rubbing restlessly against her fenders.

'I'm told my father was a ship-owner,' I said. 'But he lost his entire fleet because of the plague. So I had to start from the bottom again.'

'Good enough,' said the captain. 'I'll give you a trial passage to Trogir and back. That's our normal base port. We sail tonight.'

Thus two months later I found myself in the little city of Trogir, having completed several voyages up and down the Adriatic and with a week's shore leave due to me. So I took a room in a tenement attic by the old cathedral and sat down to supper with the landlady and her daughter just as the bells began to swing into crescendo not far above us.

'Where's your father?' I asked the girl since I could think of nothing else much to say.

She hesitated and looked embarrassed.

'Dead? I'm sorry,' I said.

'No, actually he's a leper. He's out there on the island of St Lazar, at Palmezana.' She pointed out to sea, but I knew the island anyway for I had passed it often enough.

'That's a shame,' I said, 'But nothing to be ashamed of. My father died of the plague in Perugia and so did my mother soon after I was born, leaving me an orphan.'

'Poor boy,' said the mother, pouring me some more wine. 'My husband was a silver miner up at Srebrenica until he got ill. And he served King Dusan himself when he was young. But those days are gone.'

'Indeed,' I said.

'Now we are poor and just clean up the houses of the rich Venetian merchants,' she said.

I nodded sympathetically.

'You can stay here between voyages, if you like.' she went on.

'Thank you. I will pay my way,' I said and the daughter blushed.

New York, Mar 21st, 2120

'He's due this week,' said Ariadne.

'I hadn't forgotten.' I replied. 'Are you scared?'

'A little. Not of having the baby, just of being made to have a section or something. I want it to be natural.'

'I'm sure it will be.'

'Let's go to the Rockies for it.'

§

By the time I'd done two return voyages to Trogir I had the girl waiting for me on the jetty every time.

Colorado, Mar 25th, 2120

COLDS had a Mat Unit every two hundred miles along the main roboroutes, so we headed for our old favourite Colorado Springs and the palatial mat unit at the Broadmoor Garden of the Gods where all the nurses were Native Americans. There they had the little chapel of Cosa Nostra where the Turin Shroud had been housed in a bullet-proof case. It had been bought from the people of Piedmont for a billion dollars after Fiat went into liquidation back in the 2090s. There was even one of the Dead Sea Scrolls beside it, bought by the same foundation in return for a donation to Hamas.

'Isn't it wonderful?' said Ariadne. We had a splendid lunch and then walked beyond the huge ornamental lake to a waterfall where the chipmunks gathered, then along the valley full of the spirits of Native Americans.

'Something is happening,' said Ariadne suddenly. 'Let's go back.'

Our son Mino was born four hours later, angry himself at coming into the world, but a joy to Ariadne and to me. And, when I was finally ejected from the ward with the other ineffectual fathers by a nurse called Two Dogs, I thought about how this little boy was descended from an ancient stone-age man who had been murdered somewhere near the Danube, from a strange Greek so-called hero Theseus, and from countless other unknown men and women who had striven from birth to death doing their best.

That night a probe reached the planet Pluto for the first time and before heading off on a forty-five-year trip to Centauri reported that Pluto had three more moons than we had previously known. They showed the second remake of Schindler's List on late-night television and Interpol uncovered a massive child abuse farm on the outskirts of Manila. Then another new day began.

§

Though I was not of noble blood they were so short of men that I was allowed to train for the cavalry. Thus at quite a young age I took part in my first and, as it turned out, my last battle in the year 1389. I was with the light cavalry brigade at Kosovo where we were hopelessly outnumbered by the Turks and in our first charge against them about half the men in my section were killed by the Ottoman archers. I survived and charged a second time, but took an arrow in my right arm just above the elbow. I saw our prince Lazar killed and I saw the Sultan killed. I saw thousands killed, mostly Christians, but also Muslims. There was nothing more I could do, so I dismounted and lay amongst the bodies for about five hours till all the living had gone away and the dead had started to rot.

Colorado Springs, Mar 22nd, 2120

Time to catch the Denver Express, Ariadne, baby Mino and me heading out into the world and feeling for a short time we were the centre of it. Everyone on the coach said he was a wonderful baby. But that very night an intercity roboid in Japan left the track at 300 mph and hurtled into Okinawa Bay with all its passengers. The two-hundred-years-old fashion house of Armani, now based in Bermuda, launched a new range of must-have leggings which the management believed would save the firm from liquidation. In a bloodless coup the Muslim Sisterhood had seized control of the Saudi Republic.

§

My wife had always warned me against being a soldier, and as it turned out, quite correctly prophesied that it would end in disaster. The last thing I could bear was going back to Srebrenica with a wounded arm and wounded pride. So I headed in the other direction to see if I could make my living some other way.

New York, Mar 28th, 2120

I note that exactly fifteen hundred years ago the Prophet Mohammed set out on a journey from Mecca to Jerusalem riding a horse with wings and guided by the Archangel Gabriel. Today I just went to the ink-refill centre.

A previously top-secret incident-report from the Pentagon dated March 28th, 2070 was released now that the fifty-year censorship period was over. The CIA

computer decoded it in rhyming couplets to make it seem
more user- friendly. Our duty man thought it would do
no harm.

Just for a lark to test the alarm,
But some simple subaltern down below
Thought his moment of glory had come, so
He launched a missile at 404
Which was soon heading smartly for Singapore.
It was caught on their radar a few seconds later
As it levelled off above the equator.
They fired their anti-missile missile
Within a minute, sat back with a smile.
Its beam locked on at 406,
But our men still had several tricks;
We jammed the beam and quickly sent
An anti-anti-missile which bent
The beam straight back to where it started from,
So it became a boomerang bomb.
Meanwhile they launched another ten
And alerted more anti-missile men.
For a minute more we plotted in sections
The course of missiles in both directions.
Our planes beneath a radar screen
Attempted to intercept, but were seen.
Their first bomb hit us at 408
And after that it was all too late.
Two million killed or there about
Just make sure no news leaks out.

   Top Secret,

An official inquiry has now been authorised to investigate the causes of this incident and decide the culpability of the various personnel involved, despite the fact that they are all probably in care homes or dead. Meanwhile there are still Grade 4 warnings of possible nuclear conflict in several parts of the world, most notably between the two halves of the former Peoples Republic of China which are both currently ruled by unstable military juntas. The Belinda Gates Foundation has sent envoys to both sides in the hope of reducing tension,

CHAPTER FIFTEEN

MADNESS, BADNESS AND SADNESS

Wherever God erects a house of prayer
The Devil always builds a chapel there.

D. Defoe

New York, Mar 30, 2120

'You get some sleep, 'said Ariadne. 'You're a working man. You need your sleep'

It was three in the morning and Mino had been hungry. I had made fairly useless efforts to help, like fetching a recycled diaper from a table two feet away. And I'd tucked a bit of dressing gown over Ariadne's shoulder when she opened the side of her nightie to let Mino have his fill.

'Not at all.' I said. 'We're in this together.'

'Yes, but this is my job'

'Well I suppose I do have to make some tricky phone calls tomorrow.'

§

'You're a Bosnian witch, 'snarled the miller of Srebrenica, who was trailing his usual cloud of white dust, although his face was red with anger because I'd pushed his groping hand away from my breasts.

'Just because I don't want you personally doesn't mean I'm a witch, 'I said. It was now five years since my husband had disappeared off to the Ravens' Field at Kosovo. But the sweaty, nose-dripping whiteness of the miller held few attractions for me.

'You'd rather consort with Bogomil demons,' he shouted. 'And foul creatures which crawl up their own backsides.'

'Here's the money for the flour,' I said and gave him two dinars.

'We'll see what the holy brother thinks about you, 'he said, pocketing the money nevertheless. 'He has ways of proving that you're a witch.'

I could have cheerfully thrust him into the twirling wooden cog-wheels which were whipped round by his frothing waterfall. I was far from pleased by his threat to report me. The black friar came to our village once a month and posed very peculiar questions to any woman who fairly or unfairly had become unpopular with other villagers.

'Silly little bitch

Your mother is a witch.'

He had trained the children to chant this ditty and you only had to pick a leaf of digitalis or some other useful herb and the fingers started to point. You could trust no one.

'I heard you fell into the lade and didn't drown,' went on the wretched miller.

'Of course I didn't drown. It's only two feet deep,' I replied angrily.

'The tsar of Serbia doesn't like you heretic Bogomil Bosnians,' he persisted.

189

'That's nothing new,' I said. 'I suppose it counts for nothing that my husband went off to fight for him five years ago at Kosovo and never came back.' I pushed past the miller and headed down the steps with my bag of flour. But as I went into the street I saw the dreaded figure of the black friar and for a few seconds the ghastly vision of the ducking stool sapped all the strength from my legs, so that I could barely move.

New York, June 24th, 2120

'I don't feel well,' I said about three months after Mino was born.

'What's wrong?' asked Ariadne.

'I don't know,' I said. 'I just seem to lack motivation.'

'You're jealous, aren't you?' she said as I stared at Mino sucking pleasantly at a breast which I had almost come to regard as one of my possessions. 'You are, aren't you, you selfish sod?'

'Of course I am,' I said, grinning. Then: 'No, just a joke,' I added, lying for the sake of self-esteem. 'It's business getting me down again.'

'Well why not give up and do something else?' she offered.

This was not really the kind of reply I wanted. I was looking for sympathy, not unsolicited advice to undertake some high risk, brain-sapping change of lifestyle. Less hassle to be a mediocre survivor in a routine job than risk ending up as an ex-high-flyer in Cardboard City.

'We need the money,' I said. 'I just have to soldier on.'

'Well cheer up, then.'

190

Often I would think of the belligerent bacilli that were probably gnawing away at my most vital organs at that very moment and it hardly seemed worthwhile going on.

'Do you know there's a higher rate of suicide amongst e-pod traders than in any other profession except dentistry?' I said.

'No,' said Ariadne. 'Why don't you just go out for a drink with some friends?'

'We could get my mother to babysit.'

'No. I'm happy here. You go yourself. At least you're not one of those old-style men that always want to stay in and recycle diapers.'

So I went out and wandered along the streets where the cable-duct repairers in dayglow jackets sweated their overtime and I came by chance to Cardboard City where thousands lived to escape the fresh-air and water charges. They survived by cleaning old microwaves or reassembling bits of old computers. SETA (Self Erected Temporary Accommodation) dwellers, they were called officially and there was a full degree course in SETA Studies now at the Bronx University. It covered topics such as ethno-sociological trends for long term SETA residents, an analysis of cardboard construction techniques in the art vieil period, role play in same-sex SETA relationships and isometric data on SETA convergence probabilities. I wondered if people were not quite happy in Cardboard City, apart from the coldest part of the winter. Supposing the administration bulldozed the whole of New York and got everyone paid plenty to work and rebuild it; would we be happier?

I went into the Icelandic Theme Bar and asked for a double White Death. I'd be happy enough in a cardboard shack except that I'd miss my bit of garden. As I sat sipping my drink I remembered vaguely being in an especially beautiful garden where all the trees were hanging with delicious fruit and the sun slanted through the moist fronds making a pattern on the brown back of the woman. She turned and offered me an apple and I saw as if for the first time that she was hugely attractive. In fact she was Ariadne. But she went away from me.

§

'You're the dirty son of a Christian then, are you?' asked the janissary captain, his thin-lipped mouth inches from my face.

'I suppose so,' I said. I didn't know what we believed in. But certainly six weeks earlier I had been snatched from a family that was more or less Christian. Nor, I have to say, had any of them made any risky moves to prevent my abduction. The village head man had said that one in every four must go and I think my parents secretly preferred to keep my two brothers. As for being a Christian, forget it. Why bother? I'd had an hour's instruction in the Koran every day for the past six weeks and the Prophet offered a good deal to soldiers, dead ones that is: guaranteed entry to paradise with as many houris as you wanted for as long as you liked. Strictly as per instructions from the Archangel Gabriel who had visited the Prophet in his cave. Same archangel that told the Virgin Mary she was pregnant. Must be right.

'And you, Castriota,' went on the captain addressing the next new cadet beside me. 'You're another of the Albanian scum.'

'No, I'm a Serb,' said the boy, whom I knew as George or sometimes Iskander Beg.

'Who cares?' went on the officer. 'Forget where you came from for you'll never see it again, any of you. You are slaves of the Gate,' he snarled. 'Soldiers of the sultan till the day you die. Which could be quite soon if you're not careful. You will not even leave the barracks of Edirne until I'm convinced that you have absolutely no loyalty of any kind to anyone but the sultan and the Bashi Bazouks. I don't care if it takes years. But it'll be a lot easier for you if it just takes weeks. Soon we will have conquered the whole world. There'll be no Christians left. No infidels. Right, Castriota?'

'Right, captain,' said my friend George.

'You'll get on, boy. Now you, Ali Then,' he added, turning on me again. 'Stand to attention. Stop fidgeting like a bitch in heat. You have been clothed and fed by the kind permission of His Sublime Majesty the Sultan Murad II, who killed his own father and brothers when they stood in his way, so one more or less untrainable cadet in the janissaries is neither here nor there.'

I knew of course that he was just trying to intimidate me for I could see through his technique, but it still worked. I would obey his orders to the death.

George Castriota became a firm friend and we served in the sultan's army together for twenty-odd years, from Antioch to the Red Sea and both of us were good at it. In time I learned George's secret, that he was none other than the son of the king of Albania and longed to escape to help his own people. And so he did in the end, and I helped him to do it, for I stood in for him on a forty-eight-hour guard duty in Thessalonika while he disappeared. Later when we captured Constantinople I heard he had beaten the Turks in several skirmishes and was quite a hero amongst his own people, but I never saw him again.

I enjoyed a couple of women after the storming of Medina, then lost an arm fighting down near Jeddah. So at last I was released from the janissaries and I spent all my gratuity within two months on wine and whores. Then all I had left was a pitch in the smelliest part of the market square and a begging pot to rattle at the passing camel drivers. But I have Paradise to look forward to, don't I? That was the promise.

Juneau, Alaska, June 30th, 2120

I had to take the jetstream up to Juneau to sort out another awkward sitka contract and was shocked to see that the former Mendenhall Glacier was now no more than a trickle, quite a tepid one at that. But my old friends the Thenians laid on a great barbecue of salmon, so I didn't miss Ariadne all that much and felt rather guilty. To punish myself for this infidelity I turned my wrist-top to the news.

Talks had broken down yet again in the attempted merger discussions between the Ten Ayatollahs and the Proto-Catho Primates. The sticking point was once more the Archangel Gabriel, the point at issue being whether he had acted as a divine double-agent, first of all making the key announcements in 1 BC about the pregnancies that led to John the Baptist and Jesus being born, but then changing sides to take important messages to Mohammed. Was he a traitor? Was his message to the Virgin Mary in 1 BC a set-up so that he could muck up the Jews or, if he was genuine at that point, had he deliberately misled Mohammed six hundred years later? Surely he couldn't have been on both sides? The interfaith conference had been adjourned with acrimony and the Ayatollahs were threatening to reactivate their nuclear warheads.

§

Maybe Allah is merciful after all, for I have found a girl who doesn't mind a man with only one arm. Perhaps she is not beautiful in the conventional sense, but to me she is perfect and her mother has a house on the outskirts of Jeddah.

Baranof Island, Alaska, June 20th, 2120 cont.

I stopped off for the night at Baranof Island to see an old colleague and once again had this odd feeling that I had been to the place before. For some reason the little Russian church at Nichilnik Kenai made me have some sort of belief in God which I don't feel in other churches.

195

Rubbish. By tomorrow I'll be in Seattle and on the
overnight roboid home. At least I should be grateful not
to be on the wrong side of some great genocide or plague.
Grateful for small mercies instead of obsessed with
underachievement. I watched the small lake outside the
hostel window where there was a notice instructing guests
about behaviour towards birds.

The duck sat on her eggs, it seemed an age
When suddenly their oval loveliness was trashed,
Beaks broke the perfect shells with thrusting rage,
The new impatient ducklings dashed
Around the pond and linking wakes
Snatched every crumb. At last on test-flight day
They trailed her high enough to see the lakes
Beyond, then turned, just flew away.
A few months later meeting by the pool
They cut her dead, beat her to every crumb.
They'd never asked her to be such a fool
As to sit on those eggs. Why be so dumb?
PLEASE FEED ALL BIRDS RESPONSIBLY.
Can we not have minds of our own?
Do birds not have minds of their own?

CHAPTER SIXTEEN

DOUBLE KIDNAP

The greatest of evils and the worst of crimes is poverty.
B. Shaw

New York, Jul 7th, 2120

'Call me eccentric if you like,' I said to Ariadne one day as she nursed young Mino. 'But I have a slight fascination with religion.'

'Oh,' she responded without interest and I suppose she was really concentrating on the little fellow's efforts to belch.

'It's sort of comforting to think there might actually be some purpose to this life, a god or something,' I went on.

'Isn't this enough for you?' asked Ariadne, pointing to Mino who was grinning after a particularly satisfying burp.

'I like the procreation bit,' I said.

'Well, he's not needed in that department now, Mino, is he?' she said, addressing our infant son. 'Not for a while anyway.'

It was true. She had rejected my overtures in the last few months. Not that I was desperate for it, just desperate to be wanted.

'Why has the idea of god survived at all?' I asked. 'When almost every event in the world for the past thousand years seems to prove conclusively that there is no god helping humanity to get along, if anything maybe one that does the reverse. What's the point in going on?'

'What's the point in going on then?' repeated Ariadne with more than a touch of impatience and she poked me in the ribs. 'It's not like you to be a pessimist.'

'Maybe I'm at male menopause already.'

'Rubbish.'

'But if the world's just a tiny speck in the middle of a vast black hole with millions of tiny specks so faraway we'll never see the… where's the boss? Where's he hiding?'

'You mean where's she?'

'Whatever.'

'It could all be just chemistry,' she said. 'Much better if it was love, though.' She folded a diaper and dusted Mino's bottom with baby powder.

'And yet on our speck alone there are thousands of different species of spiders who've been building umpteen varieties of intricate web designs and using advanced engineering skills that have taken millions of years to perfect, just to trap a few flies for their supper. And even flies are damned clever. They're more reliable in the air than Boeing 7'7's. It's all too ingenious to be an accident.'

'Daddy waddy's in one of his moods,' said Ariadne to Mino, tickling his tummy.

I note that this very day five hundred years ago it rained frogs in Weil Stadt, a small town on the edge of the Black Forest. And today it was announced that the former nation of Chad had been turned into one vast solar panel which provided enough energy for three neighbouring countries.

§

'There's only one thing wrong with Zanzibar,' said Ibn Batta, my trading partner, as we came away from Friday prayers in the coral mosque. 'The women are all black. But you get used to them and you can have as many as you like.' He winked and led me to his house by the harbour.

Ibn Batta's front door was only yards from where the nearest dhow bobbed on the tide. For some years, without ever having met him, I had acted as his agent in Jeddah, organising the sale of his ivory and slaves. Now I'd left my brother in charge in Jeddah, so that I could help develop the supplies from Zanzibar.

'I haven't been home to Oman for twenty years,' said Ibn Batta. A mild breeze stirred the hot, smoke-laden air of the little town and the dusty palm trees responded with a lazy wave. 'How is it in Jeddah these days?'

'A struggle sometimes,' I said. 'But my father lost an arm fighting for the sultan and got nothing but a begging bowl for his pains. So anything's better than that.' I pointed to the minaret questioningly.

'No need to bother,' he said. 'We're usually too busy here.'

I left a bag in his house and we carried on around the harbour where the falling tide left a scummy green scar against the jetty and the rows of dhows stretched downwards on their mooring ropes.

'Come here,' said Ibn Batta. 'We've got a new load of slaves just ferried over from the mainland. You can see what condition they arrive in and how we have to fatten them up for the voyage to Jeddah.'

We strolled over to a compound near the docks where manacled Africans were herded, the women on one side, the men on the other. Many had outlandish body-markings; some had big rings in their ears or noses. Even by Jeddah standards the smell was terrible and many of them were shouting or wailing.

'We usually keep them here about a month to calm them down and tidy them up for the market,' said Ibn Batta. 'Now, you need a personal servant, so you can have your pick, Ben Ali Then. She's a nice one over there, look.' He pointed at a surly black slave girl, then went on, 'The one rule is never to take the manacles off two at the same time,' he said. 'Not even Allah protects fools.'

New York, Aug 5th 2120

It's exactly five hundred years since the little ship Mayflower set sail from Plymouth, England. Those people had real guts. We just play at it. There are times when I almost suspect that Ariadne is shallow. These days she pays less attention to my ideas.

'Unbelievably clever, chemistry, the whole thing,' I had been saying. 'Perhaps just to create the basic elements and then let them battle it out with each other, so they marry and become compounds, then cells and then higher animals and then Mozart or Einstein. Why will nobody discuss it with me?'

'Try the Geyser Theme Bar,' said Ariadne. 'You need a White Death or two to get things in perspective.'

I took her advice, but after only one Death I headed off to the Iskcon Temple in 49th Street. There were banners out to celebrate the 143rd anniversary of the death of guru Bhakivedanta Swami, founder in New York of the International Society of Krishna Consciousness (ISKCON). Born in Kolkotta, no one but he had ever given such clear answers to the ultimate questions. Hare Krishna. Except perhaps the one in my mind: once you've fulfilled the urge to procreate your species, should you not just roll over and die like a drone bee? What else is there? No wonder there were only fifteen churches left in New York State and half a dozen in Italy since the Vatican moved to Chile because of lack of support.

I went into the temple and heard Dr Joe Smith deliver a fine oration on the famous guru and was greatly uplifted by his sermon on the meaning of life and self-sacrifice.

Then I left by a side door, feeling guilty for being away from home for so long. As I did so Dr Smith darted out of the staff door, brushed quickly past two beggars and by a short head beat an elderly lady to the only robo-taxi waiting in the rank.

'We need someone to go up river and organise the slave-catchers,' said my father.

Luckily the idea half appealed to me, for I was bored with the luxuries of Zanzibar and had always longed to visit the home of my mother far to the west. I also had another motive which I revealed to no one. For there had always been rumours about a rich gold mine up the river, yet nobody from Zanzibar had ever found it. So I took one native servant with me to the mainland and headed up the River Wami by canoe.

'Just two days up the river and no further,' said my father, but after three days there were still no signs of my mother's tribe, so we kept going. Then we saw canoes coming downriver laden with new slaves, so we knew we were right and we kept going.

New York, Aug 8th, 2120

'Cheer up ,' said Ariadne, an evening or two after my visit to the Iskcon T'emple.

'If only business was less erratic,' I said, still rather morose from post-natal depression or just plain jealousy of the midget son getting all the attention. 'There's that Tom O'Connor, an e-pod trader in the Long Island Irish Republic ,who gets a steady flow of work from the Reagan Heritage Trust producing antique furniture. All because the buyer's Irish. I need that kind of connection to give me a dripping roast.'

'Have you tried bribes ?'

'Not worth it, you never know who's on the closed circuit. Nothing is secret,' I said. It is hard to avoid cheating these days. I had a good new source of low price cedar in the Arab-Israeli federation at Arafat City and I put in a very competitive price for all the replacement wooden huts in the new Dachau Theme Park outside Munich, but I still didn't get the job. The same thing happened with the floors for the new palace of the playboy emperor, Saddam Hussein V of Euphrasia. I was amazed that anyone could better my price. And worst of all I missed out on the new oak beam contract for the Rodham-Clinton Mausoleum in Arkansas. Nothing seemed to go right for me.

'Don't you think Mino's lovely?' asked Ariadne, holding him up.

'Yes,' I said.

'Maybe he'd like a little sister.'

'Maybe,' I said.

'I suppose I would need some help with that.'

Suddenly my business problems seemed less important.

§

My father never went back to Zanzibar. After several years of wandering he found gold in Kibali, but much good it did us. There was so much gold around Kisanga that it was barely worth the trouble of digging it up. To make matters worse he had paddled all this way looking for the place where the slaves came from to be sent to Zanzibar, but now we found that the slave-hunters in Kibali sent them the other way down a different great river that ran towards the setting sun. So I and my brothers lived in constant fear.

New York, Aug 15th, 2120

I realise I have no chance any longer of becoming a great leader of mankind or even a minor celebrity, for it takes me all my time to avoid bankruptcy and keep a small family from destruction or humiliation. I used to think that I alone really understood the problems of the world, if only I could persuade others to listen. It was no consolation that Mohammed only converted a few friends till the last years of his life and Jesus probably not much better. By the time he was my age Alexander the Great had conquered almost the entire world but was a dysfunctional alcoholic with a suspect sex life. Why bother competing?

'What are you thinking about, Theo?' asked Ariadne.

'Nothing,' I answered.

§

It was a difficult time in Shama. The Imo tribe had always hated us for having better land than they had. Our god was a woman, theirs was a man. We had round tattoos and short bodies, they had square patterns and tall bodies. We forbade the eating of reptiles, they loved them. But even for a Baza I was different still, for I had paler skin and a longer nose than most because my father's father had been a great merchant on the faraway coast.

When I was fifteen I was betrothed to a Baza warrior about two years older than myself, but almost immediately afterwards the war started and nearly all the men, including my father and my betrothed, were killed by Imos. So we women were rounded up and marched to the river in chains and they exchanged us for beads and cowry shells.

For about a month we went down the river, which got wider and wider. Then we had to wade out to a big canoe and were paddled to an even bigger boat that was tied to the water by a long rope. This boat had eight pieces of cloth that hung above it and flapped in the wind, but we only saw them once every two days, because most of the time we were shut in boxes and only sometimes allowed to walk in the air. There was a grand chief who wore a huge white collar and was called Surgeon Whorkins. He would stand by his wooden circle and laugh at us. But the rest of the time we just had to lie on the wooden floor and I made my elbow red with scratching. I was so mad.

We were on that boat for a very long time and several of the women in my box died and were thrown into the sea. Many times the water got very angry and tried to knock down the boat. Sometimes we were very cold and wet, other times it was so hot down there that we could hardly breathe. But I survived. We got off the boat in a different land and never saw the boat or Surgeon Whorkins again.

New York, Sept 1st, 2120

It is an ironical fact that you think you're unhappy till a
real disaster strikes and then you realise you were quite
happy after all and should be grateful. It is also a fact that
if you worry about disasters it is usually the one you least
expect which actually happens. Thus I used to worry
about our block collapsing due to tunnel subsidence as
the area was riddled with old sewers and long-empty
cable ducts, but the wretched place is standing to this day.

It had been a slightly better day for me as I won part
of the order for the Rodham-Clinton Mausoleum repair
after all, the replica Whitewater rafts section. As if to fit
the script that very evening the current president was
impeached for taking Mafia cash to allow massive drug
imports into Seattle. The South China Republic had at
last acknowledged its pollution problem and renamed
the Yellow River Black until it was decontaminated. So,
buoyed up by this, I agreed to go shopping with Ariadne
and Mino in his e-pram. Cutgroce was a place I loathed,
with its one-way aisles and closed-circuit spies, but it was
the cheapest store for baby food and paper diapers.

As was my want I loitered amongst the wine shelves.
There were two bottles of 2113 Chilean Grenache for the
price of one, plus a free picnic glass with every one litre
bottle of White Death. Then suddenly there was a shriek
from Ariadne. I ran over and she was standing by an
empty pram.

'Baby snatchers,' I said and immediately pressed the
nearest store alarm button. 'I'll head for the check-out.'

I was too late of course. Baby snatching had become quite a common crime due to the number of childless women in New York, and they were quite clever at it. They'd be geared-up for a quick dash, avoiding all the closed-circuit cameras and straight through the express check-out with just one loaf of bread and a prepaid cash card all ready.

And of course they would have stocked up at home with a month's supply of baby food so they wouldn't have to go out until the furore had died down.

'I only looked the other way for half a minute,' sobbed Ariadne, when I got back having found no trace of Mino.

'Don't worry,' I said, although I was already panicking myself. 'It wasn't your fault. We'll get him back.' But in reality I felt seriously pessimistic.

'The trouble is he's such a good baby,' she went on. 'He won't cry for anyone to hear him.'

'We will find him,' I said and bitterly regretted all those moments since Mino came onto the scene when I'd shown petty jealousy and grumpiness. And I should never have become absorbed in the price of Chilean Grenache.

CHAPTER SEVENTEEN

SUGAR AND SPICE

The beaten road
Which those poor slaves with weary footsteps tread
Who travel to their home among the dead.
P. Shelley

New York, Oct 2nd, 2120

We hardly slept that night. Ariadne cried a lot and I gave endless reassurance without believing it myself.

§

'Do you like cutting sugar, Baza?' asked the master, Mista Sambrooksa, sweating beneath his broad-brimmed hat, as he always did during the day.

'Yessa, Mista Sambrooksa,' I answered dutifully, for apart from eating and sleeping I knew no other form of life.

'And do you believe in the Wuntrue God?'

'Yessa,' I said again, because that was the name of the god we were all told to believe in and if we disagreed we were beaten.

'Good girl.' he said and flicked his boot with his swagger-stick as he marched off to the residence, leaving me to slash away at the hard green stems with my sickle. My eyes blinked with sweat when I tried to see Turtle Bay in the distance, the place where I'd first come to this awful land.

'Watch out,' said the girl Momba beside me, as the master's son came round the edge of the field. He wore no hat and he sweated even more than his father.

'Come into my office when you've finished that row,' he said.

The girl Momba raised her eyes expressively to the sky behind his back.

'He'll be going to show you his funny white body,' she said. 'It's more fun than cutting sugar, but not much.'

New York, Oct 5th, 2120

Ariadne and I had spent an extremely unpleasant few days. She was distraught, she couldn't sleep and she would wake me up at all times of the night to tell me it was her fault that we'd lost Mino and look for reassurance which I could only supply by dint of lies. In turn I started making input errors on my e-pod and lost money on several deals.

The Cutgroce security men made a token effort to help us trace Mino and we wasted hours watching clips from their closed circuit. In those days Manhattan PD were so overstretched that their budget only allowed for one man-day per child-abduction case and they weren't really very interested. So by the end of that awful week I realised I would have to try to do the job myself. At least, if I gave all my time to it, I would avoid Ariadne's constant questioning and it might even produce a result.

In the morning I headed round to Cutgroce and asked for the manager.

'How can I help you, Mr Thens?' he asked smoothly.
'Still no news of little Mino'?'

'No,' I said. 'So could I possibly get direct access to your till transactions for the last four weeks? I reckon the snatcher might use this store regularly and she'll have stocked up on baby food and diapers in advance.'

'Do you think that's likely, Mr Thens? Surely not. And I'm afraid till transactions are data protected.'

'This is an exception,' I said. 'A matter of life or death. If you prefer it I could organise a search engine to focus the number of baby snatches at Cutgroce branches worldwide. That might throw up some damaging statistics.'

The manager looked mildly alarmed, as I intended, though I was far from sure of my bluff.

'Well I suppose I could lend you a terminal for a few hours if you must,' he said grudgingly.

'More than' a few,' I said. 'I'll start now. Better just let me take a copy-stick of last month's trading and I'll apply my software to it at home.'

So I took the stick home and shut myself away with the laptop, winning the first hint of a smile from Ariadne as I rushed past. There were about 90,000 transactions for the period, so first of all I screened out all of them that didn't include baby food. Then I took out all which were for under twenty New Dollars, for I knew my quarry had been preparing for a siege. She might have built up stocks over several visits, but she couldn't have resisted getting a reasonable quantity at least once. This took the tally down below a thousand and of those about a quarter were duplicates. There might just have been a match with a single purchase of a loaf of bread or something similar on the day of the snatch, but I assumed she wouldn't have been crazy enough to use her loyalty card when making a dash with Mino in one arm, so I didn't even try. I just did a print-out of the remaining loyalty-card names and addresses and made a preliminary underlining of all those who called themselves Ms.

§

'Damn mulatto,' said Mista Sambrooksa Thathud and kicked me, though some people said he was my half-brother. 'I suppose with training you might make a half-decent servant.'

'Yassa.'

'What do you think, Jenkins?'

'I'm sure your judgement is excellent Mr Sambrooke,' said the seaman we knew as Captinjenkins of the ship *Rebecca*, a strange little man with half his left ear missing. 'She's quite pretty if you like that sort of thing,' he added. 'I think I could get a good price for her in Campeachy or even Savannah.'

So I was sold and sailed away in the *Rebecca*. Captinjenkins liked to stare at me, but luckily he didn't want to do anything and I ended up in Savannah with a new master Mistakernel Oglethorpe. He wasn't the kind of man to touch black women, never. We just picked

211

cotton for him and he spent a lot of time killing Indians, but slaves he treated quite well.

The main thing bad about Savannah was having to go to the chapel of the Reverendwesley, because he always frightened us so much.

'We're all sinners. I'm a sinner,' he'd say. 'You will all suffer everlasting torment in the dreadful fires of hell,' he'd tell us and go into horrible detail of how we'd be tormented by flames and beasts. Though I was often very tired after a day picking cotton or cooking in the kitchen there were many nights I couldn't sleep for worrying about hell. It made me itch. It wasn't until the Reverendwesley went off in a ship that I took a man for myself.

New York, Oct 6th, 2120

It took me a whole day to visit the first six women on my Cutgroce print-out and it passed without any hint of success, so on the second day I decided this was too slow and hooked into the COLDS register of births and deaths. I tried a correlation between my Cutgroce list and childless women on the register between thirty-five and forty-five and this produced ten names including two I'd already visited.

The first three I managed to track down and all had full-time jobs. It took all morning, mainly waiting for lifts in decrepit multi-storey blocks. Ariadne did another two and we met to compare notes. She was exhausted, red-eyed and miserable. We sat briefly in a park commemorating the last white president and looked

up at the huge Euthanasia Tower. I'd read about it. Some
Korean entrepreneur had made a fortune out of it in the
last century. People who wanted to finish with life would
pay a reasonable sum for admission and it was all very
well organised. They had a legal section on the ground
floor where you could adjust your will; sign off your death
tax assessment, then adjourn to an excellent bistro bar.
There was a flower shop and an area for the counselling of
any relatives or hangers-on who wanted to accompany the
client. Next there was a clothes hire store and changing
room, then an office to check out organ donations and a
big box for your watch, jewellery and any remaining loose
change, then an obituary dictating lounge, a chapel and
book of remembrance and finally a choice of departure
modes; gravity, water, gas or drugs.

'I hate that place,' said Ariadne.

'You're probably right,' 'I said. 'Though it might prove
useful one day. Anyway its time to finish off this list.'

§

'You're a bastard, Theneau,' said the chief fur trader,
downing a tumbler of neat rum. 'I don't deny it,' I
answered, doing the same. 'I'm not proud. My father was
a New Orleans soak and my mother an escaped slave
from Georgia. She walked all the way here from Savannah
in only six weeks, dodging British troops on one side and
Spanish on the other. Quite a woman she was.' I paused
and he looked at me, but said nothing.

'How much are you going to give me for my skins, you
old devil?' I asked.

'Another drink before we talk about money,' he said, signalling to the waiter. 'Enjoy the hospitality of Baton Rouge.'

'I can always sell my skins to another trader. Don't just think you can make me drunk and I'll drop my prices.'

'Of course you won't,' he said, shunting the glass across the grubby table top.

I felt my coin pouch and prepared myself to be patient. If I could get ten francs a skin I'd be able to pay off the money-lender and still have a sound base to make a real run at the cards. Last time I'd lost. This time I'd win. Then buy a woman and settle down.

'Have you heard the news?' came a voice. 'What?'

'Louisiana's been sold to the United States,' said the barman with an evil smile. 'They don't like mulattos.'

'Sounds like your days here are numbered, Theneau,' said the buyer. Then:

'I'll give you five francs a skin today. Or two tomorrow, whichever you like.'

'Bastard,' I said.

'Two francs today, then,' he said. 'And you better be out of town tomorrow.'

New York, Oct 6th, 2120 cont.

'There are only two more to go,' I said to Ariadne. 'You come with me. Maybe we'll go back to the drawing board after this.'

We went to a shabby block of seventy-five storeys and waited nearly an hour for the lift up to a graffiti-covered corridor on the sixtieth, the floor scattered with assorted old needles and cigarette buts. There was one tiny shop with its shutters closed and a Tannoy which told us that more people were dying of cancer than ever before, because heart attacks had been almost eliminated.

Then we had to walk up two flights to the sixty-second, hearing the glad tidings that the Neo-communist Party had made sweeping gains in the Taiwanese general election and angry ferrymen had blockaded the world's biggest cod farm on the Dogger Bank. Dr Joe Smith of COLDS Foundation had launched a new moral crusade to return to the standards of the twenty-first century. An as yet unnamed New York churchman had been arrested on a spousal assault charge after his common law wife had been found wandering in the street with a black eye.

'Its number 6283,' I said. 'Along here.'

'Listen,' said Ariadne. 'I can hear something. It's a baby.' She paused for a second and put her hand to her mouth. 'It's Mino. I'm sure it is,' she said.

For a moment I think I was worried that Ariadne might just be hearing what she wanted to hear, for the crying, so far as I was concerned, had been very faint and could have been any baby, but then I saw that she was in absolutely no doubt. And for the first time in two weeks her face showed real hope.

The door in front had a spy hole, so I thought there was little chance of the woman opening it for us. Equally if we called the police it would take them a good six hours plus lift-waiting time. So I decided to cheat. I pressed the fire alarm and surprisingly the circuit was in working order. It might land me a thousand-dollar fine, but it would be worth it. Half a minute later the woman came out of her door with Mino and I put out my arms to stop her while Ariadne grabbed Mino. We headed back to the sixtieth floor and five lift-loads later we were out in the street. Ariadne's eyes were still glistening with joy and no one seemed to be pointing at me as the cause of the fire alarm.

§

What with the Tlingit natives on one side and the Russians on the other, Sitka wasn't the most comfortable place for a half-black American trapper to make a living, for both sides wanted all the ermine for themselves. But I did well enough, especially in the winter when the stoat's skin goes white and fetches a good price to make fancy collars for the aristocrats. And I married a half-Tlingit, half-Russian wife, so I kept the peace with both lots. In the summer I mostly went fishing on the Taku River in my kayak.

New York, Oct 7th, 2120

Mino was back in his own cot and all was well with the world. For once I had achieved something and for a while I was content.

This was also the day the largest ever unmanned battle took place both on land and in the air, with drone bombers attacking each other and at the same time firing on drone-tanks which in turn used anti-air-drone rockets against their aerial tormentors. Both the Kazakhstan and Uzbekistan governments claimed victory and there was only one human casualty, an Uzbek drone-tank controller who had attempted against orders to recover one of her charges when its wi-fi was hacked by the enemy. It was also the day when same-sex marriages were made illegal again in Alabama.

Above all it was the day after I had played the role of a world-class detective, but of course all I had really achieved was to raise us from horrendous depression to humdrum normality. Perhaps that is the nature of happiness, like the momentary flowering of a poppy after eleven months and three weeks of self-abnegation. As the plaque on St Patrick's Cathedral says:

Let's start by saying that to believe
In one god is a good deal less absurd
Than worshipping say six or seven.
I climbed Olympus years ago and heard
Not a whisper of Jupiter or Mars in heaven.
We scoff at gods with horse's legs,
Six arms, white beards or elephant's heads,
But why should he oblique stroke she be white,
Clean-shaven, male and English-speaking? Quite.
Immortal, invisible, by definition inhuman,
No eyes or even urge to look at suffering,
No ears and deaf by design to cries of pain,
No hands to flick the on/off switch for rain
Or earthquakes, no wish to ease our situation,
Yet in the web of mortal minds
There is some circuit of aspiration,
A common kindness to which our knees could bow
Matching the needs of flowers to grow.

So keep the cathedrals in good repair;
They're far from perfect, but at least they're there.

PLEASE NOTE HONESTY BOX BENEATH THIS
PLAQUE AND GIVE WHAT YOU CAN FOR ROOF
REPAIRS. THANK YOU.

CHAPTER EIGHTEEN

BIO OR MONO

All civilization has from time to time become a thin crust

over a volcano of revolution.

H.H. Ellis.

New York, Oct 19th, 2120

Everything had been absolute disaster for nearly a week, a period of torment, yet when the torment was removed the happiness only seemed to last a few hours. No sooner had we got Mino back than there was a collapse in Siberian tundra prices due to huge stock mountains after the extra-long hurricane season. Then on top of that came news of an acute shortage of Colombian hardwoods due to the escape from a private zoo of two breeding pairs of beavers that had been genetically modified to adapt to sub-tropical conditions.

§'

'Name?' asked the border control policeman at Okhotsk.

'Thenski,' I said.

'You don't speak very good Russian.'

'My father was a Canadian.'

'Where from?' he asked, writing very slowly in his book.

'He came from Fort Nelson to Talkeetna. I think I was born in Edmonton. I came to Alaska a good ten years ago to trade in furs. Our family have been trappers and fur traders for generations.'

I looked round the little office. The policeman, who had the eyes and cheekbones of a Mongol but the mouth and chin of a Russian, sat rather pompously at his little desk and the usual lithograph of our beloved Tsar Alexander II hung on the timber wall behind him. More discreet was a cheap miniature icon of the child martyr St Gleb with a silver-foil frame. An icy wind daggered beneath the ill-fitting door.

'You trappers get around,' he said. 'So why don't you want to stay in Alaska and be an American? Most of the others do, except the criminals.'

'Look at me. I'm half French, half mulatto, half something else, I don't know what. I want to stay in Imperial Mother Russia. Americans make me feel uneasy.'

'How come your name is Thenski?'

'My father's name was Theno and my mother was Minski. They mixed the two.'

'So you want a visa to stay in Kamchatka?'

'Yes,' I replied.

'How are you going to earn a living?' he asked, barely looking up from his pad of forms.

'Trading,' I said. 'Up till now I've mixed general store business with my trapping.'

'Are you sure you're not Jewish? You look it.'

'I don't think so. Not so far as I know.'

'I'll put you down as a Jewish merchant to be restricted to Provideniya. That's the best I can offer. Otherwise you stay in Alaska and become an American.'

'Thank you.'

'Do you need lodgings? I have a spare room for three roubles a month. My little wife died a year ago, bless her soul, but my daughter makes good borshch. It will be simpler for processing your visa if you take official lodgings.' He winked.

I handed him three roubles. Besides, I always had a fondness for well-made borshch.

New York, Oct 21st, 2119

'Give me a kiss, Mrs Thens,' I said , basking in my new-found success as a private investigator. 'We've been through a lot. Let's get a babysitter and go out on the town.'

'No, sorry, Theo,' said Ariadne. 'I can't bear to leave Mino out of my sight for a second. I still have nightmares about kidnappers. Let's stay in for a while and ring for a takeaway.'

So I tapped an order into my wrist-top for two four-cheese pizzas, a bottle of ice-cold Lambrusco and some apple pie. Half an hour later it arrived in the mini-hoist and I swiped my card over the e-meter.

'I need to report that baby-snatcher to the police,' I said. 'She might try it' again.'

'I think she's suffered enough,' said Ariadne. 'I hate her, but I'm sorry for her as well. Let's forget her.'

We were silent for a moment. 'There's a new plyboard mill being built in Quebec,' I said. 'They'll put a micro-thin layer of hardwood on a flexible softwood centre, so

221

it could be good business for my veneer niche. I'll have to pop up there and present my credentials.'

'Then I'll just stock up with food before you go and put the chain on the door,' said Ariadne. 'I'm not going out while you're away, that's for sure.'

I hugged her. 'Don't worry,' I said. 'Lightning doesn't strike twice in the same place.'

§

'Steward,' yelled the colonel from compartment 23.

'Yes, sir,' I answered, rushing along from my cabin at the rear of the coach.

'What's your name?' he asked. He was a rather overweight cavalry officer with a red face, an untidy grey moustache and distended tunic.

'Thenski, sir,' I answered. 'Can I get you something?'

'A large iced vodka, Thenski, and some decent caviar.'

I came back with his order. 'Just initial the bar chitty here, sir, and you can settle your account when we get to Moscow,' I said. I'd had passengers from the Third Obranski Regiment before and they had a tendency to forget their mess bills, given half a chance, particularly if the war had gone badly and this time it certainly had. They had let the Japanese capture Port Arthur, so all the officers' career prospects were under a cloud. Plus, if they didn't pay their bar bills the railway company would take it out of my wages.

'There you are, sir,' I said, presenting him with his drink on a silver tray, balancing myself carefully as the train began to gather speed out of Khabarovsk and we started on the long climb towards the Stanovoy Mountains.

'Sit down a minute, Thenski,' said the colonel, putting aside the copy of the *Protocols of the Elders of Zion* which he had been reading. It was well-thumbed. 'I'm a senior colonel,' he went on. 'And I've led my regiment out here, but I'm not a snob. Unless you're a Jew. Are you?'

'No, I'm not, sir,' I said. 'My grandfather was a Canadian who moved to Alaska.'

'Pour yourself a vodka. Put it on my chitty.'

The engine five coaches ahead of us coughed and spluttered as it began to tackle the long gradient.

'No thank you, sir. I have to stay awake till Zega. I'd better stick to tea.'

'Why does a decent looking guy like you work on the railways when you could be in the army?' he asked, resting a ringed hand on my knee. I'd had this before with officers on their way back to Moscow, particularly after a few vodkas, particularly from the navy men after they lost half their ships sunk at Tsushima. Outwitted by a bunch of nips who had only recently started to build metal warships.

'I like the travel, sir,' I replied. 'And, if I can share a secret, it suits me to have two wives, one in Vladivostok and one at the other end of my route in Krasnoyarsk.'

He took his hand away from my knee and I stood up.

'I see,' he said and stroked his moustache nervously.

'And I think I am maybe half Jewish,' I added, subconsciously scratching my elbow. 'That slipped my mind for a moment.'

He recoiled and picked up the *Protocols* again, wiping the rim of his vodka glass with his hanky.

No tip from that one, I thought, as I went back to my cabin, opened the window and breathed the cool clean air sweeping across the flat vastness of Siberia. Then I thought of my west wife in our little hut in Krasnoyarsk with the two children and I braced myself to go and make up all the bunks, while the officers guffawed along to the dining car at the rear of the train.

Quebec, Oct 28th, 2120

Ten days after Mino's happy return I took the express roboid to Quebec and met the chief buying officer in the new plywood mill.

'I'm Charles Theneau, chief buyer,' he said, stretching out his hand languidly. 'Welcome to the French Republic of Quebec.'

There was something vaguely familiar about him, but I couldn't place it.

'Didn't we meet at one of the hardwood conferences?' I suggested.

'I doubt it,' he replied. 'I've been in pet-foods management most of my career. Unless you've been to Baton Rouge. I come from an old aristocratic family. There was a governor of Louisiana called Count Theneau about three centuries ago. You might have seen me in the media down there. That could be it.'

'Remarkable,' I said. 'And so is your plant. State of the art.'

'He smiled. 'Korean bank loans, Sudanese technology. Takes only one man per shift to run the whole plant,' he added smugly. 'Plus around fifty software engineers on standby. Now let me see your samples.'

I picked out my swatch. 'This was from the last wild papingo tree in the whole world,' I said. 'But we kept the seeds and now have a whole plantation nearing maturity. Wonderful balance and texture.'

'Nice,' he agreed, tossing it aside. 'But what's important to me is getting a knot-free finish. I need accuracy to within a thou over a three meter sheet.'

'No problem,' I lied. 'I'm the main agent in North America for Brazmahog,' I added proudly. 'They planted a million hectares of hardwood in the 2090s. The quality is guaranteed.'

'That's impressive,' he said, as if he knew what he was talking about, which I knew he didn't. 'But I'm afraid I can only let you have cost plus one and a half per cent.'

This was a crippling margin, even by the tough standards I was used to. Why did he have to lead me into making a pompous statement on quality and only then choose to humiliate me on price? That sort of percentage could disappear altogether if they were a week late paying. Especially if Brazmahog was the supplier. Anyway I had come all this way to get an order, so something would be better than nothing. So I took him to lunch in a bistro in the old French quarter of Quebec called Les Collines d'Abraham, where despite protesting that it was company policy not to accept hospitality, he ordered the most expensive dish and the best wine, a full bottle of course, of which I only drank one glass. Two hours later I was on the off-peak non-status roboid back to New York.

When I got home the door to our apartment was triple locked and on the chain.

'Thank God you're back,' said Ariadne through the gap, and when the chain was off I got a hot wet hug. 'I've been so worried,' she said. 'I just can't get that woman stealing Mino out of my mind.' She was crying. 'Why are you so late?'

'Stop worrying,' I said. 'I'm here now,'

§

It was difficult to get a job in those days unless your father had the same one before you, so naturally I joined the railways. By that time, when I was about six, we'd moved to Omsk, so I was brought up near the huge marshalling yard where the huddled steam engines sweated and coughed into the night. I was a footplate trainee at fifteen and qualified for a ten-wheel loco by the time I was twenty. I had my own regular shift on the Omsk to Perm run six times weekly. It was work I enjoyed, especially when I was promoted to twelve-wheelers. On top of that, when the Patriotic War started they didn't call me up the way they did most of my non-railway friends. I was just transferred to driving troop trains.

So I spent three years pulling full trains to the front, mostly the Masurian Lakes direction near Elk in Poland, then half empty ones or hospital trains on the way back to Minsk. That was until the late spring of 1917 when even a fool could see we were losing the war. Then I was called in by the transport sergeant at Minsk, where I had a billet with my wife Katerina. By this time the Germans had beaten us so badly that Minsk was almost on the front line.

'Corporal driver Thenski,' said the' sergeant. 'I've got a special shunting job for you, from Breslau.'

'Breslau?' I queried. 'I thought that is behind the German lines. What are they playing at?'

'That's why it's special. No questions to be asked. There's a sealed train coming from Switzerland and you take it straight through to Petrograd, Finland Station. No stops.'

He gave me the papers and then gave me three darts to throw at his poster of General Hindenberg, which already had thousands of holes. Beside it was another poster for the Belarussian Workers Soviet that had no holes in it at all.

Then he said, 'Off you go.'

So I headed for a 4446, not my usual type and a newish one at that, a superb beast, and I had real fun all the way to Breslau. No problems there either. Just followed the signals to a quiet siding and shunted into a couple of darkened coaches with Swiss markings, hooked on in half a minute and the reverse signal came to green before I even had a chance to pee out the cab door. Ten hours later I was in Petrograd.

It was only two months after this that I put three and three together and realised I was the one who had brought Vladimir Ilyich back to Russia. Not that I was ever very interested in politics or a great reader of the

Spark, though there were always copies in the drivers' rest room.

So now I'm back on the Minsk to Vilnius line and the only difference is that officers and men now go in the same coaches. I've noticed this wobbly bit of track west of Grodno before, and I don't like it. Everything shakes even if I slow down. There's a noise. My engine starts to go upwards. So steep that some hot coal spills backwards out of the boiler. And still up.

'Katerina Thenskaya, God save you,' I muttered.

Now I'm falling again and the coal is following me downwards.

New York, Nov 20th, 2120

For three weeks the guy in Quebec refused to take my calls and I didn't know if he was going to give me any business. Orders were poor generally, and with Ariadne still very jumpy every time the phone or door bells rang, it was hard to stay calm. The threat of software hacking and credit reduction became a serious worry again, yet I felt it was my own fault and I couldn't share the total inanity of my work with Ariadne. I was so bored I was even tempted by the tele-fruit machines, a vice to which many of my fellow e-pod workers tended to succumb, loading their e-tops with cash and playing for days on end. The software was very ingenious, because it always held out the hope that a big win was just round the corner. It lured you to go on, even giving you the artificial sound of coins pouring onto a metal trough when it thought you needed a minor win to keep you hooked. At least two hardwood specialists that I knew went bankrupt doing this and had gone into rehab. The trouble was that when they came back into the market they offered any margin just to snatch an order, so it made life even harder for the rest of us.

Then at last the first order from Quebec came through.

'I don't know why you were worried,' said Ariadne. 'You always get orders in the end.'

She was right. I do get stressed over nothing and something always turns up in the end. But Ariadne had far more faith than me; I was always bedevilled by a deep sense of insecurity, always expecting disaster. Perhaps it was inevitable, being descended from royalty, albeit the king of a tiny state, that I should feel inadequate by comparison, a chronic underachiever, although from what I'd heard of Theseus he had been far from perfect, ditching the woman who had saved his life and making himself so unpopular with his own citizens that they flung him off the throne. So why bother? I didn't know the answer.

'Can't we buy some lottery tickets?' she asked. 'It would be great for us to win a million, and we deserve it.'

'That's what everybody thinks,' I said. 'And it never happens. I know several e-pod traders who've been put into lottery detoxification centres or ended up in Cardboard City. Half the charity money now goes to lottery dependency clinics.'

'That's crazy.'

'Anything to counteract stress. Lots of my contacts want to abseil off skyscrapers or go bungee jumping from high tension cables or play Kalashnikov roulette in disused railway tunnels. They even take out overdrafts to go on terror holidays with live war games and suicide rides.'

'Why don't you just think about your families and stop being so self-important?' asked Ariadne, dusting Mino's bottom with a professional flick.

New York, Nov 21st, 2120

Today it's exactly five hundred years since the Mayflower reached Cape Cod with its cargo of a hundred and two would-be settlers. Now those people really were achievers. Why can't we do things like that these days?

§

'Comrade Thenski, you don't have your own land any more,' said the official from the Agdept. 'It's part of a collective. Your job is to remove all the walls, trees and hedges that divide up this land. It should make three fields of fifty hectares each. All to be planted with rye.'

'But my family cannot just live on rye,' I said. 'What we can grow is flax and sugar beet. Our summers are too warm and humid for rye.'

'You'll just have to try. Orders from Moscow. All small farms round Minsk are being eliminated for the greater good of the working class.'

So I did as I was told and my pretty little farm with its fruit trees and vegetable plots and pig sties became just an invisible patch on the huge new collective. My widowed mother had been allotted this farm after the October

Revolution when my father was killed in a railway accident. Our land was on the hillside looking towards the Svislach River; it was hard to work but it had served us well.

But, as I knew all along, destroying our hedge rows to grow huge hectares of rye simply would not work. Nor did we have our fruit and vegetables any more, let alone space for the pigs. I shouldn't have complained of course, but I did. So we got nothing. It would probably mean the gulag.

New York, Dec 2nd, 2120

'If you want money you have to put up with a certain amount of stress,' I said to Ariadne with just a touch of self-pity.

'It's all this worrying about things when all that matters is people,' she said. 'What's the point?'

'Let's go out,' I said. 'We're getting claustrophobic. My mother will look after Mino. Let's get her to come round.'

An hour later she appeared with her embroidery-by-numbers kit and said, 'You go out and enjoy yourselves' as if she thoroughly despised us for even thinking of such self-indulgence. We ignored her and went out to the new Titanic Theme Bar where we had Chilean champagne in real flutes. The restaurant floor tilted gently first one way, then the other, the grand piano rolled backwards and forwards with a girl playing 'Abide with me' as we danced in several inches of tepid water. Ariadne was almost in tears. 'Nice steak,' she said. 'Even if it's not meat. It must be ten years since I last ate real meat. I should have let you take me out sooner, I know I should. But I couldn't bear it.'

'Don't worry about it,' I said.

'We're all just silly little specks of dust on the side of a bigger speck of dust,' she said. 'Aren't we?'

'Yes,' I replied, gulping hard at my Peruvian Rioja. 'After all, most pain only lasts an instant. My theory of relativity is a man in pain running fast would seem slower than a man strolling along in a happy, pain-free trance.'

'I don't 'know what you're talking about,' said Ariadne.

'I'm just relaxing for a change, that's all. Let's go for another paddle-dance.'

We stayed another half hour, and then went out into the street and the cable flash e-headlines read PROPHET CHARGED WITH SPOUSAL ABUSE. I looked at the screen. It said Dr Joe Smith, who had recently launched a major new crusade for moral reform and return to mid-twenty-first century values, faced six charges of hitting his wife and one of attempted rape. He claimed that he was totally innocent on all charges.

'Funny world,' I said as I closed the front door on my mother and gave Ariadne a hug, but that night I found it hard to sleep. My fancy alarm clock decided to speak:
I pray, that means I sit and think.
I stare, I scratch, I doze, I blink,
I wonder if I have a maker,
Some fleshless transcendental fakir
Who stops and starts the world at leisure
And doles out misery or pleasure,
Who says 'Your time is up, you're dead

Or you can be a mouse instead.'

Then it pinged and said, 'Goodnight.' I was tempted to extract its battery and send the silly gadget for recycling. Then at last I slept, at least I think I did.

'Are you awake?' asked Ariadne.

'Sorry, I thought you were asleep.'

'Give me another cuddle.'

I did. Then I put the battery back in the clock and set it for seven thirty. It was quite clever, for it knew how to send a signal to the kitchen to turn on the coffee and the toaster. But it had no talent for understanding a person's psychological needs. It muttered a dry apology for waking you up early, but there was no sincerity in it.

CHAPTER NINETEEN

A HALF CAUSE OR A HOLOCAUST

'Exterminate all the brutes!'
J. Conrad

New York, Dec 3rd, 2120, 7.30 a.m.

The alarm wakened me with its usual fake good wishes and I let Ariadne sleep on while I caught up with my virtual paperwork.

§

'But we're not practising Jews,' said my mother, not entirely truthfully, for when it had suited them her parents sometimes went to the synagogue. 'I'm a poor widow. My husband was sent to the gulag for complaining about having to give up his land to the commissars.'

We'd been sitting in the extremely cold waiting room of Bialystok Station for six hours. I'd just passed my test as an engine driver in Minsk and thought I might get a job in Poland.

The Polish immigration officer laughed.

'These things happen,' he said unsympathetically and stamped our visas.

'Bloody kulaks, I suppose.'

'No,' said my mother. 'Except for my husband our family have always worked on the railways.'

A week later we were settled in a two-room apartment in the east end of Kracow and I'd been given a month's trial with the state railway company. In the workers' canteen I ostentatiously ate pork sausages to show what a true Slav and a Catholic I was, and I joined in the group which poked fun at all the Jewish ticket clerks.

For a year I did quite well and I had just been promoted to the Lublin–Warsaw express run when the war started. Six weeks after that we'd been conquered by the Germans, but at that time I still preferred Germans to Russians, so I wasn't too worried. For a while I was put on garrison trains, then had a stint of troop shuttles to the eastern front.

'Why don't you eat pork, mother?' I asked one evening.

'Because my mother never did,' she said. 'It's nothing to do with being Jewish or not. Any more than for a boy to be circumcised.'

'But you don't go to Mass.'

'Of course I don't. Your father and I were always Orthodox until the revolution. Being in Poland makes no difference. Pure Russian. Anyway you don't go to anything, do you? I think maybe beneath it all you're really a communist like the men who killed your father.'

'No, not really,' I said. 'I thought they did a lot of good all the same, but they didn't need to send Dad to the gulag.'

'I'm glad you have a bit of loyalty left.'

Six months later I married a Polish girl from Krakow and the three of us managed to move a bit further away from the ghetto, but the stares of the policemen kept getting harder. Most of the obvious Jews had now been moved out of the city.

'I think you're at least half a Jew, Thenski,' said the foreman in the engine shed.

'Not me,' I replied. 'Never been to a synagogue in my life, gaffer.'

'Maybe not,' he said. 'But we have special assignments for people like you. They don't want you going to the eastern front any more. Spoils the atmosphere. No, there's a new run. From now on you're three times weekly to Oswiecim. The rolling stock's a bit past it, but good enough for what you'll be carrying.'

I left his office relieved that I hadn't been sacked or conscripted and took myself off to the remote siding whose number he'd given me.

'Jewish factory workers being shipped south,' said a clerk with a clipboard. 'Nearly finished loading.'

To my surprise I saw Germans cramming extra people into each truck and then padlocking the doors, but I asked no questions.

'Work makes free,' said one of the Germans and winked at me.

I winked back and ten minutes later I had the long train lumbering slowly out of Warsaw towards the southern trunk line.

'Good trip, dear?' asked my little wife, smiling when I got home two days later.

'Not bad,' I said.

'What's that smell?' she asked.

'They gave me a bunk right beside the rubbish incinerator,' I said. 'Its ponged my boiler suit.'

'It sure has,' she said. 'Never mind I'll wash it before you go off in the morning.'

'I brought you this,' I said handing her a little gold bracelet, which I'd found in one of the trucks.

'That's lovely,' she said.

'Now that my job seems a bit more secure I think we should move up nearer the Wista,' I said.

'We're so lucky,' she said and hugged me.

But I was still worried. There was an SS colonel who screamed at me if my train was ten minutes late after a trip of three hundred miles. He always stared at me and I am sure he thought I was a Jew.

New York, Feb 10th, 2121

'I fancy guacamole, fajitas and ice cream,' said Ariadne when I got home.

'You mean Mino's little sister fancies it all,' I said, patting her stomach.

'What about the Aztec Theme Bar then?'

'And by the way we have a new regular babysitter,' she said and stood aside to reveal sitting behind her a woman who seemed vaguely familiar, but appeared embarrassed by this sudden exposure.

'This is my new friend, Mary,' said Ariadne. 'Remember flat number 6285? Well she's kindly paid the fire-alarm fine for you. Isn't that nice of her?'

For a moment I was stunned.

'Anyway she loves Mino just as much as we do,' went on Ariadne. 'So she's going to come round often, aren't you, Mary?'

'If Theo doesn't mind,' said the woman.

'Delighted,' I said, astonished, as I had so often been in the past, by the extraordinary qualities of my wife.

'I've been clearing out all the cupboards,' Ariadne went on. 'Getting ready. Can we go to the metro-coup first? I want a clean start. Mino can come with us.'

So we rented a skip-van and loaded it with bags mostly of my favourite treasures from the past, but also a few of Ariadne's, and headed west along the main road with wires that blossomed with airy fragments of pulverised plastic. North America's largest and most sophisticated refuse acceptance centre was not my most favoured destination, but this was not a day for arguing. A thousand hectares of biodegradable reconstitute had been converted to a hydrogen-driven sustainable orangerie. The car and appliance compressor was the most powerful in the world – it could reduce old dishwashers to the size of a match box. The six-lane sewage recycling plant was supporting the national collection of rare hostas as well as a protected colony of giant willow warblers. Beyond that, in a grass-fringed pool beside the uranium reprocessing area, there was a platform where celebrities were brought to enjoy publicised tastings of the water as a demonstration of its health-giving purity.

We swiped our membership cards at the barrier sensor and fed our assorted rubbish into all the proper vents, separating out all the different colours of glass and plastic and the different types of paper.

'Now let's go and have some fun,' said Ariadne. So we went to the multi-kid acclimatisation centre where young and old are meant to bond in ball pools, on bouncy cathedrals, in mini-bungee jumps, water flumes, on roller moguls. Both adults and children win points for competition which can earn you a ten per cent discount on your next visit. We did well enough until Mino baulked at the two-year-old's assault course and I was so incensed by the supercilious stares of the other fathers that I whispered horrible threats in the little boy's ear until at last he tearfully embarked on the first obstacle. Luckily it was closing time, so he was spared being driven any further, but I was left feeling very guilty.

'Which turning, left lane or right?' I asked after we left, happy but close to exhaustion.

'You've just passed it,' said Ariadne, laughing.

'That's not bloody funny,' I retaliated. 'That'll be an extra ten-minute drive right down and back up again to the tunnel turn-off.'

'Grumpy daddy,' said Ariadne, infuriatingly relaxed. I fumed inwardly, and then drove on in silence.

'You've just passed it again, you idiot,' said Ariadne twenty minutes later and she was right.

'You could have reminded me,' I hissed through clenched teeth.

'You're always so pompous about being a better navigator than me, I didn't dare.'

I sulked all the way home.

'Don't bother coming into the house if that's the way you feel,' said Ariadne, blinking back tears.

'I won't,' I said, slammed the door and headed for the Icelandic Theme bar. I ordered a large White Death and sat there scratching my elbow to watch the True Confessions Programme on the big screen. There was a man who said he'd raped the Virgin Mary and a minor celebrity who had worked in a torture chamber in Guantanamo Bay, plus the usual clutch of child abusers. They were all awarded telegenic forfeits like wading chest-deep across a sewage farm or spending a fortnight in a deep freeze. Some of them got huge cheers when they finished their ordeals and became short-term national heroes. That was maybe why they confessed in the first place. It all began to seem remote and I sidled out without saying goodbye, went home, crept into bed beside Ariadne and apologised to the back of her head.

'Don't be stupid,' she said and put her hand in mine.
I dreamed:
How pleasant it is to be well-adjusted,
Liked by one's peers, respected, trusted,
No sense of feeling insecure
Just because one's short or poor,
No pang of class inferiority
Because one's less able than the majority,
Nor any temptation to feel superior
Because one's licked the right posterior,
No overwhelming sense of guilt,
No crying over milk one's spilt,
No driving compulsion to join the elite

No feeling that life's incomplete,
Alone, a failure and rejected
Humiliated and dejected.
Never.
Of course not.

There is a major outbreak of the Zeta variant of Covid 63, mainly in Canada and the USA. It his highly infectious but not fatal. However it reduces most patients to a permanently vegetative condition. There is as yet no effective vaccine but several candidates are at trial stage. Meanwhile there is the usual lock-down.

I think that I have at last decided what God is. Without a capital G. Nothing original or very clever, but it half satisfies me. So. God is not a he or a she but an it. Not my father or mother, not my king or lord. Nor can you pray to it for favours. It is just an invisible, speechless, nebulous feeling common to all humans, at least normal adults, whatever that means. It may not be eternal, immortal, but it has probably been in existence half a million years, yet it can easily self-destruct as it has regularly throughout human history. For old times' sake – and give credit to St Paul – let's say it has three main features: faith, hope and charity, all of which can make humans feel good and friendly with each other, but all three are fragile and can go horribly wrong. Faith can morph itself into lunatic obsessions and malevolent ideologies. Hope can morph into competitive greed for wealth or conquest. Charity, usually called love, can morph into sexual abuse and corrosive jealousy. So I can see myself sitting in a wooden pew in an old cathedral and praying not to God, but to humans to treasure those special feelings and not allow them to become dangerous mutations.

In Germany and the Czech Republic there has been another walk-out of female robots, complaining of unequal wages and lack of promotion compared with male robots. There are also widespread allegations of sexual harassment. The strike is backed by the IUFR (International Union of Female Robots) but boycotted by the IUMR..

CHAPTER TWENTY

TWO KINDS OF FAMILY

I have striven not to laugh at human actions, not to weep at them, nor to hate them but to understand them.

B.Spinoza

New York Feb 20th, 2121

Life was getting complicated again. I had overstocked with Siberian tundra just before the price fell and I had real problems getting rid of it. Luckily Korea had blocked all incoming news, including world timber prices, so I managed to offload most of my stuff there at not too drastic a loss.

§

I was on the way back from Oswiecim when we were stopped by the signals outside Munich. I asked one of the track menders what was wrong.

'The Russians are getting close,' he said. 'If I were you I wouldn't go back to where you've just come from,' he added, winking.

What he said rang true for I'd sensed a new nervousness amongst the ordinary troops. For months I had been petrified by the idea that they thought I was a Jew and now I was petrified by the idea of being one of those blond-haired Arians.

The signals changed and I drove my train into one of the sidings in Munich.

'Wait here,' I said to my fireman. 'I'll find out what's happening.'

Half the station had been bombed, the cafes were all closed and there was a feeling of panic about the place. I thought of my little wife back near the Wista and I thought of myself being trapped by the Russians. Everyone said they took no prisoners. So I thought I would head south for a week or two to keep out of the way. I looked round at the few trains which were getting ready to move and found one that was heading for Austria.

'Need an extra fireman, mate?' I asked the driver.

'Hop in,' he said.

Two days later I was in Milan and found a berth as a fireman on the Milan to Genoa line.

After that I tried to forget about my old life. On alternate nights I had a bedsit in the hospice next to the cathedral and soon afterwards several other German refugees turned up. One of them I could tell had been an officer and he reminded me of the colonel who had shouted at me so often in Oswiecim. His name was Ricardo Klement and he was clearly desperate to get to South America. The bishop encouraged him and there was a steady trickle of seamen who came up from the docks for a meal. That was how I found out that there was a ship bound for Buenos Aires that was short of a couple of stokers. I had done the job on the railways and a coal-burning ship was not much different. So I volunteered and so did Ricardo Klement, who came as my assistant until we had passed the Straits of Gibraltar.

New York, Mar 20th, 2121

More complications. I had miscalculated a quote for luxury champagne boxes and the client refused to let me cancel the order, so I was faced with a significant loss, meaning effectively I would have no income for at least a month. I spent a whole day searching the small print for a let-out, but to no avail. Ariadne knew something was wrong, but I was too ashamed to confess my incompetence. Then suddenly I realised that I had miscalculated my miscalculation, using the wrong code for changing Eurodollars for dollars. Just one button to the left of the one I'd meant to hit. Panic over.

So I checked the online version of *The Laughing Times* to see if there were any prize games. There was one if you joined a club for drone delivery of vintage cider. It read:
Win a luxury cruise
To the island you choose
With lovely views
And plenty of booze
Terms and conditions of course apply
In case by accident you die.

§

'Commander Thenjo, come in,' said Coralda, the admiral's wife, one of the most sought-after beauties in Puerto Belgrano, if not Buenos Aires itself and a close friend of President Videla. Her husband was officer commanding

245

a couple of prison hulks on the River Plate, but he always wore exquisitely tailored uniforms with several tiers of medal ribbons and he took her as a trophy to all the embassy parties. He was also boosting his salary considerably with the income of two requisitioned corned beef factories.

Coralda led the way through to her patio, hips swaying. 'I was so sorry to hear about your father,' she said. 'So sad. Such a kind man. So calm considering the way his life was disrupted.'

'He couldn't win,' I said. 'One side said he was a Jew and the other that he was a war criminal. But he was a railway professional, through and through. He just happened to be running rail services to Auschwitz and Treblinka when the war ended.'

'Well I know the Perons had a very high regard for him. He ran the Patagonia line at a profit, the only man ever to do so. Not a strike all the time he was there and they always said that the Bahia Blanca express ran on time. Ridiculous to suggest he was a war criminal just because he did a professional job.'

'Absolutely,' I replied. 'And how are you?'

'Great. Jaimie's doing a short cruise on the Belgrano, so I have the place to myself. And I need someone to take me out to dinner tonight...'

'Well...'

'And Jaimie's beef factory, darling. Rumour has it his tender for supplying the navy was too high. That's ridiculous. You're in charge, aren't you? Surely you're not going to let down an old friend.'

New York, August 20th, 2121

Just before little Medea was born the timber trade went through another really bad patch, as did most other trades. The sovereign debt crisis in Germany had caused a severe loss of confidence in Europe. Senior executives were sent to the New World Bank in Soweto City to sort it out and halt a run on the Eurodollar. Pensioners had taken to the streets again in several cities and the Hang Seng had dropped by a quarter. The problems of the area formerly known as the New World were proving too deep-rooted for the buoyant Fourth World Economies to re-energise. Massive job creation projects like the hydraulic lifting of Venice above the new water table had run into funding problems, as had re-dredging the Thames, which had been reduced by silting and rubbish to a foul muddy trickle winding through London. There had also been a spectacular collapse of the Lunar Investment Company, a Mafia subsidiary running a number of loss-making mineral extraction plants on the moon, so that had not helped investor confidence either. The decision to have three compulsory changes in clothes fashions instead of two each year had only postponed the problem for a few months.

I was having a frenetic time trying to get one of the contracts for Amundsen City, the biggest construction project since the Seine Barrier. The South Pole was the only area left in the world cold enough to stage the winter Olympics and I was tendering for a wooden ski jump tower.

'Angola will win all the medals as usual,' said Ariadne cynically. 'When did a white girl last win a medal?'

It was true that Angola now just had a vast single-sex population due to their intake of muscle-enhancing drugs and they were fanatically dedicated to all forms of competitive sport.

'Twenty-eight years ago,' I said.

'See what I mean?'

'I better get on with my costings.'

'Why do I have to be saddled with a man who loves nothing but his wrist-top?' said Ariadne. 'You do nothing else. You've got no interest in culture. You don't even work hard. You just sit around most of the time waiting for orders.'

'That's not fair. I have to make money to keep Mino in bouncy suits and pay for his line-dancing class. You stay at home, but you don't work. You just defrost food in the microwave. What's the point?'

'You don't even love Mino. You're jealous, you've said as much. Or me for that matter.'

'Not when you suddenly attack me for no reason.'

'Perhaps it's the only way to get your attention. It's a cry for help.'

I went to hug her, but she shrank back.

'I hate you,' she said.

'This is the end,' I retorted. 'I've had enough.' And I stalked out and walked along the Hudson where a line of cruise ships had been converted to floating prisons. I hadn't had an order for ten days and Ariadne attacking me was the last straw. She had no understanding of the competitive pressures under which I had to work. No wonder e-pod traders tended to feel they were low achievers and suffered libido loss.

I bought myself a large White Death and watched the Cablenews. There had been a meeting of the G80, the eighty richest nations in the world, in the world's tallest building at Arafat City. There was the usual count-down of twenty-two months to the final elimination of fossil fuels in the eighty top economies round the world. The week's world lottery winner had collected the country of Slovakia as her roll-over jackpot.

'Disgusting,' said a man beside me as the news showed some White Death addicts running amok in the lido resort of the Malvinas. Then the buzzer went on my viz-mobile and it was Bonzer, the Vienna contact for Brazmahog.

'You want an order?' he asked. 'Then get off your butt and come over here. Three Danube cruise boats, each with five teak decks. A great contract, but they need to see you first. That swindler Theneau from Quebec's been trying to muscle in on the act with fake teak, so you better get here fast.'

'Okay,' I said, finished my White Death and headed back to the apartment.

§

I had no choice but to resign my commission in the Argentine navy and, worse still, I had to leave the country. Coralda Aleza had told the new junta that I'd made her pay me ten thousand dollars to clinch the navy beef supply contract and had added that my father was a war criminal. The first bit was certainly an exaggeration, as was the second to my mind. In fact all I'd had from her was a dinner party and a free fortnight at her hacienda.

'Don't worry, Thenjo,' said her husband, the admiral. 'I've fixed up an interview for you with a blue-chip multinational. You won't regret resigning your commission.' And he winked.

I performed very adequately at the interview and to my surprise was offered a salary twice the level of my naval wages to become export services director for the pharmaceutical division based in Bogota. Amongst the perks was a company flat with a mega-jacuzzi, and an electric self-dispensing golf caddy.

'Glad to have you on board, Alfredo,' said the chief executive on my first day, shaking my hand over his huge mahogany desk. 'You'll have the use of the pad in San Diego as well, since you'll be up there so often. That's where we need your skills. Keep the motivation going in all our depots and make sure the staff know there's somebody from head office that cares. We expect to do very well with the next generation of Covid vaccines.'

'Yes,' I said.

'You're married aren't you? I'd base your wife in San Diego. She'll like it there.'

She did and that was where we brought up our family. Within two years I was regional director of Co-pharm which became the second largest pharmacy player in California. We developed an excellent new drug to combat chronic fatigue syndrome – it was mostly caffeine in fact. We also made huge profits from heroin derivatives used as prescriptions for substance abuse cases, which was by far our largest market niche. And being a boy from the pampas I did well on the side with a beef processing plant in Arizona. Life was good to us till I fell foul of a Mexican cartel that reckoned we were taking away their business. One of their bullets hit my spine. I'm alive but paralysed from the waist down.

New York, Sept 3rd, 2121

Just as I was organising my e-tickets for Budapest I had a medic-alarm on my wrist-top from my mother. Waves of guilt swept over me that I'd put my career and to a lesser extent my new family on my top priority list and hadn't been to see her for three months. So I grabbed a copter-taxi and went to see what was wrong.

'Sorry, Theo,' she said when I got to her apartment. 'I had a bad dream that you were going far away and not coming back. I had a panic attack and started to think I was having a stroke. I'm a silly old woman.'

'No, Mum,' I said. 'I've let myself get too busy. I should have been round sooner.'

'Well thanks for coming. Now be off with you. Give that lovely grandson of mine a kiss. Don't leave it so long next time.'

'I won't,' I said. But did I mean it?

As I sat dozing in the robodrone the intercom announced:

'In the interests of safety please pay

Attention to what I have to say:
If for some reason air pressure drops
An oxygen mask automatically flops
From the rack above. But don't ever try
To help your neighbour, instead apply
Your own to your mouth, then adapt your position
For standard emergency landing condition.
Your life jacket is securely located
But please make sure it's not inflated;
The route to your emergency door
Is shown by coloured lights on the floor;
Mobile phones should be off, cigarettes extinguished
And high-heeled shoes, if worn, relinquished;
Leave all hand luggage and proceed
As directed by cabin staff with all good speed.'

But there were no cabin staff, not even a pilot, so it was self-service.

We were expected to learn all this by heart in class 4 primary school.

I dozed off and woke up to find myself four stations beyond my proper stop.

CHAPTER TWENTY ONE

ABOVE AND BEYOND

Born down in a dead man's town
The first kick I took was when I hit the ground.
B. Springsteen

New York, Sept 3rd, 2121

'Sorry, I was being stupid,' I said to Ariadne when I got home. 'Now I've got a chance of some business in Europe, but I've got to go across and check it out. I'll try and make it quick.'

'You'd better,' she said as we hugged. An hour later I was on a Boeing 997 heading for Budapest via the Cairo hub.

Budapest, Sept 5th 2121

'Panic's over,' said Bonzer when we met outside the Buda Metro. 'They're giving us each a half of the contract. I'm sorry you've had a wasted journey, but that wasn't the way it looked yesterday. I called you but you'd already taken off.'

'Great,' I said sarcastically, but actually I had no real anger for we had after all won half a contract and there was something else. I had felt drawn to come to this place and with twenty-four hours to spare before the next flight home I felt I wanted time to myself. So I wandered a few miles down the river where it was nearly a mile wide and there were decrepit old cruise boats tied up, speed boats for hire and canoes. Suddenly I felt an irresistible urge to cross the river in a canoe by myself. It was as if it was something I had always wanted to do.

'Medium life jacket,' said the bored teenager letting out the canoes.' Be back at eight.'

I paddled from the bank through the slow-moving shallows, with water dripping down the paddle onto my trousers. Then suddenly I found myself in faster water and had to make a real effort to avoid being swept downstream. Only by aiming the canoe about forty degrees upstream could I manage to go in a more or less straight line to the other side.

After what seemed like an hour of strenuous effort I at last found myself approaching the far bank. As I stepped out into the water and pulled the canoe onto the sand I felt exhausted and my legs were shivering. Then I found an indent in the bank and began to light a small fire to heat up my can of meatballs. But I felt uneasy, as if I was unwelcome in this place. It was as if there was someone always behind my back waiting to pounce on me and even after I'd taken my meal I still had a totally irrational fear. But there was no one there and after half an hour I dragged down the canoe and set off back again.

§

'So you're Alfredo Thenjo II,' said Capo Angelini, boss of the Chicago Cosa Nostra.

'I've changed my name to Alfred Thens,' I said. 'I don't want to be identified with Mexican scum.'

'But you have good contacts in Bogota, like your late father?' he asked.

'Yes I do. And some helpful ones in Washington too,' I added.

New York, Sept 10th, 2121

'Thank goodness you've got some good orders for once,' said Ariadne, who was looking extremely plump and had only a few weeks to go. 'It makes you easier to live with.'

'I know. Sorry,' I said. 'It hasn't been easy for you.'

'No.'

'And I've got a part-time extra job as a post-disemployment-syndrome stress counsellor. It's not much more money, but it's regular.'

'Great,' said Ariadne and hugged me. 'It's not the money, it's in the caring sector. I always thought you would be good at that.'

So we went to the Aztec Theme Restaurant to celebrate. I ordered a couple of large Montezuma's Revenges and we started to read the menu. Suddenly there was a disturbance at the other end of the bar and we saw Rev Dr Joe Smith caressing a bottle of Venezuelan Brandy.

'Beware, the end of the world is nigh,' he shouted, lurching to his feet. 'Prepare to meet thy god. Love him. Do you know that Jesus was a direct descendant of Prince Gautama Siddartha otherwise known as Buddha?'

'No,' I said.

'Do you know that half the buildings on this planet are empty and there are two bedrooms for every living soul in the world, yet still millions are homeless?'

'Is that so?'

'There are six and a half billion homeless,' he said and staggered out.

'We're very lucky,' said Ariadne. 'We should never complain when life is so easy for us compared with so many others.'

'Let alone compared with animals. Or insects who only live for a couple of days. Two TexMex specials,' I added to a passing waitress. 'And a half litre of your Atahualpa Red.'

'Wait a minute,' said Ariadne suddenly, wincing. 'Let's go to the Mat Unit instead. Give them a phone first.'

With only a middle-sized feeling of panic I spoke the number into my minimobile. Just at that moment my eye caught a familiar face on the wall-mounted cable-screen. It was Dr Joe Smith, announced as the world's leading authority on dysfunctionalism, who had been convicted of shop-lifting and e-mailing selfies to twelve year old girls. The age of consent had just been reduced to thirteen.

§

'Not you again, Fred Thens,' said the Los Angeles police officer as he slipped the cuffs onto my wrists. He only managed to do so because two of his burlier colleagues had me pinned to the ground. 'It was only a year ago we put you away the last time.'

It has to be said that my career as a professional criminal had been dogged by mishaps of this kind. I blamed Bobby Kennedy and the crackdown on organised crime. I had made a huge effort to work my way up as the main cocaine dealer in San Diego. But there was far too much competition as well as obsessive persecution by the police.

New York, Feb 28th 2122

Ariadne and I had a good year. Little Medea was born and she was a sweet little girl with long brown hair and a splendid temperament like Ariadne, who seemed totally happy swabbing the children's bottoms and cooking little meals for them. We would take the two of them to Central Park and they'd hold out seeds for the pigeons and laugh to see them perch on their arms. We heard that Joe Smith had been released from custody and been appointed dean of the Saddam V of Euphrasia School of Clinical Pederasty at UCLA.

Then I too had an unexpected bonus. I was voted the *E-Pod Magazine* Timberman of the Year by my peers, a huge honour for lifetime achievement in e-pod trading.

'You deserve it,' said Ariadne with a kiss, her eyes bright. 'Okay, I always thought you could have done well in the caring sector too, but you've made money for us to have a nice home. I'm really pleased.'

Kwazulu Natal, Apr 10th, 2122

As my prize I was awarded a two-week family trip to see the new willow plantations in South Africa, paid for by the International Willow Foundation. So ten days later we boarded a B797 at Rodham–Clinton International and flew overnight to Zuludurban. It wasn't too bad a flight, but as usual there was one of the those computer alarm scares when there is always just the nagging doubt that the plane might actually be in trouble. As it was the sight of five hundred oxygen masks decanting simultaneously from the ceiling and homing in on our mouths, while at the same time our seat life-jackets automatically half inflated, was sufficiently unnerving to make me buzz the robo-steward for a couple of White Deaths. As the connecting flight approached Nkrumah Airport in Ghana and we crossed a wide bay and looked down at the Heritage Department's ethnic canoes crawling over the sea like water beetles I had the uncanny feeling I'd been there before. Then at last after a short wait we headed over Africa to Tambo and, as still happens on these occasions, we all cheered the robo-pilot hysterically when he managed a normal landing.

Two hours later we took the train up to Chosamaritzburg where we were shown round the Witch Doctor Theme Park. The authorities were making a huge effort to exploit the revival in ethnic medicine and top witch doctors were now making huge salaries throughout the world. Because of its high success ratio the park attracted large numbers of substance abuse patients from outwith Africa and its bone-based anti-allergy pills were now the country's biggest export earner after gold, diamonds and willow.

'This is great,' said Ariadne, enjoying herself as the four of us joined a circle of admirers around a chalk-faced Zulu lady who was tossing small bones on a patch of dried mud. Suddenly a bejewelled Frenchwoman leapt to her feet and shouted, 'I am cured' and threw all her e-cards into the centre.

That evening as the sun went down over the blue jacaranda trees we sat outside our family rondavel and watched the zebras grazing peacefully.

'Are you happy?' asked Ariadne.

'Yes,' I said. 'Are you?'

She nodded, smiling as Mino pointed to a large ape which had sidled up to our picnic table. 'You usually want more,' she said, looking at me. 'You never seem totally content.'

'Well I would like to go for a swim,' I said.

'I knew it. You always want more, even when you've got everything. Okay, we'll go for a swim.'

And we did as the moon dunked itself in the foaming ocean. It was perfect. Ariadne looked superb in her diakini and the children were ecstatic as we cradled them in the warm water. I thought it was the best moment of my life. But still I wanted more.

Ten minutes later I happened to pick up a newspaper and on the front page was a piece about a cruise boat disaster on the Danube. Seventy people had died when the passenger deck of the boat had caught fire, apparently because the timber supplied had been reconstituted without the addition of fire retardant. The timber

259

suppliers who had guaranteed fireproof wood were
expected to be sued for massive damages.

I knew that for a few days I had been too happy, yet
wanted more, and now I was right back in the abyss. For
some totally unknown reason I said to myself, 'That's
what comes of not respecting the Stones.'

§

'Sit down, Thens,' said the chief interviewer at the college,
a tight-lipped woman of about forty. 'Your father was
murdered by the mob in San Diego, correct?'

'More or less,' I admitted, my palms prickling with
sweat and my elbow itching. 'It was never proved who
did it. And he was straight as a die. He made a major
contribution to the development of a drug that finally
cured arachnophobia.'

'Right,' she acknowledged with little attempt to
disguise her cynicism. 'Now, you've chosen to major in
Lottodynamics. Why?'

'I think it's the subject for the future,' I said. 'I'd like
to study different lottery operation techniques round the
world. They're going to be the primary source of income
for regenerating the world after the 2120 bank crisis.'

'And your secondary subjects?' went on the second
interviewer, a narrow-shouldered little man with glasses.
'You're asking for Russian and Actuarial Studies.'

'Yes,' I said. 'I'm specially interested in the death
statistics in the nuclear contamination areas throughout
Russia.'

'And you're computer literate in Windows 2050?' he asked.

'Certainly,' I said.

'And was your father a man or a woman?'

'A man, definitely, though I believe one of my grandfathers was a woman.'

'And how many substance abuse problems have you had?' went on the female interviewer, who it turned out was a professor of psychogenetics, a subject in which I later became very interested.

'Only two,' I answered. 'Though my father never believed in locking the cabinet where he kept all his heroin samples. It was a matter of principle to train me.'

'What do you regard as the greatest danger facing us as we enter the 2060s?' asked the male again.

'Well, one that concerns me is the silting up of the Amazon,' I said. 'If it's reduced to a muddy swamp because of ex-forest erosion our entire eco-system has to be at risk. Global cooling will become a major problem and the ice cap could come as far south as New York.'

The lady professor smiled indulgently. 'That rather depends on which school of thought you support,' she said mildly. 'Never mind. You've passed your viva, Mr Thens. We look forward to your joining us next semester. Your late father kindly left a major donation to cover your fees.'

New York, Sept 5th 2123

'You're going grey,' said Ariadne to me one day. 'And fat.'

'Middle-aged, you mean,' I answered. 'It was the Danube law suit that started it. Eighteen months of worry before it went to the International Court of Arbitration at Soweto. Damned lawyers. And damned insurance companies. I pay a huge annual premium to cover me for professional indemnity and as soon as there's a hint of a claim they start looking for incendiary exclusion clauses.'

'They paid something in the end.'

'But I lost half a year's income in the process. And started losing hair. And comfort eating in a big way.'

I wasn't the only one who'd had a bad year. The sea was nearly up to 42nd Street. The Golden Gate Bridge had been irreparably damaged by an earthquake. Bulgaria and Scotland went bankrupt. The fifth moon colony was finally abandoned as uneconomic. There was an outbreak of seventh variant CJD disease in eastern Europe.

'What's life going to be like for our children after we're gone?' asked Ariadne.

'Fine, 'I said. 'They'll have problems just like we've had, but they'll be okay.'

'Are you happy?'

'Most of the time, except when I'm working. I like eating and sleeping and the other thing... How about you?'

'Yes. Most of the time I just worry about how Mino and Medea will cope.'

'Why worry?' I said, and hugged her. 'We've done our best. What more can we do?'

New York Oct 25th, 2156

I seem to have stopped writing things in my diary. Nothing important seems to happen any more. Maybe Ariadne and I are getting old.

§

'What a lovely baby. What's he called?' asked the lady from below us on floor 191 of the condominium.

'Theo,' said the proud Mrs Thens, as I cleaned the drive on my laptop and punched in the birthday of my first child born in September 2089. So far it had been a difficult year for me: there had been a major campaign against meat eaters and most of the few remaining cattle breeding countries had been compelled to limit bovine methane emissions by ninety per cent.

'Does your husband help much?' she asked, pointing at me and obviously expecting the answer No.

'He gets us a nice supply of beef, that's all you can say for him,' said my wife, winking at me.

'Just as well CJD Sixth Variant's gone away then,' said the neighbour.

My wife shrugged. 'Yes if business keeps improving we might be able to move to a real house in Brooklyn,' she said.

'Lucky old you,' said the neighbour, as if she regretted having asked, and she walked away down the long corridor in a dudgeon as she had long since given up such aspirations. Life on the 190th floor had its limitations.

That year, 2090, had been a difficult year for me, for the beef industry had shrunk drastically due to the methane problem. This was despite the introduction of carbon capture barns and persuading people to eat venison instead. I had not dared to tell my wife, who was so happy with the baby. I was glad that we now had a son but I could not imagine what the future for him would be like.

New York, Sep 10th, 2173

Just happened to find this old diary in a cupboard I wanted to tidy. Life used to be more exciting. Maybe we should go a trip somewhere. I'll look up the robocruise timetable. Maybe to Canada again.

§

I walked nervously into the headquarters of Cable International in Washington DC. I'd done quite well to get on the shortlist for this job, but now I had to impress the chairman, Peter Murdoch VII, no easy task. As I waited in the marble-lined reception area the big screen showed the latest news. Marine archaeologists were exploring the long submerged city of Amsterdam. Siberia had finally been abandoned when its remaining two nuclear power plants had gone irredeemably out of control. A five-hundred-mile exclusion zone had been applied for the next eighty years.

'Come in, Mr Thens,' said the receptionist. 'Mr Murdoch will see you now.' She smiled without warmth and used both hands to smooth her skirt over her thighs. She tapped the glass door and let me in.

'Welcome to Cable International, Mino,' said the hereditary tycoon, barely rising from his vast leather chair. 'I was so sorry to hear your parents were amongst the victims of that terrible roboid crash in Canada. Such a waste. I met your mother once. She looked after my grandfather's geri-unit. Lovely woman.'

'Don't worry,' I said. 'They died as happy as any couple I know.'

'I think I met your sister Medea once,' he went on. 'Charming girl and remarkably young to be running ten care homes.'

'She's done well,' I said.

'So have you,' said the tycoon. 'Now, we have a vacancy in our rhyming news department. It has become very popular with our readers and I think you would fit in well.'

That evening COP83 announced that average world temperatures would fall by another half a per cent within the next two years. The British government has installed a reclamation base on the island of Jersey, which has been uninhabited since 2095 due to large areas being submerged beneath the English Channel. There is a new production of *The Sound of Music* on Broadway with the role of Maria being played by a trans soprano. Three polar bear cubs have been spotted on the coast of Baffin Bay. It is now five years since the last outbreak of Covid75 and compulsory vaccination in most countries has been ended. Things are looking up

POSTSCRIPT

Ah, Pythagoras, metempsychosis, were that true
This soul should fly from me, and I be changed
Unto some brutish beast.

C. Marlowe

The official diary of Theo A. Thens comes to an end
at this point, but subsequently I tried to relive the
metempsychotic visitations I had from my long-gone
ancestors and traced the long circuitous route by which
they had in the end arrived in New York. Often I had
dreams about these people and recorded them as best
as I could manage. What follows are my jottings about
the places and people with whom I felt I had some
connection and what I found out about many of them on
the internet or in old books.

Chapter 1Somewhere in Northern Europe c.40,000 BC, probably near Ulm in Germany.

My first ancestors had no name for the places where
they lived; no names existed then, but analysing what I
remember about them in my dreams I have concluded
that the most likely region where they first made contact
was in northern Germany and that they gradually moved
southwards looking for animals to hunt.

The mention of a caveman who painted stones with
different coloured dots and carved little mammoths out
of bone suggests that at this time my ancestors may have
been living in the big cave at Hohle Fels near Ulm, where

archaeologists have found such artefacts and they indicate a date for this episode of around 20,000 BC. The cave is 49 feet long and also found here were bone flutes and small statues of lion-men. DNA analysis of bone suggests they were Magdalanean people of the upper Palaeolithic era similar to the Red Lady of Miron, whose skeleton was found in Cantabria, Spain.

Various thinkers who helped me form my thoughts are mentioned, including the French philosopher Renée Descartes (1596–1650) saying 'cogito ergo sum'. I also liked the ideas of Carl Jung in Switzerland (1875–1961) who said something about collective unconsciousness. Ron Hubbard (1911–1986) was the founder of a cult based on Dianetics. The novelist John Buchan (1875–1949) wrote a book called *The Path of the King* which follows a family tree spread over a thousand years in which the individuals are quite unaware of their predecessors, yet there is some kind of hidden link. The Greek mathematician Pythagoras (570–490 BC) had the idea of the transmigration of souls without any genetic link and not just restricted to humans. Joseph Smith (1805–1844), founder of the Mormons or Church of Latter Day Saints, preached the idea that human souls never die but transfer randomly down the generations; hence the Mormon desire to trace everyone's ancestors so that their souls can be baptised and redeemed long after their deaths.

Chapter 2

Near Budapest, 10,000 BC

The story of the man who built a canoe and crossed a wide, fast-flowing river may have referred either to the Danube near what is now Budapest or the Elbe, a story that is re-echoed in Chapter 18.

The Alps and beyond, c 1500 BC

Thereafter there is the memory of crossing various mountains until we come to mention of stone circles. Since there are virtually no such monuments surviving east of France this could only have been the Little St Bernard Pass where a circle survives 2188 m above sea level south of the Mont Blanc Massif and to the north of the Aosta Valley leading down into Italy. It is extraordinary that people could have erected such megaliths in such an inhospitable location, the spot where Hannibal is alleged to have crossed the Alps, so these people must have been very determined and very tough. The probable date of the first stones was around 1400 BC.

Chapter 3

Via Slovenia to the Balkans, c. 1400 BC

The tribe then for some reason seems to have migrated back through what is now Switzerland towards Austria or what is now Hungary where it crossed the Danube, then into Slovenia, gradually heading southwards,

Greece, c. 1300 BC

Over several generations we moved further south towards Greece and ended up in Athens, where my first named ancestor, Theseus, became a hero and king until he made himself unpopular and was deposed. Apparently he had two fathers, an earthly one, Aegeus, and an immortal, Poseidon the sea god. Ruins of his temple, the Theseion, and alleged burial place still stand in the market place at Athens. Some of the events of Theseus' reign are depicted in the statues which once adorned the Parthenon and are still controversially in the British Museum.

Chapter 4

Crete, c. 1280 BC

There is no archaeological proof that the ruins of Knossos in Crete were the home of King Minos or the site of the so called labyrinth in which young Athenians were sacrificed to a monster bull, but certainly the Cretans had created a substantial empire and Athens may well at this time have been under its control. The legends of Theseus' victories over the Amazons and the Centaurs provided good material for the decorations of the Parthenon.

Skyros, c. 1260 BC

The place where Theseus supposedly committed suicide on the island of Skyros can still be seen. The attractive well-wooded island lies almost in the centre of the Aegean Sea east of Athens and is now a popular place for holidays. Some scholars argued that Theseus did not throw himself off the cliff at Skyros but was pushed by King Lycomedes, who was also famous for sheltering Achilles by having him dressed to look like one of his daughters, one of whom in gratitude he made pregnant before heading off to the siege of Troy. The estimated date of this event was around 1265 BC. One of the Jupiter Trojan asteroids, Number 9604, is named after Lycomedes.

Chapter 5

Troy, Turkey, c. 1240 BC

The site of the ancient cities of Troy was famously discovered at Hisarlik south-west of Istanbul and close to the entrance of the Dardanelles by the German amateur archaeologist Heinrich Schlieman and most people believe he found the right place. The fact that some Greeks from Naxos took the Trojan side in the famous siege is not surprising since the island of Naxos is closer to Troy than to mainland Greece. The most likely date for the horse episode was around 1240 BC. Whether King Priam of Troy, his son Paris and his daughter-in-law Helen were real people is not certain, but they figure prominently in Greek literature, particularly in Homer's Iliad.

Tiryns, c.1200 BC

The huge cyclopean stone walls of ancient Tiryns can still be seen at this UNESCO site just north of Nauplion in southern Greece. Again we find a Naxian apparently on what might seem the wrong side in a war, but Tiryns was being attacked by the very same people who had won the war against Troy. Archaeological evidence suggests that the last great palace of Tiryns was built around 1200 BC and was captured first by the Argives and later by Spartans.

Grotta, Naxos, c. 550 BC

The town of Grotta is now a part of the main city of Naxos, which has the same name and is now an attractive seaside holiday resort on this lovely island. The tyrant Lygdamis (fl. 546 BC) is the first character in this account for whom we have real historical proof of his existence, seen in this diary as the villain of the story although he seems to have been in his time an able dictator who helped his Athenian ally Peisistratus to become tyrant of Athens in 546 BC, thus providing us with an approximate date for these events.

Chapter 6

New Naxos, Eastern Sicily, 530 BC

New Naxos in Sicily was founded by Greek migrants in about 735 BC and lay between modern Catania and modern Messina on the east coast where a rocky outcrop of cooled volcanic lava called Cape Schiso stretches out into the sea with a sheltered anchorage to the north. Only a few tumbled stone walls remain of the ancient city which was captured by the tyrant of Gela in 415 and came under the rule of the despotic Hieron of Syracuse (478–467 BC). The River Alcantara lies to the south.

Himera, 480 BC

Gelon (d.478 BC), the tyrant of Syracuse and Gela, won a major victory over the Carthaginians in 480 BC, the same year as Sparta lost the Battle of Thermopylae against the Persians. The defeated Carthaginian General Hamilcar (fl. 510–480) committed suicide. Large numbers of skeletons have recently been excavated at the site of the battle at Himera on the north coast of Sicily. Gelon was succeeded by his brother Hieron (d.467 BC)

Syracuse, c. 415 BC

It is known that the Athenian siege began in 415 BC and the people of New Naxos so hated those of Syracuse that they supported Athens, with disastrous results. The prison quarries of Syracuse can still be visited. The Athenian general Nicias (470–413) was captured and executed.

Somewhere between Malta and Carthage c. 350 BC, Carthage was founded around 800 BC by Phoenician settlers who built two large harbours on a point dominating all sea traffic passing between Sicily and the African coast. It had a fleet of 250 warships and its massive city walls stretched for 24 miles. It was destroyed twice, first by the Romans in 146 BC after two long and bloody wars, then by the Muslims in AD 698. The ruins are now a World Heritage Site, and can be seen in a suburb of modern Tunis. In 217 BC, as it prepared to attack the Romans, Carthage founded a colony in Spain, New Carthage or Cartagena (now a major Spanish naval base) which in turn helped found another new Cartagena in what is now Colombia (also a World Heritage site for its surviving walled city.)

Chapter 7

Pella, Macedonia, 336 BC

Some ruins of the new palace built by King Philip II (382–336) here survive north of Thessalonika. It was the birthplace of his famous son Alexander the Great (356–323), who was blamed by some for the plot to murder his father in 336 BC, thus giving us a precise date for the incident recorded here. The palace complex was on the island of Paxos, on a lake which at this time was on the coast. The River Axion, now sometimes known as the Vardar, is 240 miles long and rises in Macedonia, entering the sea just west of Thessalonika. Alexander's mother Olympias became queen in 375 and was supplanted by Cleopatra (not the one who later ruled Egypt) in 337; hence the plot for Alexander to secure the succession.

Bactra, 328 BC

Bactra, now known as Balkh, lies in Afghanistan but at this time was attached to the Persian Empire, having previously been an important centre for Buddhism. Alexander the Great captured it in 328 BC. It was here that he married Roxana, the daughter of his former enemy, the King of Balkh. Ruins of the Mound of Rustam, the ancient fortress, survive as does the superb seven-domed mosque from a later period.

Babylon, Iraq, 326 BC

The ruins of this famous city on the Euphrates are now in Iraq, south of Baghdad. Alexander conquered the area in 331 BC after the Battle of Gaugamela and in 326 BC his army rested here on its way back from India. His behaviour was becoming increasingly erratic, perhaps due to heavy drinking and the pressures of constant warfare. He died here three years later. Ruinous mounds, the remains of the great Babylonian ziggurats, survive beneath the former summer palace of Saddam Hussein.

Chapter 8

Alexandria, Egypt, 320 and 275 BC

Underwater archaeologists believe they have found remains of the famous lighthouse, the Pharos, built in 280 BC and largely destroyed by an earthquake in AD 986. The city's founder, Alexander, had conquered Egypt and become the new pharaoh. When he died in 323 BC he was succeeded by one of his generals Ptolemy I (367–283) whose dynasty ruled Egypt until the death of Cleopatra (the mistress of Marc Antony) in 31 BC.

At sea off Carthage, Tunisia, 250 BC

This incident could be dated around 250 BC during the First Punic War between the Roman Republic and Carthage.

Lake Trasimene, Italy, 217 BC

The fourth-largest lake in Italy Trasimene is surrounded by fishing villages including one Sanguinero, which recalls the bloody battle here in 217 BC when some 16,000 Romans were killed by the Carthaginian army under Hannibal (247–183) during the Second Punic War. Hannibal had famously brought his army and his troop of elephants by land through Spain and the Alps to conquer Italy. Initially he completely outfought the Roman army but due to the attrition of his own army over several years and the stubborn resilience of the Romans he was ultimately defeated.

Chapter 9

Perugia, Umbria, Italy, 210 BC

Perugia, situated some 90 miles from Florence on the upper reaches of the River Tiber and then known as Perusia had been an Etruscan city captured by Rome in 295 BC. Little survives from the Roman period except the Etruscan Gate, which came from the pre-Roman period but was refurbished by the Emperor Augustus.

Rome, Italy, 133 BC

The ruins of the Roman forum are of course one of the most famous tourist sites in the world and the scene here took place at the time of the murder in 133 BC of the popular politician Tiberius Gracchus, brother of Gaius Gracchus (184–121). It was the custom that Roman soldiers who had completed their term of military service would receive a proper allocation of farmland on which to retire.

Pistoia Italy, originally Pistoria, 62 BC

The attempted military coup by the notorious rake Catiline (108–62) is well recorded, as is his attempt to murder the consul Cicero (106–43) and the probable involvement of the young Julius Caesar (100–44). Pistoia was the town where Catiline, with around 10,000 men, gave battle against the Roman Republic in 62 BC; it is in Tuscany some 19 miles north-west of Florence on a tributary of the River Arno. The battle was recorded by the historian Sallust who seems to have been a relative of the Sallust, who was one of my ancestors and who fought and died along with Catiline when their force was overcome by regular troops under the Consul Antonius. Pistoia is these days a delightful medieval city

The coast of Egypt, 48 BC

The precise location of the spot where the great Roman general Pompey (106–48) was murdered in 48 BC by a Greek henchman of Pharaoh Ptolemy is not known, but it is believed that Pompey's enemy Julius Caesar was genuinely upset and after this event took the side of Cleopatra against her half-brother.

Chapter 10

Tiberias, Israel, AD 25

The new palace of Herod Antipas (20 BC–AD 39) was near the thermal springs on the shore of the Sea of Galilee. A son of Herod the Great (d.AD4) he is best known for his persecution of John the Baptist who condemned his second marriage to Herodias as she was the widow of his own half-brother. Her daughter was the allegedly exotic dancer Salome. The new town was built by Herod in AD 20 and named after the Emperor Tiberius as a piece of deliberate flattery. Remains of a Roman amphitheatre survive but no sign of Herod's villa except the thermal springs.

Dover, Britain, AD 43

This second Roman invasion of Britain in AD 43 inspired by the Emperor Claudius (10 BC–AD 54) resulted in the conquest of most of what is now Great Britain, though ultimately the Roman province of Britannia was kept within the limits of Hadrian's Wall.

Rome again, AD 64

This incident coincided with the great fire of Rome of AD 64 during the reign of Nero who finally committed suicide in AD 69. Famously Saint Paul (c. AD 4–64) was one of the Jews rounded up to be executed for their alleged act of arson but others thought it was a planned piece of slum-clearance authorised by Nero himself.

Trogir, Croatia, AD 130

At this time the town of Tragurium was a fishing village set on a small island off the coast of the Roman province of Dalmatia. It was originally founded by ancient Greek colonists and today it is still an unspoilt medieval town a few miles north of Split. Off shore are the islands of Phar and Brattia. This incident was during the reign of Hadrian (76–138) around AD 130.

Trogir again, AD 185

This career took place during the reign of the paranoid emperor Commodus (180–192) whose mistress Marcia had him strangled by her favourite athlete Narcissus. There were clearly plenty of opportunities for ship owners to help supply the legions garrisoned in all the Balkan and Eastern European provinces of the Roman Empire

Split, Croatia, AD 308

Parts of the magnificent palace of Diocletian (244–311) who retired here in AD 305 survive embedded in more recent buildings in the city of Split/Spoleto. Diocletian had conducted the last major persecution of Christians in the Roman Empire just a few years before Constantine made Christianity its official religion. Diocletian, who had been born nearby, devoted his final years to gardening and philosophy.

Aquincum/Budapest, Hungary, AD 326

The incident referred to here seems to have occurred just after the publication in AD 325 of the Nicene Creed by the Emperor Constantine, (272–337) followed by persecution of all who failed to accept the new Christian doctrine of the Trinity. Remains of the Roman frontier fortress of Aquincum on the river called Danuvius after an obscure Roman god still survive in the modern city of Budapest. The lower reaches of the Danube were known as the Ister. Those who disagreed with the theory of the Trinity were known as Arians and led by Bishop Arius (256–336), who was allegedly poisoned. This began a period of fierce persecution and inter-sect warfare.

Chapter 11

Carnuntum, Bavaria, AD 408

The remains of the Roman frontier fortress of Carnuntum stand close to the Danube in Bavaria near the village of Bad-Deutsch Altenburg and form part of an archaeological park. The Goths under Alaric (370–410) seem to have crossed the Danube in a number of places and rapidly advanced into Italy where in AD 410 they famously captured the imperial city of Rome. Alaric was a Christian, albeit he did not accept the Nicene Creed, and would not let his troops destroy the city.

Ravenna, Italy, AD 480

Ravenna, an ancient city built on stilts on a group of small islands in a lagoon, became the capital of the Western Roman Empire in the period AD 402–476, after which it was held by Odoacer, the Visigoth King of Italy (431–493) who deposed the Emperor Romulus Augustulus, last of the Roman Emperors based in Rome in 476, but was himself defeated and killed by the Ostrotrogoth Theodoric the Great (454–526) in AD 493 who became Emperor in Constantinople in 496. Ravenna was thus taken over by the Byzantines in AD 540, the period when its magnificently decorated churches were built. The incident described in the diary here was probably around AD 480, well before the famous plague of Justinian in AD 541.

Near Nantes and Tours, France, AD 498

Farming near the mouth of the Loire could have provided a reasonable living. Pigs, carrots, apples and grapes all thrive there.

Tours on the River Loire was an important city of Christianity due to the fame of its fourth-century bishop, St Martin (316–397) and several important battles fought there. It was the royal capital of the Valois from the reign of Louis XI and until that of Henri IV the capital of France. All that remains of the first church of St Martin is the Tour Charlemagne in the Place de Chateauneuf. The upstart Frankish King Clovis (c. 466–511) married the saintly Clotilda here in AD 493.

Tours, AD 541–549

The Plague of Justinian, called after the Emperor of that
name (fl. 527–565) is the first pandemic recorded in
history and peaked in AD 541 after first being identified
in Pelusium, Egypt. It was caused by the bacterium
Yersinia Pestis, also responsible for the Black Death, and
was attributed to rats on ships between Constantinople
and Alexandria. Its intensity was blamed on a series
of poor harvests which were in turn later blamed on a
volcanic eruption in Indonesia which blocked out the
sun. Its spread was exacerbated by the constant troop
movements and unhygienic camp conditions due to the
wars of the Emperor Justinian, who was aiming to reunite
the territories of the old Roman Empire. It is estimated to
have killed between 30% and 60% of the populations of
Europe, North Africa and the Middle East.

Tours, AD 656

The future King Dagobert II of France (c. 636-679) was
regarded as unfit to succeed to the throne when his father
died in 656, so there was a plot to have him tonsured
(monks could not become kings) and exiled to Ireland to
keep him out of the way. The Bishop of Poitiers arranged
for him to be accompanied by the deputy prior of Tours
who was being punished for his sins. The ex-prior is
assumed to have died in Ireland not knowing that a
daughter had been born as a result of his misbehaviour.
Dagobert, however, was brought back to France and had

a few tempestuous years as king before being murdered in 679.

Poitiers, France, AD 735

Poitiers in the Poitou region was the site of the hugely important Battle in 732 when Charles Martel, the Hammer (c. 680–739), founder of the Carolingian dynasty, defeated an invasion by Saracens or Arabs based in what at this time was the Muslim colony of Spain. Its Grand Notre Dame church became a major pilgrimage destination.

Chapter 12

Aix/Aachen, Germany, AD 795

From ancient times this spa town near the Belgian border was famous for its numerous hot sulphur springs, which is why the then King Charlemagne (c. 742–814) chose it around 790 as one of his favourite residences. After a significant period of conquest, including an invasion of Italy to support the Pope, he was crowned Roman Emperor on Christmas day 800. Aachen subsequently became the location for coronations of Holy Roman Emperors for several centuries.

Chartres, France or Leuven, Belgium, AD 811 or AD 891

There seems to be some confusion whether the battle mentioned appears to be the one at Chartres in 811 or the one known as Leuven won in 891 against the Vikings by a French force under Arnulf of Carinthia(c. 850–899), after which the River Dyle was apparently blocked with Viking corpses. Arnulf had in 887 staged a coup to dethrone his uncle Charles the Fat to become king of Francia and he was later briefly Emperor (894–896). Leuven became an important centre of the Duchy of Brabant and later the home of Stella Artois Beer. Chartres retains its spectacular cathedral, almost destroyed in World War II but for the pleas of an American army officer.

Soissons, AD 923

Charles the Simple (c. 879–929) was by any standards an ineffective ruler of West Francia which was now threatened by two major external forces. East Francia now had its first German king, Henry the Fowler (876–936) while Charles the Simple had foolishly allowed the Vikings to settle officially along the Channel Coast, thus creating the new duchy of Normandy in 911, which would in due course start spreading eastwards. The fact that Charles had six daughters but no sons, and had a crush on the effete Hagano, made him more of a target and led to his dethronement. However, his replacement Robert I (860–923) was killed just a year later in the act of winning the Battle of Soissons in 923.

Falaise, Normandy, AD 1026

Falaise in the Calvados region of Normandy, 20 miles south of Caen on the River Arne, was a major base of the Dukes of Normandy and the birthplace in 1027 of

William the Conqueror, whose mother Arlette or Herleva was the daughter of the local blacksmith; hence his earlier nickname of William the Bastard.

Outside Rome, Italy, AD 1083

It is difficult to place this event in context as it was a confused period in papal history, but the most likely scenario was that this was in fact the great Pope Gregory VII (1073–1085) at a low point in his career during his long confrontation with the German emperor Henry IV, when Rome had to be rescued in 1083 by the ruthless Norman leader Robert Guiscard whose troops did so much damage that the Pope was subsequently ejected from Rome; he died two years later.

Clermont Ferrand, AD 1095

Pope Urban II (1035–1099), was a Frenchman from Chatillon-sur-Marne who was prior of Cluny and Bishop of Ostia before being elected Pope in 1085. Ten years later in November he preached his famous sermon announcing the idea of a crusade to rescue the Holy Land from the Seljuk Turks. It certainly raised the reputation of the papacy but also provided the motivation not just for the official crusades, but for hundreds of others right up to George W Bush and the invasion of Iraq, resulting in many thousands of deaths due to fighting and collateral damage such as trashed harvests and disease transmission.

Chapter 13

Larnaka, Cyprus, AD 1186

Larnaka still has nearby one of the great stone keeps built for Guy of Lusignan, who became the crusader King of Cyprus in 1186.

Megiddo or Hattin, Israel, AD 1187

The massive archaeological site of Megiddo, sometimes believed to be Armageddon, in Israel seems to have been the place where this skirmish took place. It may also have been the site of the Battle of the Horns of Hattin won in 1187 by the Kurdish general Saladin. The Horns of Hattin just west of Tiberias in Galilee, Israel, are a small extinct volcano sometimes believed to be the site of the Mount of Beatitudes.

Constantinople/Istanbul, AD 1204

The diversion of the Fourth Crusade to capture the then Christian city was organised by the Venetians and was seen as an unjustifiable misappropriation of the Crusading ideal...

Perugia, Italy, again, AD 1297

The outbreak of flagellant processions in Perugia in 1297 followed a series of bad harvests in the area and began a whole succession of such outbreaks throughout Northern Italy that later spread into Austria. Perugia was an ancient Etruscan city that became the capital of Umbria and its Cathedral of San Lorenzo in pink and white marble was rebuilt around 1345, half a century after the events described.

Chapter 14

Venice, AD 1320

The Riva della Schiavoni in Venice was a long quay built from the mud of the estuary in the ninth century and named after the Slav or slave labourers who had done the digging. It is now a popular promenade and at the time of this incident a standard place for merchant ships to unload their wares including slaves.

Trogir, Croatia again, AD 1350

Trogir in Croatia became a virtual colony of Venice around 1420 and its Cathedral of San Lorenzo was rebuilt at about the same time. Originally founded on an island by the ancient Greeks – its name means goat in Greek – the town had been captured successively by the Romans, Goths, Saracens, Hungarians and Dukes of Dalmatia

Kosovo, Kosovo, AD 1389

The famous battle of the Field of Crows at Kosovo Polje took place in 1389 between the Serbian kingdom under Prince Lazar (1329–1389) and the Sultan Murad I of Turkey (1326–1389), resulting in a disastrous defeat for Serbia and the deaths of both leaders.. The site is some three miles from Prishtina, the capital of the modern state of Kosovo and became a symbol of Serbian nationalism during the twentieth century.

Chapter 15

Srebrenica, Bosnia, AD 1420

In recent years more famous for the massacre of Bosnian Muslims by Serb Bosnian troops, the mountain town of Srbrenica in eastern Bosnia was captured by the Ottomans in 1440 when its Franciscan monastery was converted to a mosque. The incident described in the diary here suggests that there were also Dominican friars in the area looking for heretics, perhaps Bogomils. There were many German miners in this area then looking for silver that was sent down to the port then called Ragusa, now Dubrovnik.

Edirne, Turkey, AD 1430

Formerly known as Adrianople, this city in the European part of Turkey was founded by Hadrian in AD 125 and captured by the Sultan Murad I in 1361, becoming the capital of the Ottoman Empire until 1453 when the Turks also at last captured Constantinople/ Istanbul. Naturally it was a major training centre for the crack regiments of janissaries, most of the recruits young Christian boys collected or kidnapped from almost every village in the Balkans. Our hero in this section seems to have been much the same age as his friend George Castriota, later known as the great Albanian leader Skanderbeg (1403–14-68).

Jeddah, Saudi Arabia, AD 1460

Jeddah remains the chief port providing access for Muslim pilgrims to the holy cities of Mecca and Medina. However, much of the medieval city has been demolished to make way for modern skyscrapers paid for by oil revenues over recent years. Efforts are now being made to preserve what is left of the old quarter, al Badad, where these events took place round about 1460.

Chapter 16

Zanzibar, Tanzania c. AD 1480

The site of the massive open slave market in the Stone City, which was once a colony of merchants from Oman, can still be seen near its ancient mosques. Set on Ungufa Island it is some 18 miles off the East African coast and is now included in the nation of Tanzania. Clearly our hero moved here from Jeddah about 1480, well before it was invaded by the Portuguese in 1498.

Up the Wami River, Tanzania, c. AD 1500

It is hard to trace the route followed in this account. The River Wami rises inland in what is now the Mikumi National Park near route A7 in Tanzania.

Kibali, Democratic Republic of Congo, c. AD 1560

Kibali in the Democratic Republic of Congo, north of Kisanga and near the massive seven-arch waterfall on the River Congo, now has a huge modern gold mine run from South Africa, but the excellent mineral resources of this region have latterly been a very mixed blessing due to corruption and civil war. The kings of the Congo had a reputation for selling many of their own subjects to slave traders.

The timing of our family's epic crossing of Africa seems to have been over at least two generations between 1490 and 1570.

Shama, Ghana, c. AD 1580

This is now a fishing village, but at that time its Fort San Sebastian, first built by the Portuguese, had become a pick-up point for English slave ships mainly from Bristol heading for the West Indies and North America. The probable date of this episode was around 1580. The ships captain referred to as Surgeon Whorkins may well have been the pioneering slaver and admiral Sir John Hawkins (1532–1595).

Chapter 17

Barbados, AD 1737

John Sambrooke was sent out to Barbados for four years in 1660 and his grandson seems to have been managing a plantation in the Parish of St Andrew on behalf of the Trustees of the Society for the Propagation of the Bible in London. Sir Jeremy Sambrooke (1703–1740) was a member of the influential London sugar lobby and a member of parliament in the 1730s. Captain Robert Jenkins (fl. 1730–1740) of the naval ship HMS Rebecca lost part of his ear due to an attack by Spanish coastguards in 1731 when he was allegedly bringing in contraband. This incident eight years later provided the excuse for the war in 1739 named after his ear. Thus our family had provided some six generations of slaves in Jamaica by the time of these events and Barbados regularly imported several hundred a year.

Savannah, Georgia, USA, 1738

Judging from the affairs mentioned, the escaped slave in this incident must have arrived in Savannah before the departure of the fiery preacher John Wesley (1703–1791) in 1738 when he returned to England after an unfortunate affair with Sophy Hopkey and founded the Methodist Church. The Colony of Georgia and city of Savannah were founded by the idealistic Colonel James Oglethorpe in 1733 and Christ Church where John Wesley was briefly rector still stands in historic Bull Street.

Baton Rouge, Louisiana, USA, 1789–1803

The city of Baton Rouge, now the capital of Louisiana, was founded by French settlers in 1719 and named after a red pole which the explorer Pierre Le Sieur d'Urberville (1661–1708) had noticed marking a tribal boundary in the Mississippi River. The trapper mentioned in this anecdote seems to have arrived in about 1780 when the city had recently been captured by the Spaniards, who held it till 1810. The Old Arsenal Powder magazine at Point Coupeé built in 1756 and many other buildings from this period survive.

Louisiana, including New Orleans, was purchased from the French in 1803 for sixty million francs, thus paying for Napoleon's next campaign in Europe.

Sitka, Baranof Island, Alaska USA, c. 1810

Reading between the lines it appears that the trapper Theneau had been russianised when he moved north up the Alaskan coast and settled, probably in Novo Archangelsk (now Sitka), founded by Alexander Baranof (1746–1819) in 1799 after a Russian force had overwhelmed the native Tlingits.

Chapter 18

Okhotsk, Russia, 1867

Okhostk in the Russian subarctic region of Kamchatka was founded by the mouth of the Ochota River on the orders of Peter the Great as part of his effort to create a port on the Pacific coast. The explorer Bering pioneered the hunting of sea otters for their valuable fur and it was the base of the Russian-American Company from 1799. Alaska was sold by Russia to the USA in 1867 and since then the importance of Okhotsk has declined. Its name has been given to an early culture that also flourished in Hokkaido, the northernmost region of Japan.

Khabarovsk, Russia, 1905

The incident took place on the Trans-Siberian Railway near Khabarovsk, Russian Federation. Khabarovsk, founded by Cossack pioneers on the River Amur close to the Russo-Chinese border – it was once part of China – is 500 miles from Vladivostok and 5000 from Moscow. It is now a major city on the Trans-Siberian railway and a popular stop-off. The Stanovoy Range is some 500 miles long and rises to over 8000 feet. This incident can be dated to 1905 just after the Russian fleet disaster at Tsushima and the Russian army's defeat by the Japanese at Mukden

Omsk, Russian Federation, 1917

The city of Omsk is a major junction on the Trans-Siberian railway in south western Siberia, some 1400 miles east of Moscow and one of the largest cities east of the Ural mountains. It served briefly as the capital of the White Russian army during the civil war against the Bolsheviks. It was a fairly natural place for a railwayman to live and perhaps to start farming when he retired round about 1930. Wheat, barley and sunflowers were significant crops, but the climate is at times difficult so the collectivisation of agriculture under Stalin caused considerable hardship, particularly for small peasant landholders who resisted the reforms. The incident referred to is clearly the famous sealed train in which

Lenin was smuggled back into Russia from his exile in Switzerland in 1917.

Minsk, Belorus, 1923

Minsk on the Svislach River, now the capital of Belorus, was at this time an important railway junction between Poland and Leningrad. Like other areas in the Stalin era it suffered from the enforced collectivisation of agriculture. Its small peasant farms had mainly thrived on flax, sugar beat and livestock, especially pigs, but the destruction of hedgerows to make huge collective farms micro-managed from Moscow met considerable opposition and led to a drastic loss of agricultural productivity.

Chapter 19

Bialystok, Poland, 1930

This ancient city on the River Biala in the far eastern area of Poland has warm summers and long frosty winters. In the 1930s it still had a Jewish ghetto and was conveniently on the main railway line from Warsaw to Moscow.

Krakow, Poland, 1944 This scene clearly comes from around 1944 when long train-loads of Jews were being delivered at Oswiecim/Auschwitz for extermination. While the main character in this section of the diary was only a train driver, he must have been at least partly aware of the vast gas chambers behind the camp perimeter.

Chapter 20

Genoa, Italy, 1946

It is probable that the SS colonel who had threatened Thenski at Auschwitz was in fact Obersturmführer Adolf Eichmann (1906–1962), who reappeared in Genoa under the false name of Ricardo Klement

Puerto Belgrano, Argentina, 1952

This was the largest Argentinian naval base, sited some 400 miles south of Buenos Aires in the Bahia Blanca. Clearly the escaped railwayman from Poland had used his expertise to build up a new career on the Buenos Aires–Bahia Bianca line and his son had joined the Argentinian navy in the base near his home. President Jorge Videla (1925–2013), dictator of Argentina from 1976 to 1981, had encouraged the settling of wealthy Nazis.

San Diego, California, USA, 1958

San Diego Bay was named by Spanish pioneers in 1542 and the territory of Alta California remained Spanish till 1821 when it became part of independent Mexico.

In 1847 it was conquered by US troops and became part of the USA. Frank Bonpensiero (1905-1977), a senior caporegime in the Los Angeles Mafia, moved here in the 1920s and was murdered here in a pornography sting in 1977.

Chicago, USA, 1965

Capo Donald Angelini (19262000) a mobster known as The Wizzard of Odds, was leader of the Chicago Mafia.

Los Angeles, 1966

The Mafia had come under severe attack during the campaign against organised crime by Bobby Kennedy (1925–1968).

New York 2090

My father's career as a beef trader was very erratic due to the campaign of Green parties to minimise or eliminate methane gas emissions from beef cattle.

New York, 2118–2123

This is the main period covered by my diary.

Washington 2150

This is the only dream scene that occurred some years after my death and the interview of my son Mino seems to have been with a great grandson of Rupert Murdoch (1931–), owner among others of THE LAUGHING TIMES.

Those mysterious moments that history sometimes brings forth in accordance with its unfathomable will

Stefan Zweig

REVIEW BY THE LITERARY EDITOR
OF THE LAUGHING TIMES

Most autobiographies dwell on success
And talk about failures very much less,
But the late Theo Thens is remarkably frank
About each fault and juvenile prank.
His life in fact was quite mundane
Except when he felt less than sane.
He does not boast of his family tree.
Just the ups and downs of his pedigree,
Full of princes, peasants, rich and poor,
But what every one of them had to endure
Was the pain of hunger, war and disease,
The heat of the sun. the cold of the seas,
With life's typical allocation
Of misery and frustration,
Occasional sparks of joy and pleasure,
With moments of delightful leisure,
Then comes the end and the end of this book
Open the cover and have a look.

If you enjoyed this book, please consider leaving a review at the online bookseller of choice.

Thankyou

and don't forget to check out other Sparsile titles at www.sparsilebooks.com

Further Reading @ www.sparsilebooks.com

CHILDRENS/YA

Two Pups
Seona Calder

The Few

The Black Dog
Cathy McSporran

I Wanna Be Like Me
Kenny Taylor &
Grisel Miranda

CONTEMPORARY

The Promise
L. M. AFFROSSMAN

Red Road Green
Jonathan Franklin

Gamebird
Adrian Keefe

CRIME

Drown for Your Sins

Dress for Death

Civil Guard
Diarmid MacArthur

HISTORICAL FICTION

Simon's Wife

The Unforgiven King
L. M. Affrossman

Stumblestone
Clio Gray